FRIENDS & MOTHERS

FRIENDS & MOTHERS

LOUISE LIMERICK

Thomas Dunne Books
St. Martin's Press ❦ New York

THOMAS DUNNE BOOKS.
An imprint of St. Martin's Press.

www.thomasdunnebooks.com
www.stmartins.com

Design by Dylan Rosal Greif

Library of Congress Cataloging-in-Publication Data

Limerick, Louise, 1970–
    Friends & mothers / Louise Limerick.—1st U.S. ed.
      p. cm.
    ISBN-13: 978-0-312-35512-8
    ISBN-10: 0-312-35512-2
    1. Postpartum depression—Patients—Fiction. 2. Women—Fiction. 3. Self-realization—Fiction. 4. Motherhood—Fiction. I. Title.
PR9619.4.L56 D95 2007
823'.92—dc22

                                                                    2006048863

First published by Pan Macmillan Australia Pty Limited

First U.S. Edition: May 2007

10 9 8 7 6 5 4 3 2 1

For Michael, for his patience, persistence, and love
For Ellen, Peter, and Kate Rose
For Mum and Dad, my brother and my sisters—all.

ACKNOWLEDGMENTS

I wish to acknowledge those who helped me deliver this book. In Australia: Cate Paterson, Brianne Tunnicliffe, Julia Stiles, and Tara Wynne. In the United States: Kathleen Gilligan, Sara and Bob Schwager, and Faye Bender. My heartfelt thanks to you all.

FRIENDS & MOTHERS

JOANNA

EVER SINCE EVELYN CRACKED, I'VE BEEN DYING for cake. I crave it when I get up in the morning and I pour my regulation ten ounces of cereal into my bowl. Ten ounces isn't much, you know. I think I'll have to find a variety without raisins. They weigh too much. And the half a cup of skim milk only just settles the bran dust. I look into my bowl, and I know that I'm too hungry for cereal. I'm aching for cake. Not the add-an-egg dehydrated variety in a cardboard box. What I want is much more substantial. Packet mixes never fill those empty places. The light texture dissolves like spun sugar on your tongue and smears the inside of your mouth with a waxy film of almost flavors. Almost banana. Almost blueberry. Almost chocolate. Actually, the chocolate's not too bad. If I was going to bake a packet mix, I'd choose chocolate. One of those fancy American chocolate cake mixes that make you drool. One of those double-layered, rich, choc-frosted cakes. Bloody hell, I can almost taste it!

Last night, after I'd eaten my grilled steak and steamed vegetables, I saw that ad. You know the one—the little kid is standing on the stairs watching his mother ice a Betty Crocker chocolate cake in the fluoro-lit kitchen. That cake looked so good, the saliva in my mouth was nearly drowning me when I thought about licking the rich buttercream . . . But what gets me is why a stay-at-home mom would be giving her kid a packet-mix cake for his fifth birthday and frosting it like it was an act of love. Do you know how I could tell she was a stay-at-home mom? She looked like me. It could have been me sitting there, with my drab brown hair, in my sloppy old clothes, in my 1950s, never-been-redone Formica kitchen.

Anyway, working mothers buy their five-year-olds sponge slabs from Woolies that feed twenty. The slabs come with a big yellow banana in blue-striped pajamas dancing through an inch and a half of Vienna cream frosting. The cake tastes like chemicals are holding it together and keeping it soft. It doesn't matter. Kids only eat the frosting anyway.

I know the kind of cake I'm dying for. It's not the kind of cake you can buy in a box, or at Woolies. It has to be homemade. The kind of cake they sell here, at the Vista Cafe. I drool like a dog when I look in that display cabinet and see those cakes. Mud cake, the top so thick with dark chocolate you need a hot knife to cut it. Pumpkin syrup cake, flecked with citrus rind and drenched in sweet orange syrup that congeals like sticky toffee on the crust. Blueberry sour cream cake, thick and buttery with a cinnamon sugar crumble and a juicy berry in every second mouthful. Vanilla slices, caramel tarts, melting moments . . . My heart's rocketing around in my chest as I stand looking at those cakes. Then I remember the weigh-in tonight. I order my skinnychino and I go outside where I can't see the cakes, not with my eyes open anyway.

I sit outside under a large white market umbrella, at a table with a mosaic of blue and green tiles embedded into the top. The tiles make a pattern that looks like waves frozen in the act of uncurling. I look at the tiles and try to think about the sea. It doesn't work. As I lift my three-year-old onto my knee, the waitress brushes past us with a tray loaded with coffees and cake. Warm apple teacake. Lightly crusted on the outside with sugar and strewn with soft wedges of apple. The rich butter curls slide down the soft yellow crumbs and unfold onto the plate. I'm drowning. My mouth fills with water and I can barely breathe.

I can't afford to eat cake if I want to lose ten pounds. Least of all that teacake oozing with butter. Sixteen points! That's nearly my whole day's food quota under my Fat-Trimmers points plan. So, when my skinnychino arrives, I try to make the sweet froth last as I juggle Sam on my knee.

"More frop," he says, grabbing the spoon, and he makes me spoon so much froth into his mouth that I'm going to have to order another skinnychino before the others get here. And maybe a babychino for him, just so I can at least get the sugar kick from the chocolate sprinkled on top. Even just a little taste of something sweet . . . but it's like throwing matchsticks into a fire and it never satisfies me for long.

Sam's a big boy for three. Long legs and big feet, puffy inside his sandals. Smelly feet too. He sweats a lot, especially in the heat. Even though it's March now, there's still enough heat in the mid-day sun to start him sweating. As he leans back on me and his Popsicle trickles down my arm, I smell the savory sweat in his hair. That smell and the quick beat of his heart remind me of the rabbit I owned as a child. I remember holding that rabbit up to my face and inhaling the smell of grass and sun and sweat. I remember feeling its heart beating against my cheek. I look at him, Sam, my only baby now that Jake's at preschool. I stroke the soft pink cheek and stare at the long-lashed eyes and I feel like I'm going to explode with love. It's moments like these when I can't understand Evelyn at all. Why doesn't she tell us what happened? Why does she just sit all closed up and silent? If it were my baby . . .

People talk. They talk about Evelyn and they say that she won't ever get better. They say she's trying to protect herself. I don't think like that. I won't think like that. She was my friend and I can't think of a reason why she would have done what people are saying she did. When I think back to the weeks before it happened, my mind's full of empty spaces. I do remember this one day when something wasn't quite right. Evelyn walked into the cafe for coffee after she'd dropped William at preschool. It was the first time I'd seen her out and about since the baby was born. Clare had been doing the drop-offs and pickups for her. I remember thinking what a beautiful baby she had. Tiny little Amy, only four weeks old. Evelyn didn't look beautiful. She looked worn-out, and while the rest of us gooed at the baby she just sat there melting in the summer sun like Sam's ice cream. She was quiet, too quiet, and when she looked at me she looked straight through me as if I wasn't really there at all. And that was just before . . . No, I mustn't. I mustn't make the connections that everyone else has been making. All new moms get tired. Amy was stolen. That's what I believe.

The day Amy disappeared, Evelyn went queer. She didn't explode. She's not the exploding kind. She kind of did the opposite. She imploded. I think that's the word. Kind of caved in on herself and shrank away until she certainly wasn't anyone I could recognize. Yet sometimes I wonder whether, in the moment before she completely lost it, Evelyn did let it all out. At least that would have been gutsy, to yell and scream and kick like a wild thing. I like to think she did but somehow I doubt it. It would be so out of character for Evelyn.

Evelyn was always too well mannered to make a fuss. In any argument she was the first to back down and could put us all to shame just by being so nice. Nice. That was my impression of her

4

when we met on the day our children started kindergarten. Evelyn was helping the teacher soothe five howling three-year-olds. She held two of them in her lap but only one of them, William, was hers. The other kid was wrapped around her neck and screaming for his mother. Evelyn was crying too. Big drops of empathy rolled down her cheeks. "I feel so silly," she said to me, embarrassed by her tears. "I just can't help myself when everyone else is doing it!"

I liked Evelyn from the beginning. I tried to prize the clingy kid loose—the one that wasn't hers. His grip around her neck was so tight that she was beginning to choke, but the kid just wouldn't come off. I was grateful when my old friend Susan arrived with her daughter, Laura. She shook her head at the chaos and took control straightaway.

It was Susan who suggested that the moms make a quick exit and go for coffee at the Vista Cafe. So a small group of us did. We had coffee and cake and enjoyed ourselves so much that we decided to meet regularly. I remember how Evelyn laughed that first day. Her green eyes glistened. She was so different then from the time after Amy was born. I can't remember what we talked about. Probably our kids. We were all going through the same stuff. I *can* remember the taste of the mud cake I shared with Evelyn. It was made with dark chocolate, not just cocoa, and it was dense and moist and . . .

It's strange how this whole business has made me feel so hungry. I don't like to analyze myself too closely but it's weird that I should have this incredible longing—for cake. Sometimes I wonder if I'm just a little shallow. On the other hand, maybe I'm so deep I can't even begin to sort myself out. All I know is that ever since Evelyn imploded—gee, I like that word—I've been dying. Day by day, a little bit more. Just dying for cake.

CLARE

IT WAS NEARLY NINE O'CLOCK WHEN I REAL-
ized that Sophie hadn't had a thing to eat for breakfast. I thought
I'd been doing well this morning. We were all up at seven thirty
and I had Sophie dressed by eight. The dressing ritual's usually
rather prolonged in our house because Sophie never wants to
wear what I pick out for her, and she takes a long time to choose
clothes for herself. Most of the time she insists on wearing long
dresses, which are very impractical for preschool, so we usually
start our day with an argument. In the end, she wins.

She won this morning when she finally decided to wear the
orange dress and the hot pink socks which, in combination with
her frizzy copper hair, make her look like she's on fire. When Sophie was finally dressed, I put on my jeans, had my breakfast, made
Sophie's lunch, and kissed David good-bye.

At eight thirty I realized that I couldn't drag Sophie away
from *Sesame Street,* so I put her cereal and juice on a tray and let
her eat in front of the television. At a quarter to nine I came into
the room, jangling the car keys, and there she was, watching Big
Bird, her mouth hanging open like a goldfish, her breakfast un-
touched.

I switched off the television, and she gave me one of her looks
with her surly green eyes. "I'm not in the mood for nonsense this

morning, young lady," I said. "We're late. We have to pick up William." I took her tray back to the kitchen and threw her pink Minnie Mouse backpack in her lap. She got off the couch and pouted at me. "You never let me do anything I want!" she grumbled as she headed for the door.

We were just pulling out of the drive when I saw her sad little face in the rearview mirror. That face has the power to knead my heart and make it yield love. Guilt consumed me. Sophie's eyes were full of crocodile tears. "I'm hungry," she whimpered. "I didn't get any breakfast." I stopped the car and raced back inside to find something for her to eat. There weren't many options. Cereal would spill in the car. All I could find were two Choc-Mint Slice cookies. "Here," I said as I slipped them into her hand. "You have to eat something for breakfast." The tears dried up instantly and, as she began licking off the chocolate, I knew I'd been had again. More guilt. My child has such a bad diet. Sometimes I just know I'm a bad mother.

Anyway, the upshot of that little episode was that I was running late, as usual. I think I've been running late since Sophie was born, and she's five now. She should be in school, but David and I kept her back a year. Correction—I pleaded with David to keep her in preschool five days every two weeks for another year. It's only March, and Sophie can already read and write. It was selfish, I suppose, not to let her go on, but once she's at school, I don't know what I'll do with myself. I can't go back to work. I can't face teaching again. Have another baby perhaps? Not a clever option.

You don't know what I was like after Sophie was born. I was a mess. Almost as bad as Evelyn. Correction—never as bad as Evelyn. I got help. I still have help. The help sits inside three little silver packets with tamper-resistant seals. The help gags me every morning and lodges bitter particles halfway down my throat. I don't mind. Everything has its price.

I know David wants me to do something with my life. I think he wonders what exactly I do with myself all day. He thinks I've joined some sort of hedonistic women's coffee sorority. A time filler for bored suburban housewives. This morning he suggested that perhaps, if I'm not interested in having any more children, I should go back to work or do something at TAFE.

"Why don't you go out and look into it today?" he asked.

"I'll do it another time, David. This morning is my coffee morning."

"Coffee? What a loafer. I wish I could sit around drinking coffee all day." He started stuffing his briefcase with papers. "But one of us has to generate some kind of income."

The truth is, David works as a solicitor and generates more than enough for our family to live on. Money is not really the issue. David hates the fact that I'm still on antidepressants. It makes him anxious to think that I'm not coping, especially now that Evelyn has been admitted to the psychiatric ward at the Royal. He worries that I will lose my grip completely and that he will be left bringing up Sophie. He thinks that if I had something else to do, besides mothering, I might manage to pull myself together and get off the drugs. Maybe he's right. The pity is, I just don't have the nerve. The thought of a job, and all the juggling it would involve, fills me with terror.

Poor David. He didn't know he was marrying an emotional disaster. He thought he was marrying a levelheaded girl, and back then, I thought so too. I'd studied art at college. Well, actually, I was supposed to be training to become an art teacher, but teaching never held much appeal for me. The art was what I really wanted to do. I consoled myself with the fact that it would take three years to qualify as a teacher, and that meant I had three years to immerse myself in as many creative mediums as I could. So I explored the subtle gradations of charcoal from peaceful grey to deathly black. I threw clay on the potter's wheel and grew vases and bowls under my hands. I made sculptures from objects that I scavenged on rambles to the local dump.

And I painted. I painted in watercolor, in acrylic, and in oil. I learned different ways to move the color about, ways to make it melt into my canvas and harmonize, and ways to make it stand out and jar the senses. Of all the mediums, paint was the one I took the most pleasure in and I liked to think of myself as an artist. But artists don't make any money, as my father pointed out. So, at the end of my course, I followed the line of least resistance and became a teacher.

Teaching seemed a safe choice. I didn't know much about the world of work, but I knew about teaching. I'd been to school. I'd even liked school. School felt secure to me. I'd enjoyed the routine, the feeling that people were looking after me. So I became a teacher and, in the summer holidays, before my first semester started, I married David.

That was an eventful time for me. I got married, I left home, and I started my career. It was not the marriage that broke me. Kindhearted David just seemed to assume the role that my equally loving parents had relinquished. But teaching was more difficult than I'd ever imagined. School was different from the other side of the desk. And I'd been educated in a cozy middle-class school. The school where I started teaching was in a poor area in Brisbane's back blocks. I went into the classroom thinking that I'd be the kids' savior. I'd share my love of art and of painting with them. They were going to adore me, just like in the movies. I didn't have a clue.

All those uncontrollable teenagers. Every day my voice rose

another pitch, struggling to be heard over the scrape of metal chair legs along the linoleum, over the ADD kid slapping his paintbrush on the table, over the girls screaming whispers into one another's ears. One day, when the grade nine boys were picking little pieces of clay off the block and throwing them onto the ceiling, and the girls were dribbling the clay slip in lacy patterns on the floor, I lost it. I felt my vocal cords twist and tighten until the squeal turned into a screech that ricocheted around the room and back to me again. And I knew then that I had to get out. I had to escape the frantic sound that came from my own throat. So I did get out. I was pregnant in a month, and I took leave at the end of the year. A baby would be easier, and I'd get some time to do what I'd always wanted—to paint. It wasn't, and I didn't.

Those months after Sophie was born were the worst in my life. I came so close . . . It makes me shudder even now. Perhaps that's why it's me, not Joanna or Susan or Wendy, who feels that Evelyn might be responsible for Amy's disappearance. You see, I've been on the edge too.

Sophie was born screaming, and she didn't stop screaming for four months. Everyone said it was because I was a nervous first-time mother. "Babies all cry," they said. "It's normal." But it wasn't normal. I'm not a fool. If all babies cried like Sophie, the human population would be in decline. Sometimes Sophie cried for four-hour stretches. Her bottom lip quivering, her face red and ugly, tiny beads of sweat sprinkled through her hair. I rocked her, and I changed her. I sang to her, and I walked with her inside and outside. It didn't make any difference. The clinic nurse told me she was hungry. Well, when she got like that, I couldn't feed her. She'd suckle a minute, then arch her back and scream as if the milk were poison. Sometimes I wished it was. Guilt again. I felt so useless. A useless mother.

I remember standing on the porch one afternoon with Sophie bawling in my ear while I stared at the concrete driveway below. I leaned over the railing with Sophie and looked into the dark cracks that ran through the grey concrete. It would be so easy, I thought. So easy to stop the noise. To let her tiny body slip down . . .

And then I felt her little clenched fist rub against my neck. I smelled her sweet sickly smell, and I felt her tiny anguished body curl against mine. The bile ran into my mouth, and I stumbled back inside. I shut the door to the porch. Locked it. I put Sophie down in her cot still screaming, and I locked her door too, then I ran into my room and threw myself on the bed and cried and cried. After an hour of this, Sophie stopped screaming. I didn't trust myself near her again, so I stayed on the bed and fell asleep.

When David came home late from work, he went into Sophie's room and found her lying in sheets damp with milky vomit. He picked her up and carried her in to me. I saw him standing there, his dark brow raised over his big brown eyes. Standing by the bed, holding Sophie, limp with exhaustion, in his arms. From far away I heard my own voice. "Sophie needs to go to the doctor. She's ill. No baby could scream so much and not be ill."

David pulled his earlobe and told me that it was late, nearly nine, and hadn't the clinic nurse seen her just yesterday and assured me that she was fine, even putting on weight.

I felt my neck grow tighter. "Look at her, David! She's wet with vomit. She screamed for four hours this afternoon."

"All babies throw up," he said, sitting down on the bed. "She probably drank too much earlier."

"She needs to go to the doctor, David." Something inside me was twisting, tightening, about to snap.

"All right," he said. "We'll take her to the doctor first thing in the morning. Now, you give her a bath while I fix us something to eat."

I stood up. This was it. I was about to break. I could feel the frustration rising inside like gall. The emotion began to spill into my mouth, bitter and choking, yet at the same moment I had a sensation of distance, detachment even. It was as if there were two of me. One person full of frustration, beating her fists in the air, and another, to whom no emotion could be ascribed, coldly looking on. It was the cold me that suggested the closet as a place to vent my fury without attracting too much attention from the neighbors. I got up and moved past David and slid open the door. I slipped behind David's suit coats, and I heard my voice sweep before me like a torrid stream growing louder and louder.

"She needs to go to the doctor. Not tomorrow. NOW, NOW, NOWWWWWWWW!"

When it was all over, David's tie rack fell on my head, and the ties slithered over me like snakes. The cold me found this final incident objectively funny and laughed a hollow, voiceless laugh. The other me folded up on the floor like a hangerless coat and cried. Sophie started screaming again, and David, practically reduced to tears himself, spoke softly.

"I've got the keys. Get in the car."

Well, we went to the doctor's that night, and I thank God every day that we did. Sophie was referred to a pediatrician, who diagnosed acute gastric reflux and put her on a course of medication that changed her personality completely. She was finally comfortable. She could feed without arching her back and cried a lot less. She even started to sleep better, which meant that both David and I finally got some rest. I started to feel almost human. Almost.

It was quieter in our house after Sophie was on medication.

She slept. She fed. She kicked her legs in the sun during nappy-free time. Quiet was something I wasn't used to. Not just the absence of noise but the absence of wild feelings beating in my breast. When Sophie had screamed and struggled I'd felt angry, I'd felt wretched. At least I'd felt something. But now? Now I looked at Sophie's smiles, tremulous fragile little movements that fluttered across her lips, and I felt nothing. Nothing at all.

Did I even like her? It was the hardest thing I'd ever had to admit. I saw how David kissed her, cuddled her, loved her to bursting. I pretended to love her too. But I didn't love her. I knew that much. Guilt consumed me. I'd committed the greatest sin a mother can commit. What mother doesn't love her own child?

The problem was that I hadn't bonded to Sophie in those first months, and even though she was much easier to manage now, I still shivered every time she whimpered. I crept around the house while she was asleep, and I hated being left alone with her. The days when David went to work were the worst. I started looking at the clock, counting the minutes until he returned and I'd have some adult company. I felt so incredibly lonely. The dark days dripped by in a mundane routine, and my old paints and easel stayed in the garage because I was so uninspired. It was unbearable.

One day I was bathing Sophie. My hand was holding her head up out of the water. She was about five months old. Perfectly pink and rosy. Objectively beautiful, with her red curls just starting to form. I slid her up and down the bath. I moved her body slowly back and forth, back and forth. She relaxed. She closed her eyes, almost slept . . . It would be so easy, I thought . . . so easy . . . She kicked her legs, opened her eyes and smiled anxiously. My heart shuddered. What was I thinking? With my own tears dripping into the bath, I whipped her out, wrapped her in a towel, and drove back to the same doctor who'd helped to diagnose her reflux.

13

I had never felt so low. I cried in the waiting room, and I sobbed in the examining room. That was the day the doctor referred me to a psychiatrist, who diagnosed postnatal depression. I was immediately put on a course of tablets that blew away the dark haze that shrouded my existence. In a matter of weeks I started to feel alive again. More importantly, I started to enjoy looking after Sophie. I began to feel love for her. Of course, because of the medication, I was no longer able to breast-feed, but after all our troubles, the bottle felt right for us. And on the advice of my psychiatrist, I started taking Sophie to playgroup, to Gymbaroo, to the shops. Anywhere. I started to get out of the house and I realized that I could still be a participant in life.

Things seemed much better after that. I realized that I had a beautiful little daughter to raise and watched her personality unfold as she grew. I went on long walks with Sophie in the stroller, and I was with her when she experienced all those commonplace things—the flyaway fluff on a dandelion weed, the feel of rain on her skin, the hilarity of a bouncy puppy off its leash in the park. I didn't see the world anew; I saw Sophie—new and delightful, in the world. I wanted to know this child of mine. Her chuckles, the dimples in her knees, the way she stuck her tongue out between her lips when she was absorbed in a game—these things were special. Occasionally I even got my paints out. No great masterpieces but little compositions that I could fit in around my domestic chores—bowls of fruit, flowers, the usual stuff.

After all this, I thought I would have been able to help Evelyn. I knew something was wrong after Amy was born. I could tell Evelyn wasn't coping because she always had that flat expression so characteristic of depressed women. I tried to get her to go and see someone, but she said she was all right. She said that the baby wasn't sleeping well and she was tired. I let it rest when I should have packed her into the car and driven her to the doctor myself.

The truth is Evelyn fell apart much faster than I did. While I had a colder, more objective version of myself to arbitrate over my worst impulses, Evelyn didn't. Postnatal psychosis is what they called it. I'd never heard of it until they diagnosed Evelyn, then I understood why she did what she did. She had no part of herself left to be rational with. That rational part had drowned after Amy's birth in a sea of bizarre thoughts and black moods that left Evelyn unable to connect either with her baby, herself, or anyone who might have been able to help her.

In the end I was too late to help Evelyn. Guilt again. My psychiatrist says that I'll never really be well until I stop carrying so much guilt with me. It's hard not to feel guilty, though. I always assume that it's my guilt that prevents me from being the wicked person I secretly know I am. Guilt is my natural impulse stabilizer.

It's a pity that guilt can't speed me up a bit because now I'm running late for coffee. Joanna, Wendy, and Susan will be waiting for me. And Susan will glance at her watch, like she always does when I arrive, because she is never a minute late. I will say, with an embarrassed laugh, that Steve hadn't dressed William when Sophie and I arrived to pick him up. Susan will nod, but she won't believe me. She'll tell me to sit down, and she'll go and get my coffee, she was thinking of ordering a second cup anyway. And I'll sit down next to Wendy and wonder if I should run after Susan and tell her that I'd really rather have tea. But I won't, and Susan will get me a flat white because she always does.

SUSAN

Monday March 18

6:30 A.M.—Shower, get dressed, make lunches

Maxine's lunch
Red box, blue bottle
Salmon sandwich
Sliced triangles, no crusts
Wafer-thins, pink
Pink Lady apple
Sliced wedges, Glad-wrapped

Jonathan's lunch
Green box, yellow bottle
Salad sandwich
Sliced squares, no sprouts
Muesli bar, chewy choc chip
Melon sliced, Glad-wrapped

Laura's lunch
Madeline box, orange popper
Honey sandwich

Sliced fingers (mine)
Cheese stick
Mandarin
Gladly left unwrapped (preschool rules)

7 A.M.—Wake children, wake Richard, drag Laura screaming into the shower, then dress her for preschool. Feed family breakfast.

Maxine's and Jonathan's breakfast
Consists of
Tinned spaghetti on toast

Laura has
Raisin Bran
Like her dad
Heavy head dragging over her bowl
Like her dad
Who's never been known
To have
ANY OTHER CEREAL
For breakfast
Since 1990
But now finds the recent increase in raisins
In the "NEW IMPROVED FORMULA"
So annoying that he may yet
Return to Weet-Bix
After ten years
So that numerous
Tiny tuppers of handpicked
Bran-dusted raisins

May yet cease
Multiplication in the pantry

7:30 A.M.—Wash up breakfast, wipe benches, make beds

Laura's wet the bed
Again
Strip the stinky sheets
Again
Wipe the plastic cover
Over with disinfectant
Again
Remake the bed
Again

7:45 A.M.—Kiss Richard good-bye, do the girls' hair

One little girl had a little knot
That grew and grew and grew
Her mother combed it out
In one brisk sweep
And broke the comb in two

Another little girl wanted a part
That was neat and straight for school
But the comb was too short
For things of that sort
And a zigzag was considered uncool

8 A.M.—Inspect Jonathan's homework, practice Maxine's spelling
list

Mother—M-O-T-H-E-R
Maid
Marriage
Maternity
Mother—M-O-T-H-E-R
Menial
Marginal
Monotonous
Miracle—M-O-T-H-E-R

8:15 A.M.—Teeth. Very important. I remember the kids who never brushed their teeth before school. Their breath reeked like rancid butter. My children stand one, two, three beside the basin and practice synchronized brushing. They take turns spitting, however.

8:20 A.M.—Brush own hair, apply lipstick, grab keys. My mother always told me that the only cosmetic one needs to apply each morning is lipstick. Lipstick is essential.

8:30 A.M.—Drop Jonathan and Maxine at school early for band and choir practice.

8:45 A.M.—Drop Laura at preschool in time to do puzzles on the red mat.

9:15 A.M.—Meet Joanna and Wendy at the Vista Cafe and wait for Clare who, even though she only has one child, never manages to make it to puzzle time at preschool or the first round of coffee.

WENDY

WENDY PULLED HER ANCIENT MORRIS MINOR into her driveway, and the engine shuddered gratefully as she turned it off. Daniel hated being picked up from school in the old blue car, and he had spent the entire trip home whining.

"It's so embarrassing, Mom," he said. "Everyone can hear you coming. Just let me catch the bus. I am in grade six, you know."

Wendy looked at his freckled face, framed by his "cool" spiky haircut, and shook her head. "As long as I have to leave work early to pick up Maddy from preschool, I might as well wait the extra ten minutes for you, Dan. Next year maybe you and Maddy can catch the bus, but this year I'm afraid you're stuck with me and the bomb."

Wendy sighed as Daniel slammed the back door and dragged his Pokemon rucksack up the front steps so that it bumped against each one. She sat lethargically in the car and watched him find the house key behind the umbrella plant and run his fingers through his gel-set brown hair before going inside.

Madeline was too small to notice that other parents drove cars that didn't backfire or let off smoke. "Mom, can I have a Popsicle? Please?" She had her arms tightly wrapped around Wendy's neck, and her lips pressed against her mother's ear.

Wendy pushed her away gently. She was too tired to argue. "Sure," she said. "Get one out of the freezer and ask your brother if he wants one too." Maddy bounded out of the car, her blond pigtails flying. She slammed her door with enthusiasm rather than anger and raced up the steps of the old Queenslander, blue like the car.

Wendy rubbed her eyes and reached over into the child litter that was strewn over the backseat: Popsicle sticks fused to the vinyl, chip packets, empty Coke cans. She grabbed Maddy's yellow backpack and climbed out. The carport was a long way from the house. Harry had built it himself, and it had a slight lean to the left.

She walked to the front gate, which was behind the carport, and tried to avoid looking over into the Easterns' yard. It made her feel tired, that yard. Tired and guilty. Since Evelyn's hospitalization, Wendy had avoided Steve. But they were neighbors. There was no avoiding that.

She reached out to her own gate, and her shoe kicked a newspaper, tightly wrapped in plastic, sending it spinning across the grass. It was not hers. She and Harry didn't have the paper delivered. Now and then Harry would buy one to read, if he felt like it, but mostly they didn't waste their money. They didn't waste anything. Every spare dollar was saved, and with her back nursing part-time, they were finally accumulating some funds to send the kids to private secondary schools. Wendy stooped over and picked up the paper. She leaned over the wooden fence that divided their yard from the Easterns' and threw the paper as far as she could into the grassy wilderness. It hit the overflowing letterbox and sent a river of mail out onto the grass.

Wendy rubbed her eyes again. Her head was beginning to ache. She looked up toward her own house and could hear the television blaring. *Playschool* was on. Her "cool" eleven-year-old son still watched *Playschool*. He would never admit it, of course. He said he let Maddy watch it so she wouldn't bug him while he was playing his Game Boy. Wendy thought she might go inside and make herself a coffee and just try to forget. Of course, it was impossible to forget. She'd tried to forget about it ever since it had happened.

She made her way across to the Easterns' letterbox and picked up the mail she had dislodged: bills, letters, junk. She picked up the newspapers too, thirty-four of them scattered in among the azalea bushes. She put the out-of-date papers in the green recy- cling bin and wondered if she could ring up and cancel the East- erns' papers, but they'd probably stop delivering them soon anyway. Steve couldn't have paid his bill in weeks. She walked through the yard, averting her eyes from Steve's workshop which was situated under the house, behind the palings where the white paint peeled and cracked in the sun, flaking onto the stumps of dead hydrangeas.

The Easterns' house was a Queenslander too, but the veran- dah, which ran along the front and the right-hand side of the house, was hidden beneath a sixties siding makeover. The house was raised high enough off the ground for Steve not to bump his head on the beams, if he remembered to duck. He seldom re- membered, judging from the streams of profanity Wendy over- heard whenever Steve was tinkering with his cars. She walked up the steps. It always amazed her that the Easterns' front steps had not collapsed, for the wood was rotten in the corners, and bare nails, rusted raw, popped out along the side so that the balusters along the railing swung loose. But the steps neither creaked nor wobbled as she trod on them, fossilized as they were by the weather patterns of the last eighty years. The steps, she knew, would remain, while the balusters were shed onto the grass like toenail clippings.

The door loomed large before her, painted so many years ago that the glossy mission brown had now taken on a dull patina of greasy fingerprints. The large prints at the top—Steve's oily mechanic's hands—the small ones nearer the bottom the result of William's sojourns into the garden with a jelly sandwich.

Wendy could hear her heart beating. She told herself it was because the steps were steep, but there were only thirteen in all. She took a moment to catch her breath, then she knocked on the door. With the force of her fist the door swung back into the half-light of the verandah, which was boarded up and completely shut against the garden by rows of opaque glass windows. Stale air rushed out at her, and she tried not to breathe it in.

The house was quiet. William must be with Clare, she thought, as she stole across the verandah boards, past the silky oak daybed. She moved toward the door, which had originally been the front door before the verandah was enclosed. It had a stained-glass panel of two entwined pink and yellow roses, but Wendy scarcely noticed the decoration in the gloom. Steve's black boots and William's trucks lay scattered around the threshold, and there was an overpowering smell of cat food. Seven opened tins were scattered around the door. Steve's old ginger Tom crawled out from under the daybed, slowly stretched and arched, then slunk across the floor and wrapped himself around her legs.

Her voice wavered as she spoke. "Steve? Are you home? It's Wendy."

There was no answer. She was about to put the mail on the floor and leave, but something compelled her forward into the house. She walked through the living room, where the television was flashing blue pictures into the dim light. It was dark in the

Easterns' lounge. Dark and stifling. Wendy had the suspicion that things were lurking in the dusty corners, among the discarded clothes and cat fur. In the kitchen, a tap was dripping onto piles of plates stacked up in the sink. She smelled cigarette smoke and saw Steve sitting crouched over on the back steps, his sandy blond head in his hands.

"Steve?"

He turned toward her and squashed his cigarette into a dead pot plant. "Huh?" Looking bewildered he squinted to see her in the dim light. "Wendy?"

"Yeah, it's me." She made an effort to sound casual. "I thought I'd bring in your mail. It seems to be stacking up a bit out there."

Steve rubbed his hand over his unbrushed hair and stood up. "Thanks. Put it on the table."

Wendy picked up some cereal bowls caked in concreted Weet-Bix and cleared a space on the table for the mail. She turned to find a space to set the cereal bowls down, but the benches were overflowing. She balanced the empty bowls on top of the toaster.

"You need some help around this place."

Steve looked at her. She was wearing her pink nurse's uniform. It hugged her waist and glided over her hips. He saw the way her dark hair was pulled tightly back from her face and the way the severity of the hairdo accentuated the puritanical look in her swimming-pool blue eyes. He stood up and moved over to the kettle, struggling to fill it up without knocking over the pile of plates in the sink. He didn't get much water in the spout before it started splashing out.

"I was about to have a coffee. Would you like one?"

Wendy looked at the coffee cups stacked up beside the sink and watched a cockroach disappear under the toaster. "No thanks.

I just dropped in with the mail . . ." That was the truth, wasn't it? She hoped he'd believe her.

Steve shrugged and waited for the kettle.

Wendy hesitated. "How's Evelyn?"

"The same, I expect. Haven't seen her since last week. She was pretty drugged. Didn't even know I was there."

"Has she said anything about Amy yet?"

"No. She doesn't speak. She won't say a fuckin' word." Steve searched his pocket and shuffled another cigarette out of the pack and lit up.

"I'm sorry . . ."

"Yeah . . . Doesn't help, though, does it?"

"How's William been taking it?"

"He spends most of his time over at Clare's. Best thing really."

Steve turned off the kettle, which was beginning to screech, and spooned three large teaspoons of Nescafé into his cup. She saw the cigarette tremble in his fingers as he lifted the kettle and poured the steaming water onto the coffee granules. Taking the cup in his hand, he turned, leaning against the counter, his chest concaved and his shoulders rolled toward her. A broken thing. An empty husk of a man with eyes so red that they wept like bruised cherries.

"Have you got anyone to talk to, Steve? Someone who'll listen?"

Steve blew smoke into the air. "I've got the police, Wendy. The police are here every fuckin' day. Talking. Asking. Listening. Why don't they get off their fat arses and find her? Someone must know something, but as I keep telling them, I know bugger all. Why waste time on me? I've got nothing to say. If I knew where my baby was, I'd find her myself. I loved that kid. I loved Evelyn too. You've got to believe that . . ."

Wendy looked at the floor. "I believe it. You loved her. Things happen." She looked into his eyes. "Mistakes . . ."

Steve's eyes held her gaze over his coffee cup. He swallowed and let the coffee burn his throat. "You know, when the police finally called me that day, it was already four o'clock in the afternoon. Said they had trouble tracking me down. Hopeless bastards. They've been hopeless, bloody hopeless since day one. They told me not to worry, my son was fine, but my wife had been taken to the psychiatric unit at the Royal.

" 'What?' I said. I couldn't take it all in at first. I think I must have started swearing." Steve laughed, a hollow sort of laugh that became a cough. He drank some more coffee. Wendy bit her lip.

"Someone else took over the call then, a woman. Someone with a softer touch, more experienced in breaking that sort of news, bloody social worker no doubt. She told me that Evelyn had some sort of breakdown in the middle of Westfield Shoppingtown, but that she was lucid enough to tell them that William was waiting to be picked up at preschool. Someone from Family Services picked him up and fed him M&Ms all afternoon.

" 'What about the baby?' I asked. 'Was the baby with her?' No one knew anything about a baby. I started to get angry then. It was all so damn frustrating, and the angrier I got the more bloody condescending they became. They tried to make me calm down. Perhaps the baby was with a friend. Could I call around and check? Could I ring them back if there was a problem? Shit! Of course there was a fuckin' problem."

Steve inhaled and turned away to release the smoke. "Bunch of idiots, the whole bloody lot!" Wendy saw that the tremble in his hand had moved all over his body. He clawed his sandy hair with his huge hand, and tears flooded his eyes. He sat down at the table, put his head on it, and began to weep. She stiffened at the sound of his deep sobs. She wanted to hold him, but instead she walked away, stood behind him at the sink. She let Steve weep while she did the dishes, cleared the table, and emptied the ashtray into the bin.

"I'm sorry," she said, resting her hand lightly on his shoulder, unable to avoid feeling the warmth of his flesh, the dumb solidity of his body. She drew her hand away again, in some pretense of straightening her uniform.

"I have to go. Harry will be home soon." And she left the dark house and walked out into the bright afternoon.

EVELYN

I AM CALM. CALM AND STILL. LIKE THE MOMENT between night and dawn. Like the soft pause between breaths. I linger in my nothingness. There is nothing I need. Nothing I desire. No one I want to be with.

My body is here, but I have gone beyond my body. I've left my body here for you to find. Sitting in the chair. Staring out the window. Watching the rain cry the tears I cannot. Forget tears. Feel as I feel. Feel nothing or you will be unhappy. You will want more.

See me watching the rain. Yes, I am alive. I breathe. See how my chest rises and falls underneath my soft lilac nightgown. Lilac is the color of dreams. I dream. I dream beyond myself.

I know what happens here, and I watch it happening from a distance. I see the nurse who comes to brush my hair. "Such beautiful auburn hair," she soothes. She likes my hair so much, I wish I could give it to her. I am no longer wearing it. It no longer suits me. It drifts in my face and tangles through my dreams like a sticky spiderweb. It threatens to enclose me completely, but I increase my momentum and swing myself out from the web, tearing at the sticky strands, releasing myself enough to breathe again, clinging still to save a fall. "Now, now," she says, "you've spoiled it and it was so pretty too."

She is older. She has grey hair and thick glasses and a soft, kind face. Maybe, if my mother had lived, she also would have worn this aged female face. A face with lines and creases and a mouth with words tumbling out. Soothing words, soft and comforting. Mother words.

I cannot remember the words she used to speak. Did she ever speak to me at all? I remember a dark shape in the kitchen. That was her. She shuffled across the floor as if she was weary from the distances between refrigerator and stove and sink. I remember her crying over onions, but she cried over pumpkin and potatoes too. She held me once, crushed me against her green dress, so that I could barely breathe. She cried over me too and I struggled out of her arms and ran out into the garden and pulled the petals off all the roses. I didn't like her crying over me as if I were an onion.

But I must not remember my mother. Thoughts of my mother are dangerous. They calcify and form a hard vessel in my mind, which pours me back into my body and that is not where I want to be. See, a tear has formed. A tear has formed in the corner of my green eye. That eye does not shed tears. If the nurse sees the tear, she will tell the doctor that something made me cry. Something.

I sigh myself away. Far away into the highest corner of the room. Now I am smaller than the spider that hides in the cornice. I am nearly as small as the dust particles skidding down the sunbeams that slide through the window. I am as small as the midge in the cornice spider's web. The midge is so small that even the spider has forgotten it. Now I am so small, I feel nothing. Nothing never makes me cry.

THE EMPTY CHAIR

WENDY SAT WITH JOANNA AND SUSAN OUTSIDE the cafe. Every week they sat at the same table because it never occurred to them to sit anywhere else. Out of habit, Susan vigilantly guarded the two spare chairs beside her. When a young office worker wanted to borrow the chairs for his friends, Susan curtly told him that both chairs were already taken. It was a half-truth. Wendy knew it. Still, she thought, the delusion that things were normal was strangely comforting.

That particular table outside the cafe had always been "theirs." Wendy wasn't sure why they had chosen it originally. Perhaps they all liked the shelter of the market umbrella with the security of the cafe's big glass window behind their backs. Maybe they were also drawn to that table because it was outside, near the rubber plant in the heavy terra-cotta pot. Somehow, Wendy thought, intimate conversations were less threatening outdoors. Outside, they had the wide leaves of the rubber plant to guard their privacy and conceal their secrets.

Wendy looked at Joanna. Joanna always sat closest to the rubber plant. It was as if she was trying to hide some of her flesh behind the succulent green leaves. A difficult proposition, Wendy decided, when even the clothes Joanna was wearing seemed to accentuate her weight problem. That T-shirt! Those horizontal stripes certainly didn't do her figure any favors. The red-and-white bands coiled around Joanna's thick upper arms and pulled over her large bust. The jeans were wrong too. They stretched over the bulge of her belly, and the zipper puckered and strained. Her mousy shoulder-length hair was loose and parted on the left; it flopped over one side of her large doughy face. Sam sat on her knee and fingered the leaves on the rubber plant. While his mother sipped her coffee, he punctured holes in the leaves with his nails and bled out the milky sap.

Susan sat on the other side of the plant. She was thin and gaunt and her face was small and sharp-featured. In that small face, her hazel eyes seemed huge, almost carnivorous, and so intense that Wendy felt compelled to avert her eyes rather than be devoured—or found out. As always, Susan was wearing dark, well-fitting clothes and a bloodred lipstick which, though applied thickly, never seemed to smudge on her perfect white teeth. When she was speaking, as she was now, her whole body became animated with quick movements, and she reminded Wendy of an excited animal in a cage. Susan's physical agitation betrayed her active mind: quick cuts and jabs with her hands, twitches around her mouth and nose, the perpetual jiggling of her small foot in her red shoe.

Wendy saw that, sitting on either side of the rubber plant, Joanna and Susan were like mismatched bookends, although somehow they balanced each other. Wendy sipped her latte and listened to Joanna and Susan talk. She was tired. Bone tired. She wished that she could close her eyes but that would attract questions from Susan—questions she didn't even want to ask herself. So she slumped back in her chair and let the conversation flow around her. Occasionally she took her foot out of her shoe to rub the back of her calf. Her legs were aching, and she hadn't even done her shift yet. She was trying to break in her new shoes, but already a Band-Aid covered a blister above her heel.

"Did you enjoy your long weekend, Susan?" Joanna casually pulled a leaf out of Sam's mouth and exchanged it for a Twistie from the packet on the table.

"Oh, you know I didn't!" Susan put down her coffee and the cup made a chink as it hit the saucer. "You know how much I 'love' camping." She smiled without showing her teeth and drummed her small, perfectly manicured fingers on the table.

Susan, immaculately presented, totally urban Susan, was definitely not the outdoor type. "I don't know how Richard manages to drag you along every year," commented Wendy, slowly shaking her head.

"Well, you know what he's like. The Boy Scout who never grew up." Susan put on her best Richard voice, serious and slightly pompous. "'Come on, Susan. We can't let the children down. We always go camping in March. It's my bonding time with them . . .'" She rolled her eyes. "His bonding. My bondage."

Wendy watched Joanna gaze longingly at a plate of sticky date pudding that had just been served to someone nearby.

"But you told me he cooks all the meals when you're camping," Joanna said, as Sam grabbed a handful of Twisties and stuffed them into his mouth.

"Only because he won't let anybody else touch his campfire! Anyway, who do you think does the washing up? Ever tried to wash up bacon and eggs in cold water?"

Wendy looked at Susan's small hands and nails with red nail polish. She found it hard to believe that hands like that actually went into dishwashing water at all. There was something incongruous about Susan and domestic life. She wondered what Susan wrote under "mother's occupation" on those forms the school sent home at the beginning of term. Wendy was almost certain she didn't put down "domestic duties" like all the other stay-at-home mothers. What had Susan once said? Something about consciously rejecting any label that pigeonholed her. Something about power and the way society used labels to exclude people . . . She'd probably been to that women's bookshop in South Brisbane again.

"At least you got out of the house for the long weekend," consoled Joanna. "A change of routine, some clean air and sunshine always cheers me up!" Sam was sucking on a leaf again. Joanna pulled it out of his mouth. "Stop sucking them, sweetie. They might make you sick. Here, have another Twistie."

Susan snorted. "Sunshine! Huh! It rained nearly all weekend and all the clothes got muddy. I think I spent most of my time in the launderette doing the washing!"

"Why didn't you just leave the washing until you got home?" Wendy hooked a wisp of dark hair behind her ear. She thought about how she longed for a holiday and how, if she had one, she certainly wouldn't spend it doing the washing. She would lie on the beach and sleep in the sun. That would cure her lethargy. Yes, that was all she needed. A holiday. Then she'd be back to normal. Was it any wonder her body rhythms were confused? She was utterly exhausted. That had to be it.

"What! And spend the next week catching up?" Susan downed the last of her coffee. "No thank you. The laundry is the place to be when it's raining. The kids come home with bags of clean clothes, and I come home with a completed novel. This year I read *Anna Karenina*. So I can tick that off my list of must-read classics."

"What about Richard? Did he enjoy his annual camping trip?" Wendy asked.

"No, he didn't actually."

"Why? Because of the weather?"

"No, because of the constipation! I forgot to remember his Raisin Bran. He moaned about that all weekend. No one wants to linger longer on those self-composting toilets, I can tell you!" Susan thrust her nose into the air and breathed in sharply.

The women burst out laughing, but at that moment Clare arrived, her face unreadable behind her sunglasses. Without any of them realizing it, the laughter stopped.

Wendy could never get used to seeing Clare without Evelyn. Evelyn and Clare had grown up as neighbors and were like sisters. Evelyn Eastern still lived in the childhood home she'd inherited when her father died. Clare had moved away, however, when she got married. Later, when Clare's parents retired to the coast, Wendy and Harry had bought Clare's old home. They did it up. Renovated the Queenslander inside and out until it looked like a grand old dame. Unfortunately their renovation accentuated the shabbiness of the Easterns' house, which sat forlornly on thirty-two perches like a bag lady.

"You have a seat, Clare," said Susan, standing up. "I'll get you your flat white. I was just going to order myself a second cup. Does anyone else want anything?"

Joanna asked for another skinnychino, but Wendy shook her head. For some reason the coffee tasted strange. The brew was so bitter and strong it was beginning to make her feel nauseous.

Clare stood beside the table. She opened her mouth, as if to say something to Susan, but Susan was already pushing through the other customers at the doorway to the cafe.

Wendy observed Clare standing beside the table in her sun-glasses and noticed that she slouched a little, as if she was tired too. Even so, thought Wendy, even with all the stress of this mess heaped on her shoulders, she still looked good. Clare was tall and slim. Wendy recalled Joanna lamenting that, when she stood beside Clare, she felt even shorter and dumpier than usual. But, Wendy mused, Clare's allure was not wholly related to her physical attributes. No, she also had an innate sense of style.

It wasn't that Clare's clothes were particularly fashionable. Most of the time, especially lately, she seemed rather hurriedly put together. It didn't matter, thought Wendy. Whatever Clare wore looked right on her. It was the combinations she used, drawing in the disparate parts to create something harmonious. Beautiful even.

Today Clare's honey-colored hair was hastily gathered at the nape of her neck with a clip. Large sections of it fell out and floated around her face but the overall effect was whimsical rather than messy. And although the sleeveless beige dress she wore over her white T-shirt was crushed and obviously unironed, Clare had wrapped a string of odd-shaped wooden beads around her neck to serve as a distraction. The trick worked, and the illusion was complete. Wendy knew that Clare had probably picked up those beads in a thrift shop. Clare could do things like that and get away with it.

Clare tried to pull out her chair, but the legs were entwined with the empty chair next to Susan's, and Clare had to yank her chair hard to pull it free. The other chair slid back and fell sideways then, scraping along the paving. Clare picked it up and sat down. Taking off her sunglasses, she began rubbing her eyes with her fists. When she lifted her head, Wendy saw that the skin around her brown eyes was puffy and red. Smiling weakly at Clare, Wendy searched her mind for a safe topic of conversation. She didn't want to talk about Evelyn or Amy, so she launched into a conversation with Joanna about the latest preschool fund-raising drive. They were discussing the virtues of Lamington cakes compared to chocolate snowballs when Susan returned with the coffee.

"God! You look a sight, Clare. Are you getting enough sleep?"

Clare put her head in her hands and stared dejectedly into her cup. "William slept over last night. I was up with him from two till four."

"What did he want?"

"His mommy."

Joanna sighed audibly and put her hand on Clare's shoulder. "Well, I think you're wonderful, looking after William the way you do. You've got a lot on your plate, covering for Evelyn. How is she, anyway?"

"About the same. They've tried a few different drugs, but she still won't even speak. They'll keep on with the drug therapy for a while, but if that's not successful, they might try electroconvulsive therapy."

"God, I didn't know they still used that!" gasped Joanna.

"Well, apparently they do. Steve's already signed the consent form."

"I'm sorry I haven't been to visit her," said Joanna. "I guess I'm just a bit afraid that I wouldn't know what to say."

"Oh, don't worry, Jo. It's not as if you can have a conversation with her and, you know, when I visit I'm not even sure that she knows I'm there. Still, I feel as if I have to go and see her. Apart from Steve and William, I'm the closest thing to family she's got."

Wendy tried to swallow but her mouth was dry. Her hand

shook as she poured herself a glass of water from the decanter on the table. "If there's anything I can do for you, Clare . . . Shopping? Picking up the kids? I'd be really happy . . . more than happy to do . . . anything."

Clare shook her head. "No . . . no, I'll manage. William's my responsibility. Thanks anyway." Clare tried to smile and, when she spoke, her voice was overly bright. "Hey! Do any of you feel like sharing a piece of cake? I haven't had breakfast yet."

Joanna was quick to respond. "I'd love to but . . ." Wendy saw Susan glare across the table at Joanna. "But . . . I'd better be good. I'm doing the Fat-Trimmers points plan, you see. I've only got eighteen points left for the rest of the day."

"How many points is a slice of carrot cake?" Clare asked.

"About twelve. But don't let me put you off. You're not fat. Go on. Have your cake. I'll eat it with my eyes anyway."

"I'll share a piece with you," said Wendy, springing up, happy to help Clare out in some small way and anxious to relieve the tight feeling she got in her chest whenever they spoke about Evelyn. "My treat," she said, picking up her purse and walking inside the cafe.

When Wendy returned with the cake, Susan was shaking her head at Joanna. "You can't just starve yourself, you know. You have to exercise. You should come to aqua-aerobics with me."

"When do you do aqua? I've got Sam to look after during the day."

"Seven o'clock on Saturday nights. It's my 'me' time. Richard stays with the kids. The whole session only takes an hour so I'm back in time to put the kids to bed."

"I might give it a go," said Joanna, stroking Sam's blond head. Sam leaned back on her and began to suck his thumb. He was tired, and his eyes began to close.

Wendy pulled her chair closer to Clare's so they could share the cake. She hadn't thought she was hungry. She had planned to toy sociably with her food while Clare ate. As a general rule, Wendy tried not to eat cakes or pastries. She found it easier to maintain her figure when she jaded her appetite with a monotonous succession of apples, crackers, and low-fat cheese. But the carrot cake was moist, plumped with currants, and covered in vanilla cream cheese frosting. The spicy aroma seduced her, the frosting melted over her tongue, and, as she ate, Wendy realized she had begun to covet more than her share.

"Are you interested in coming along to aqua-aerobics, Wendy?" Joanna asked.

Wendy swallowed. "Sorry. I work Saturday nights," she said, scooping up another mouthful of cake.

"You didn't use to," said Clare.

"I picked up an extra shift at Mater Mothers. They pay time and a half on the weekends."

"I think if I was a nurse, I'd like to work in the maternity ward," said Joanna. "I'd like to see someone give birth."

Joanna's births had both been emergency caesareans because of her high blood pressure. Wendy's own births had been fairly straightforward, enjoyable even. But, she tried to convince herself, at thirty-nine, she could leave childbearing behind her.

"You know, Joanna," said Susan quietly, "when you're in labor, I don't think the views are all that good from the other end. Since I've had my children, I've realized that there's an evolutionary reason for that huge gestational belly. It obscures your view of what's going on down below!"

Wendy knew that this was Susan's cue. Susan never let a chance go by to tell the birth story to beat all birth stories. It occurred to Wendy that men had fishing stories and women had birthing stories. Well, at least it was a welcome diversion from other more unsettling topics of conversation. And besides, Susan told her story so well.

"Natural childbirth's a mess, Joanna. Really!" Susan leaned conspiratorially across the table. "Just ask Richard. He can tell you all about it. He got the shock of his life when I was having Maxine . . . Of course," she said, sinking back into her seat, "you've all heard this story before . . ." There was a lull, and Susan lowered her eyes. "But, you'll indulge me," she said, looking up and grinning wickedly. "Won't you?" It was less a question than a command.

"Richard couldn't believe all the blood!" Susan began.

Susan was amazing, Wendy thought. Somehow she always found a new angle. A new way into the conversation so that she could tell the same story.

"I couldn't see most of it. The blood. How can anyone see anything over that huge mound? And I certainly wasn't going to ask for a mirror!"

"Lots of women do, you know," Wendy interrupted. "They want to see the baby crowning."

"I can't understand why," said Susan abruptly. She reached across the table and clutched Joanna's wrist. "Honestly," she implored, her wide eyes fixed and shining, "the whole thing is completely catastrophic and totally uncontrollable.

"I remember yelling, after a particularly bad contraction, 'How much longer do I have to put up with this crap?' And you know, I can still hear Richard's prudish whisper in my ear. 'Hush, darling! Not much longer. Be brave . . .'" Susan released Joanna's wrist, and her hands cut wildly through the air. "'Fuck you!' I screamed at him. 'I've been going fifteen hours! Tell me when it's going to stop.'"

Wendy couldn't help but be drawn in by Susan's story even though she'd heard it many times before. The drama was in the way she told it. It was as if she were reliving the whole ordeal again.

"And then came the urge to bear down. Huge seismic thrusts. But at least I felt like I could actually do something then. I could push. I was in control. And did I ever push. I pushed so hard I pooed myself.

"It was the shit that got Richard. He fainted. Keeled right over, and knocked the obstetrician and the instrument trolley to the floor. What a fuss everyone made of him. Never mind me!" Susan waved her arms around for dramatic effect. "Hey! I'm over here everybody! I'm about to have a bloody baby."

Wendy watched Clare fighting the urge to laugh. Despite the way things were, none of them could help laughing at Susan's story. Mostly they laughed *with* her, but they also laughed *at* her— just a little. Something about the idea of Susan briefly losing her control over the situation in the labor ward struck them as funny.

"Then I felt her crowning, and no one was anywhere near me. I certainly wasn't going to wait for them to glove up again. So I lunged over as far as I could, and would you believe it? I delivered her myself. I caught her with my own hands." Susan looked down at her hands incredulously, then she returned to her audience. "I even had the presence of mind to look at the clock. It was 6:15 *A.M.* What do you think of that?"

"It really is a sensational story," said Clare, finishing her last mouthful of cake. "You should write in to one of those parenting magazines. They'd pay you for it."

"I've thought about it, but Richard would be too worried that the story would reflect badly on him."

"You could be anonymous," said Joanna.

"I don't believe in being anonymous."

"Well," said Clare thoughtfully, "I admire your presence of mind. You were really together even when you were about to give birth. With Sophie it all felt kind of surreal, like the whole thing was happening to someone else. And as soon as she was born she screamed and screamed. I felt so numb that I gave her to David to hold while I watched her yelling and pummeling her fists into the air. All I could think was, 'Oh my God. What have I done?'"

"We all think that, Clare," said Susan. "I didn't sleep for two nights after Maxine was born. The first night I was too pumped full of endorphins to sleep, and the second night, when I was totally exhausted, Maxine screamed for hours because she was hungry, and the milk wasn't in. I remember thinking, The rest of my life is going to be dominated by this child's demands." Susan laughed cynically. "A pretty accurate assumption really!"

"You know, no matter what any of you say, I really regret not seeing my boys being born," said Joanna, planting a kiss on Sam, who was asleep against her breast. "After Jake was born, it was a day before I was well enough to see him. Eventually, a nurse wheeled me into the special care nursery, and I just sat there, looking at him, so small in the incubator.

"His skin was red and raw, and he was lying on his tummy, with his tiny face turned to the side. Completely naked, of course, except for a little blue hat. There were all these tubes everywhere, and he looked . . . I guess he looked like a red frog in a beanie, but all I could think was, He's the most beautiful thing—is he really mine? I kept thinking that someone was going to tell me to push off and leave their baby alone. When the nurse wrapped him up and put him into my arms, I just cried. I never wanted to let him go. Never."

Clare and Susan were silent. Wendy watched them looking at Joanna with glazed eyes. Joanna blushed, rubbed her cheek against her son's head, and stared across the table to the space beside Clare. Wendy followed Joanna's gaze and saw, in Evelyn's place, the hard metal outline of the empty chair.

Swimsuits for Babes

JOANNA STOOD IN THE CHANGING ROOM GAZ-ing at her thighs. The diet wasn't working. She had not shed a single pound in five weeks. She tried to smooth out the pouches of fat that pocked her thighs. Each little curve and hollow seemed highlighted by the fluorescent lighting in the cubicle. It was a wonder they sold any swimsuits at all. She tugged the navy costume down over her bum, but it kept riding up into a wedgy. Size sixteen was still too small. She would have to try a different shop. A shop where they sold fat clothes. She had only tried on this one so that she could get away from the shop assistant.

The kid was very thin, very blond, and very young. She had smiled at Joanna when she had walked in to browse.

"Hi, can I help you?" She stood next to Joanna and flashed her perfect teeth. She wore a tiny black midriff top with a pair of stretch denim jeans, and Joanna found herself staring at the cubic zirconia that shone in her navel.

"Um, I . . . I need a swimsuit."

The girl put her head on one side and raised her eyebrows. "For you or a friend?"

It was an odd question. Why would anyone try to buy a swimsuit for a friend? It was hard enough trying to find one for yourself. "For me . . . I thought a dark color might . . ."

The girl screwed her tiny nose and bit her lip. She said, very softly, "Sorry . . . Maybe if you try two shops up. I think Spawning Time might . . ."

"Spawning Time?" What was this kid talking about?

"They have some groovy maternity wear there."

"Maternity wear?"

"Yes, how far gone are you?" The girl patted her own flat tummy.

Bloody hell. The kid thought she was pregnant. Joanna shook her head. "I'm not pregnant!"

"You're not? Oh, I am sorry." The girl giggled nervously and spun around. "Let me see what I can find."

The girl proceeded to raid the racks. Flicking back hanger after hanger while Joanna stood, red-faced, trying to recover her composure. "What would she know anyway," she told herself. "Why, she'd only be about eighteen."

Finally, the girl found a navy blue one-piece. "Do you think this might suit? It's a sixteen and quite a big make."

Joanna glanced at the tiny piece of fabric hanging limply on the hanger. "Thanks," she said, grabbing it and charging into the fitting room, pulling the curtain shut behind her.

The more Joanna looked at her body in the mirror, the more deflated she felt. She knew she was overweight but she didn't realize she looked like she was gestating something. The problem with mirrors in fitting rooms was that they went all the way round. Suddenly, Joanna saw herself from every angle. She saw the way her rounded belly came out farther than her boobs. She saw the way her upper arms had an extra roll of loose fat, and she noticed for the first time her double chin. She bent over and peeled the tight suit off her skin and saw the way the bits of her that had been held in place by the swimsuit fell back to their natural gravity-friendly positions. She didn't have a full-length mirror at home. Was that a subconscious decision to avoid looking at too much of her body at once? At least it meant that, until now, she'd been able to maintain some shreds of vanity.

She dressed again in her striped T-shirt and elasticized shorts and gave the swimsuit back to the girl. "Thank you," said Joanna. "But I think I'll keep looking."

"Okay." The girl bit the side of her lip and looked apologetic. "I'm sorry about that gaffe I made before."

"That's all right." Joanna forced a smile.

"I guess I've just got pregnancy on my mind lately. You see," she leaned over toward Joanna's ear, "I'm four months in myself."

Joanna stared at the diamond-studded belly button. How was it possible that this girl was pregnant? Was there really a fetus growing behind that flat stomach? Joanna imagined the girl in the final month of her pregnancy. She imagined the tight rounded abdomen and the cubic zirconia butting forward where her navel pushed out like the cut stem of an orange.

"Do you have any kids?" asked the girl.

"Yes, two. My eldest boy just started preschool this year. I've still got my baby at home though."

"They grow so fast, don't they? My little girl's in grade one."

This child-woman had a baby older than Jake. Joanna was incredulous. She readjusted her shoulder bag. "Well, I better get going."

"Yes, of course, sorry again. I should know how hard it is to lose that pregnancy tummy. It took me two months to get back into my size ten jeans after Cassie was born. How old's your baby?"

Joanna edged toward the door. "He's three," she said over her shoulder.

Out in the mall again, Joanna concentrated on her breathing.

She must try to forget her embarrassment. It wasn't often that Tom offered to babysit the boys on a Saturday morning so that she could go shopping. She was here to enjoy herself. She walked past the window of Spawning Time and glanced at the thin mannequins in the window. Anorexic models with little fiberglass bellies just pushing out the swimwear in the right places. She remembered herself when she was pregnant with Sam and pictured herself next to the models in the window. She had been huge. Huge legs, puffy ankles, varicose veins. She wouldn't have sold any swimsuits.

She tried on a red suit in the Big Is Beautiful section of Myer. She bought it because it fitted and because, being the beginning of autumn, it was reduced to half price. Then she thought she'd cheer herself up by buying some makeup.

"Can I help you?" A middle-aged woman with perfect skin and a sleek brown bob approached her.

"Yes, I thought I'd buy some new makeup. I haven't bought anything since my boys were born so . . ."

"Time for a splurge then." The woman's green eyes glinted and narrowed. She was on commission, and Joanna looked like a sure thing. "We've just released a new range especially designed for busy moms like yourself, and if you spend sixty dollars or more on cosmetics in our range, you get the starter pack: beauty bar, cleanser, and moisturizer free. How does that sound?"

"Great."

"Well, what do you need?"

Joanna chose some beige makeup base, a fuchsia pink lipstick, and a pale pink blush.

"Oh, what a shame, that comes to just under sixty dollars at $57.95. Is there anything else you need? I'd hate to send you home without the gift. It's such good value."

Joanna pondered a moment. She began to feel as though she was being conned. There really wasn't anything else she needed, but she chose a waterproof mascara.

"Excellent! That takes you up to $73.90. Now before I get the gift pack, we need to have a closer look at your skin to see what skin type you are."

The woman laid a mirror down on the counter and Joanna looked into it, her cheeks saggy and her eyelids hanging flaccidly downward, with her grey eyes receding back behind them. The mirror magnified everything. Joanna peered into her own eyes with a small measure of resignation. It could only get worse. She was thirty-six.

The saleslady shook her head. "Thank goodness we've caught you in time," she said. "You could certainly use some work on your face. I think we should give you the starter pack for dry skin. And may I suggest some of our wrinkleless eye cream. You'll see the results in days, and it will certainly help to reduce that puffiness you've got there."

"How much is that?"

"Well, it is a little pricey. It's new, and the latest technological research has gone into developing the product. But I believe it's worth it." She fished around under the counter and brought up a tiny mauve jar. "It's $27.95 at the moment." The woman smiled and nodded at Joanna. Joanna swallowed. "Oh well. I'll try it." Maybe the woman was right. Maybe she had let herself go.

The woman quickly ran all the items through the till. "I don't think you'll be sorry. It will take years off your face. I use it sparingly every night." Joanna looked at the woman's smooth complexion and nodded. "Let's see . . . That comes to $101.85. And don't forget, you've got our free starter pack as well. Will that be cash or credit?"

47

Leaving the shop, Joanna clutched her bags tightly. She had bought a swimsuit and some makeup. She'd spent nearly two hundred dollars on herself. Why, then, did she feel so deflated? As she approached the Fiddler Cafe, where Susan was meeting her for lunch, the smell of roasting coffee reminded her how desperately hungry she felt. Hungry for cake.

Susan was already on her second cappuccino. She waved at Joanna, and a flash of white appeared between her ruby red lips. Joanna could never understand why superthin, superorganized, raven-haired Susan wanted to be her friend. She liked to think Susan appreciated her down-to-earth sense of humor, but she had a nagging suspicion that perhaps being around fat, sloppy Joanna made Susan feel better about herself. For Susan was beautiful, in the way that thin, immaculately groomed women are beautiful, at least to other women. Moreover, Susan, a full-time mother like Joanna, was clever.

Susan had graduated from university with honors in English literature, whereas Joanna had left school at the end of grade ten and found a secretarial job in an office in town. Despite their different backgrounds, they had found common ground in their devotion to mothering. However, while raising children was second nature to Joanna, motherhood was an acquired skill for Susan.

Susan had once told Joanna that she didn't know how to relate to her children. She said that she had no "maternal instinct." It was, she'd reflected, "a deficiency akin to a chromosomal defect." Joanna had caught the gist of what Susan was trying to tell her, but she'd never been one for big words—chromosome, that had something to do with biology, didn't it? Did it even matter? Joanna knew that Susan would overcome any problems she faced with sheer bloody-mindedness.

When it came to motherhood, Susan did her research. She

read every book on parenting and child psychology available in the Western world, then applied whatever guiding principles she had gleaned to her children. Susan set boundaries, rigidly maintained routines, and attended to her children's immediate needs with the energy of a zealot.

Joanna was awestruck. Susan had a professional approach to child-rearing, while she, on the other hand, only used her intuition to guide her. For the most part, Joanna felt she was doing a reasonable job as a mother. Her love for Jake and Sam was completely organic, and she found it easy to be demonstrative toward them. Sometimes, though, Joanna felt inadequate when she watched Susan enthusiastically putting some theory of child psychology into practice. Then, Joanna sensed the overwhelming force of Susan's maternal love and forgot about the insecurity that inspired its savage expression.

When they'd met at a community playgroup, not long after Jake was born, it was Susan, rather than Joanna, who had fostered their unlikely friendship. Susan was the one with older children and yet, over the years, she continually asked for Joanna's opinion on dealing with everything from tantrums and potty training to sibling rivalry. Of course, in talking to Joanna about mothering, Susan would expound the approach of whatever child "expert" she was currently reading. Joanna often thought Susan was lecturing her. She never contemplated the possibility that Susan might actually admire her, even envy her.

Susan was a great advocate of mothers staying at home with their children. Joanna supposed that Susan's commitment had something to do with her upbringing. Susan always said that she came from a "broken home." That is what she called it, even though her parents chose to stay together. Her mother, a doctor, had worked long hours, leaving Susan and her father pretty much on their own. Susan had resented her mother's disinterest in her, and she had been determined that she would have a different relationship with her own children.

"Any luck?" Susan asked, as Joanna sat down.

"I found some swimsuits, but it was the most humiliating experience of my life."

Susan listened sympathetically as Joanna recounted her ordeal, and, when Joanna had finished, Susan's eyes glistened mischievously. "Oh well," she said, "that's why we're going to aqua-aerobics tonight, isn't it? You can only achieve so much with diet alone. You need to exercise to really lose weight."

"I hope you're right. It would be so nice to shop for clothes anywhere I wanted to."

"Of course I'm right! Once you get your metabolism working a bit faster, that fat's just going to melt away. You'll see. Now, shall I order for us?" Susan jumped up. "I was going to have a turkey and cranberry bagel. How about you?"

Joanna looked into the glass display cabinet. There was a large hummingbird cake sitting on a stand. One piece had been removed, and Joanna saw that the banana-and-pineapple concoction was filled with cream and what looked like a mango puree. There was thick cream cheese frosting sliding languidly down the side of the cake. Joanna imagined her mouth melting around the sweetness . . .

Susan moved between Joanna and the display cabinet. All Joanna could see were her thin hips in her black Country Road boat pants. "Joanna?" Susan clicked her tongue and shook her head.

"The bagel sounds good," said Joanna with a sigh.

That evening, Joanna put on her new red suit and climbed up onto the bathtub ledge so that she could see her bottom half in the mirror over the vanity basin. At least it had some coverage. She tucked in some stray pubic hairs and stepped down. The little lilac bottle of miracle cream sitting on the vanity lured her closer. She picked it up. "Apply sparingly around the eye area before bed for dramatically reduced puffiness and wrinkles." Thoughtfully, she screwed open the lid. The product inside was lilac too. Soft and creamy and slightly scented. Joanna put a little on her finger and rubbed it around her eye, noticing, not for the first time, how loose the skin was there. Her eyes were becoming hooded. When did that start? She dipped into the jar again and rubbed some eye cream around her other eye. Her eyes began to water. She must have got some cream in them. She ignored the watering. Susan was waiting to be picked up. Joanna pulled on her shorts, grabbed her towel and her keys, and walked out to the living room to kiss Jake and Sam good-bye.

The boys were building a Duplo city with their father. She squinted to see a magical city melting over the red Persian rug. Green buildings trembled over red bridges with fuzzy edges. Yellow splodges, which must have been Jake's cars, lay scattered about.

Jake was wearing his Wiggles pajamas and the spotted dinosaur vibrated across his chest. "Your eyes look funny, Mom," he said. "They're all red."

The large blurred shape of Tom turned toward her. "He's right, love. Have you got something in them?"

Joanna wiped her eyes with her towel. "I think I must have got some of my new eye cream inside my eye. It'll be okay in a minute. See you later. I've got to pick Susan up."

Sam ran toward her and wrapped himself around her legs. "I wanna go with you," he yelled.

Tom laughed as he prized his son's hands free of Joanna's

knees. "Come on, Sam, let's build a rocket ship before bed, eh?" He picked him up while he kissed Joanna good-bye. "Have fun."

Joanna drove through the hazy suburban streets to Susan's house. The streetlights glowed fantastically, like gigantic white orbs, their rays spidering out into the dark. Street signs leaned toward her with words and numbers readable only in her memory, and the area around her eyes grew so itchy that she only ever had one hand on the steering wheel, the other one engaged in frantic rubbing.

Susan opened the door, and the car was illuminated. "My God! What's happened to you? Your face is a mess."

Joanna groped blindly for the tissues in the glove box. "I think I'm having an allergic reaction to my eye cream."

"Here," said Susan, opening Joanna's door. "You better let me drive. When we get to the pool, you can wash out your eyes in the shower."

The shower helped, and by the time Joanna got home after the aqua-aerobics class, her face was looking almost normal. She showered again, leaning her body against the wall and letting the hot water run down her back. Every muscle felt stretched and sore. She wasn't used to exercise. She put on her pink nightie and climbed into bed beside Tom. It was after ten, but Tom was only pretending to be asleep. He rolled over and pushed up her nightdress, running his hand over her belly and up to squeeze her breast.

"So, did you have a nice day?" he asked.

Joanna remembered that Tom had been looking after the kids most of the day, while she'd been to the shops, out to lunch, then to aqua-aerobics. She felt she owed it to him to be quiet about her shitty day and show some gratitude. She turned toward him and kissed him.

"Yes. Thank you. It's been exhausting though."

Tom rubbed her buttocks and kneaded the flesh between his hands.

"How exhausting?" He was pulling her nightie off now and pushing his body against her. He pushed his penis between her thighs, and she felt the warm hardness of it. It was so familiar to her. She'd never slept with anyone else. It was easier to give in now. She hugged him.

"Come on then, but you'll have to be on top."

He moved and poised himself above her, supporting his weight on his arms, his large stomach hanging beneath him and pressing on hers. "Are you sure you're not too tired?"

She ran her hand through his wavy brown hair and looked into his long-lashed hazel eyes. "It's okay. I don't mind," she said.

He kissed her mouth and pushed inside her. "You know I love you." He began to thrust.

"I love you too."

As their bodies rubbed against each other, the familiar squelching noise of two warm moist mounds of flesh meeting reached a crescendo. The image of Tom thrusting against an inflatable pool came to Joanna's mind, and she could not shake it. That's what their lovemaking always sounded like. He came before she could and sank into her. "God, you're gorgeous," he said.

She felt his semen run from her onto the bed. "Did you come?" he asked.

"No, but it doesn't matter. I think I'm too tired anyway."

"Are you sure? I could kiss you there if you like."

"No, don't worry. I still enjoy feeling you come. I'll just have a quick shower, then we can snuggle up."

"Okay. Don't be too long."

When Joanna got back to bed Tom was asleep. She was beyond tiredness now. Restless. Hungry. An image of hummingbird cake came into her mind. She crept out of bed, stepping over the nightdress that Tom had tossed onto the floor, and walked naked through the house out to the kitchen. She knew it was madness, but she just had to make herself one of those cakes. Just to smell it cooking. Just to have a tiny taste of the raw batter.

She didn't turn the light on in the kitchen. She couldn't bear either the kitchen or her own body to be defined by the stark white fluorescent beam. Instead, she turned on the light in the hall and moved about in the soft colorless room where edges were blurred and where red Formica countertops did not assault her senses. Looking out the window above the sink, she saw that the mild autumn night was softened by a full moon. She opened the window and let the moon flow in. The moonlight trickled over her body, gleaming on her full breasts, shimmering around the curve of her belly, shining against her buttocks. She was beautiful in the moonlight. The full-bodied moon took some narcissistic pleasure in her figure, lingering over her skin, delighting in the shape of her womanliness. Entwined in its pale embrace, with her own anticipation warding off the slight chill in the air, she began.

She placed quantities of soft butter and delicate brown sugar in her large ceramic mixing bowl and caressed them with her wooden spoon until they relented. She created, quietly, patiently, a softness, a suppleness, a drooping texture that slid from the spoon into the bowl, relaxed and easy. She broke eggs deftly, with one hand, the delicate shells held away from the bowl, and the yolks descending, slowly drawing in their long clear strands of albumen. She added bananas, bruised and tender, along with crushed pineapple, before finally she folded in the flour and the pungent grounds of cinnamon and nutmeg with slow, gentle strokes until the mixture was just combined. She took her spoon out of the bowl. It was ready.

She put her finger in the batter, stroked it, felt it give way. She raised a smear on her finger, closed her eyes, and put it in her mouth, pressing her moist lips around her finger, taking in the sweet batter on the tongue. It was ecstasy. It was enough.

While the cake was cooking, she made the frosting as she stood beside the warm oven. Passionfruit, cream cheese, and frosting sugar, beaten by hand until her arm was tired and the frosting was smooth and yellow, flecked with little black seeds. By now the kitchen benches were covered in flour and sugar and batter. Tiredness overwhelmed her as the tropical odors of pineapple and banana overflowed from the oven and soothed her. She stood over the bowl, licking it with her fingers, scraping every last bit of batter away. She washed up. It took a long time to clean the kitchen. Her body seemed to be slowing down. She looked at the glowing red digits of the oven clock. It was nearly midnight. She brought the cake out of the oven and breathed in the smell of her own baking. The cake was warm and risen and golden brown. It smelled of fruit and spices. Perfect.

For a moment she thought of cutting a slice, or a slab even, frosting it and wolfing it down. No one need ever know. But she was strong. Besides, licking the batter had satiated her appetite, and the desire was gone. She wondered how many points were in cake batter. Then she resolved not to bother counting points during moonlight baking sessions. She wrapped the cake tightly in Glad wrap and wrote *Hummingbird Cake—March 30* on a sticky label. She looked at the clock again and rubbed out the 0 and changed it to 1. Then she wrapped the whole cake in foil and wedged it in the deep freeze, somewhere between the pumpkin syrup cake she'd made last week and the mud cake she'd made at the end of February, after Amy disappeared. She put the frosting in one of her last remaining Tupperware containers of an appropriate size, shoved it in the freezer, and went back to bed.

She snuggled naked next to Tom's warm body and closed her eyes. The house was still full of the smell of cake. That was how she liked it. Sleep drifted toward her, carried in the aroma of the hummingbird cake, and she cut herself a slice at last and closed her eyes.

VISITORS

I SIT IN THE FRONT OF MY CAR BITING MY thumbnail down to the quick and staring at the concrete greyness that surrounds me. What am I going to say to her now that I am here? I came ready to shame her for her treatment of William, of Steve, and even of me, but now I am actually outside the hospital, my bravado has disappeared. In the back of my mind, I hear my mother's voice, "Clare, don't be so inconsiderate! After all the poor girl's gone through, show a bit of sympathy. Please!"

I wish my mother was still alive. She would know how to handle Evelyn. She would cajole and soothe and comfort. And I would watch with jealous, pouting lips, just as I used to do when we were children, when Evelyn seemed to be stealing the maternal affection that rightfully belonged to me.

Back then, Evelyn would come into our house, complaining of some little scrape or cut or some petty injustice I had done to her, and my mother would enfold her in her arms. Mom was never too busy or too tired for Evelyn. Mom would hold Evelyn when she cried and never even mind that Evelyn's nose was running and had left little snotty trails on her best dress. And when Evelyn was finished weeping, and happily sitting at the kitchen table with a cup of sugary tea, Mother would come and cup her hands around my face. "Why such a sad sack, Clare? You've got no reason to feel so miserable. No reason at all."

I sigh over my recollections, and as I reach under the seat for my handbag, I feel the guilt creep through me again. As a child I always felt so damn guilty around Evelyn. Guilty when I didn't want to play with her and Mom had to insist, guilty when I refused to walk with her to school, guilty when I opened presents on my birthday in front of her.

On my sixth birthday, Mom and Dad gave me a beautiful Cry Baby Sue doll with sky blue eyes that really closed and curly blond hair you could brush. If you fed her from her special bottle, she cried real tears. I carted her around with me all day and put her carefully back in her box before I went to bed. When I got up the next morning, she was gone. We looked everywhere for that doll but we never found it. I knew that it was Evelyn who took it. Out of jealousy? Out of spite? She never owned up to it, and Mom, out of kindness, never forced her confession. On my seventh birthday, Mom bought me a Sweetheart Barbie doll and gave Evelyn another one, exactly the same.

Well, I decide, clutching the handle of the car door, perhaps it is time Evelyn shouldered some guilt. She can't just do God knows what with her baby girl, dump William on me, and retreat into some form of psychosis. She just can't get away with it anymore. For the first time in my life I admit to myself that I actually don't want to be "nice" like my mother. Sorry, Mom, but we've all suffered too much for the sake of Evelyn's disturbed childhood. To hell with guilt! I take a deep breath and open the car door. It is time to face her. I want to break her, and I decide that the best way to do that is to confront her about her responsibilities to her son.

I walk into the ward and register my name at the desk. It's a secure ward, and the nurse accompanies me down the white-walled corridor. The whiteness of the space makes me feel uneasy. Like an empty canvas, the space is soulless, a backdrop for whatever raw emotion is projected onto it—fear, dread, anger, hate. The nurse smiles thinly and lets me inside Evelyn's room.

She is sitting in the corner in her lilac nightdress, her face pale and sunken. Her wiry auburn hair cascades down her shoulders. If I were to paint her hair, I would use a blend of magenta and a touch of cadmium yellow. For a moment she seems to register my face and her emerald green eyes stare at me, but then her gaze recedes, turns inward, and her eyes become as lifeless as two small stones.

"Hello, Evelyn," I say in a lighthearted voice as if nothing at all has happened. I sit down and pull my chair closer to hers.

"I thought that I'd come and chat to you about William. It's been a while since you've seen him, and you must be wondering . . ." She is watching me. She is watching my mouth open and close, but is she hearing what I am saying?

"Tomorrow I am going to take William and Sophie to the museum. William told me that he's never been there before. I wonder why you've never taken him. Sophie just loves the place!"

Evelyn turns her head away and looks out the window, but I see that her fists are clenched and her knuckles are white and I am motivated to continue my monologue in the hope that some of what I say will permeate her thoughts.

"Of course, I suppose you have your reasons for not taking him to the museum, and maybe I should try and work out what those reasons might be. Perhaps you'd like to tell me? You could save me some trouble . . .

"Well then, I'll take your silence as acquiescence. I thought we'd go early in the morning. There will be less of a crowd." I keep rambling because there is something flickering in the corner of her eye. I hear my mother's words again, playing on my conscience. "Clare, how can you be so cruel?" Shut up, Mom! It's not only Evelyn who's hurting now.

"After we go to the museum we might do a bit of shopping. Steve gave me some money to buy William a few new pairs of track pants. Last year's ones are far too short. He's grown half an inch in less than three months—since you've been here. Steve measured him the other day, against the door frame in your kitchen. He's big for his age, isn't he?"

Of course Evelyn does not respond. I can see, however, that she hears at least some of what I say because she begins rubbing her clenched fists up and down her thighs.

"He might be tall but he's still only five. He really misses you, Evelyn. He cries at night. During the day he's quiet. Sophie bosses him around a lot, and he never complains. But when he's sleeping over with us, and I walk past his room, I can hear him sobbing. It's too much for him to bear, Evelyn. He misses you, and he misses Amy too. If only you could tell us where she is."

She is biting her lip now and rocking back and forth in her chair, her fists still clenched and her eyes still staring out the window.

"Of course, you of all people should know what missing someone is like. How old were you when . . . ?"

She looks at me. Stares at me with cold, hard, emerald eyes and puts her hands over her ears so that she can't hear any more. All the time she is rocking back and forth in her chair and I can hear a strange high-pitched whine, not really a human noise, more like the soft drone of an insect. Where is the noise coming from? I look along the window ledge to see if there's a bug trapped inside, trying to get out, but there is nothing. I search

Evelyn's face, which is blank and expressionless now, and I realize that Evelyn is making the noise herself, behind her teeth.

CLARE IS HERE. IN THE ROOM. SITTING ON THE the green vinyl chair where Steve sits when he comes. She talks. Am I listening? Sometimes I hear words among words. These words are not mine. They are not the ones I seize and squash as they float through my mind like bits of refuse on a still sea. The words belong to Clare. She expects me to listen as I used to do. She talks to my face like she used to do, and she doesn't see that I am not inside my green eyes. I am behind her, hanging suspended into nothingness. I am the fly with the brittle wings trapped in the web behind her head. I am motionless, and the blood is dried up inside me. Soon I will break, piece by piece, into the air and make dust on the floor because the spider that meant to eat me couldn't be bothered. The dust will be wiped up by the cleaning lady with the pink socks and the dirty fingernails. Tomorrow.

Tomorrow. What is it that Clare is saying about tomorrow? She is talking about William. My son. How strange that a fly who is brittle and bloodless should have a son. A son made of flesh and blood. She is taking William to the museum tomorrow. The museum. The words make me want to pull away the threads that bind me and fly into her face. Not the museum. Don't take my flesh-and-blood child to that place of dried skins stretched over bones. He might as well come and see me here. But I don't want that either. That is why I've left him with you. You are someone who is alive.

Clare sees that I have come back into my old body. She sees that I am in front of her now, and she keeps on talking about William. She tortures me more than my analyst, and her words punch my ears.

Big. She says he is big. The moment he turned five he was bigger than me. How could I mother him after he turned five? My mother went away when I was four, and I haven't had a birthday since then.

Missing. This word bothers me. Who is it that is missing? I am missing. That is true. I am not where they come to find me. I am suspended in the spiderwebs that hang from the ceiling. Some days I am a fly. Some days I am a beetle. Some days I am a moth. I am never the spider. That is someone else.

Missing. What? William is not missing. He is with you. Remember? He is with you so that he can keep on growing. He can grow past me now that he is with you. I never knew how to take him any further. And Steve was always too busy. Like my own father. Too busy to bother.

Missing. The word continues to fire. Missing me. Of course William is missing me, but please don't bring him here. The person he is missing is not here, and William would not recognize the fly or the beetle or the moth. He would not love the insects I've become. He will love you. In time, Clare, he will love you. And, when he does, there will be no need for me even to be an insect on the wall. And you will love him too. Just like you love Sophie. You will be his mother then. You will be a good mother just like your mother was.

Missing. The baby is missing, you say? What baby? I don't have a baby anymore. She is gone. Please go. You are hurting my head. You are making it ache, and the sounds you make keep coming even when your mouth is shut. The sounds spin inside my head and spike through rememberings I buried long ago. Rememberings of Mother. I do not want to remember Mother. I must not remember the day she went missing . . .

Missing. The day has been full of sun and cicadas. Mother

62

gives me a plate full of snacks—frosted cookies, watermelon, salami sandwiches—and I sit by the letterbox and wait for my father. I eat my food and wait. I make a fairy house out of a ring of pebbles on the concrete path, and I wait. Daddy doesn't come. The sun bleeds into the clouds, and I am tired of waiting. I look in the kitchen, the bedroom, the bathroom, but she is . . .

Missing. I cannot find her grey shape anywhere in the dark house. I have tears in my eyes, and I run. I run down the back steps. The paling door to the laundry under the house is locked but I know where the dog squeezes through. It is dark under the house. It is dark and spidery but, in the darkness, I can just make out the grey shape of Mother. She is hanging. She is hanging on her own thread from the beams under the house. She is a spider. I touch her shoe, and it falls off. Her foot is still warm. I pick up the shoe and squeeze under the palings and I run.

I run to the rose garden, and I break all Mother's rosebushes with her own shoe. I break the green stems. I pull off the leaves until my hands are full of thorns. When Clare's mother sees me standing in the rose bed, destroying the flowers, she jumps the fence and runs to me. I am covered in blood and dirt and spiderweb, but Clare's mother holds me close. She takes me home and gives me a bath. Only the dirt and the blood ever washes off.

Stop! Stop! I know who is missing. You are torturing me. How I hate you. Right at this moment I hate you. I do not want to feel any more. I am tired. I am going back to the web. I will thrash until the threads are wrapped around me again. You might as well leave. You can stay and sit if you like, but my visit is over, and it is lonely when you are the only visitor in the room.

I WALK OUT OF THE HOSPITAL DOORS INTO the golden winter sunlight, and I can't shake that strange insect noise that is droning in my ears. I get back into my car and turn the radio on. Classical music floods the car, and the insect noise is drowned out by more melodic sounds. I can't help feeling a small sense of accomplishment because both she and I know that I almost dragged her back today.

When I started talking about William, I caught her off guard. She came back into her face for an instant, and I knew that she heard some of what I said. Her doctor has told us that we mustn't upset her too much. He says that as Evelyn recovers from the shock and stress of whatever has happened, and her medication is adjusted, she will come back to us. She will get better. It will just take time. Until then, she must have peace and quiet and calm. Well, what about Amy? What about William? That little boy cries himself to sleep every night, and Steve is so wrapped up in his own self-pity that he's totally useless. Useless.

I merge onto the overpass with all the traffic, and I think to myself that I can get through to her. I can shake it out of her and find out what happened to Amy. Everyone assumes that Evelyn killed her. The ultimate crime. The bad mad mother, consumed by depression, disposes of her newborn child, then conveniently forgets that she ever had her. Well, I won't let Evelyn escape that easily. I don't think Evelyn killed Amy, although for some reason she'd like us to think she did.

William needs a mother who's not locked up in an institution. No one can replace Evelyn in his eyes. I should think that, of all people, Evelyn would know that. If Evelyn continues her bizarre behavior, however, a psychiatric institution is precisely where she will stay. Even if the police find enough evidence to charge her, she won't be fit to stand trial. She will stay in that psychiatric hospital until we forget she's in there. Until we all stop visiting. Until we just let her go. That's what she wants.

She wants to be left alone. She wants me to raise her child for her. As if I were somehow stronger, more competent, more loving, less exhausted than she. I'm making a mess of it in my own way. No matter what I do, Sophie will grow up slightly damaged because I was too neurotic, too controlling, too cold. But that's not the point, is it? At least I'm doing it. I'm raising my own child. That has to count for something.

God, I need a strong pot of tea. I won't go home yet. It's not quite time to pick up Sophie and William. I think I'll stop at one of those cafes in Rosalie and order a pot of orange pekoe. Maybe I'll splurge and have a piece of cake too. I feel like I need some comforting. It's been traumatic seeing Evelyn again. I wish I could extract her from my life. We are hopelessly entangled, Evelyn and I. I know too much of her past and too little of what goes on inside her head.

I get out of my car at Les Gateaux Grands. Strange, isn't it, that a piece of cake and a cup of tea can be so comforting? Chocolate, oysters, smoked salmon, all those things quicken your desire. But cake? Cake makes you forget. It satiates. Maybe that's what Marie Antoinette meant when she said to the starving peasants, "Let them eat cake." She knew, you see, as only a woman can, the power of a piece of cake and a cup of tea.

CLEANING OUT THE COBWEB

Thursday May 2

10:30 P.M.—CAN'T SLEEP. Writing it all down to try to make some sense of it.

4:00 P.M., last Friday (April 26)
BEG Wendy to let me have the key to clean the Easterns' house while Steve's away for the weekend. Wendy says, "Don't bother!" (Steve doesn't care about house.) INSIST. Argue that state of place is bad for William's physical and emotional health. (Argument appeals to her sense of hygiene as a nurse. So she gives me the key.)

Wendy says, "Susan. It's really good of you to want to help Steve but don't expect him to show any gratitude." SMILE benignly and leave with key. Couldn't give a FIG about Steve. Never liked him. A vain slob when Evelyn was home. Even worse now. Spends most nights sobbing at pub counter while being plied with rum and Cokes by dubious-looking female person. (Behavior witnessed by Richard, after work, at 6:30 P.M. on Friday March 22. Have told Richard that UNDER NO CIRCUMSTANCES is he ever to buy Steve a drink.) Can't abide weakness or stupidity in anyone. Steve obviously thinks he can afford to be spineless and idiotic because he's got Clare to look after his son.

Saturday 27 April
Clean Steve and Evelyn Eastern's house. (Not to be interpreted as act of Good Samaritan but as act of HYGIENE FANATIC OBSESSED by recurring nightmare.)

RECURRING NIGHTMARE = Me, Susan, trapped inside the stifling atmosphere of the Easterns' house. Surrounded by discarded objects, food scraps, life's general refuse. Frantically looking for something. What? Not her. It ought to be. What I'm looking for is an old English literature assignment I did for EN271 at university eighteen years ago. God knows why my final paper is at the Easterns', but I'm filled with dread that if I don't find that assignment, I'll fail the subject. Of course, I never failed anything at university.

Anyway, I'm pushing away furniture. I'm lifting up crates of dusty bottles and stacks of newspaper, trying to find my assignment before the five o'clock deadline. I'm simply positive it's in the house somewhere. It has just been overlooked, and if I can organize the Easterns' mess, I'll find it. But I can never organize the Easterns' mess.

The kitchen benches are full of dirty dishes, stacked in teetering piles. I have to clean up the kitchen because my assignment might be here, wedged underneath some crockery or a heap of rotting food. I need to fill the sink with soapy water so that I can start washing up, but the sink is already full of plates smeared with runny egg. I take them out one by one and balance them carefully on the leaning piles, but when I look back into the sink it's still full. I can never empty it. My task is endless.

I move around the house in circles. Achieving one objective always requires me to initiate another, and somewhere, hiding in this intricate web of refuse, is my final paper. The search seems to consume the hours and when it's nearly five o'clock, I still haven't found my paper. I wake up. I'm covered with sweat, and I know I won't be able to get back to sleep.

Still Saturday, 8:15 A.M.—Richard says he'll look after the kids. (Anything to stop me grumbling about lack of sleep. Says I haven't been this bad-tempered since Laura was a baby.)

8:45 A.M.—Arrive at Easterns' house. Pick up the mail. Letterbox already overflowing. (At least they've stopped delivering the papers. Steve probably hasn't paid the bill in months.) Notice that the grass needs cutting. BADLY.

8:50 A.M.—Stand uneasily outside house. Unable to move for some minutes. Mouth dry. Sensation of SPIDER CRAWLING under shirt. Lift up shirt. Brush at skin crazily and find nothing. (Decide that skin irritation is psychosomatic response to extreme anxiety provoked by appearance of house.)

APPEARANCE OF HOUSE—With its siding-covered facade and closed-in verandahs, the house used to look sad. Now it looks sinister. It's cold and secretive, hiding in a yard full of shadows. It looms. Large and leaning. Is it something to do with the strange tilt it acquired years ago when Evelyn's father had it restumped? Clare told me that after Evelyn's mother hanged herself, Evelyn's dad had the whole house restumped. He didn't raise it and build under like most people did in the seventies. He cut three feet off each support. Clare didn't tell me why, but I can guess.

9:00 A.M.—Finally resolve to stop procrastinating and walk up the front steps.

9:01 A.M.—Notice that Steve still hasn't fixed the front steps! Broken balusters swing and creak in the wind. House needs painting too. All paint is faded or peeled away to a nondescript grey. (No wonder that dark, brooding shape haunts my dreams.)

9:02 A.M.—Open door. TERRIBLE STENCH! Saliva rushes back into my mouth, and I start retching. Damn cat has been locked inside. SHIT and urine all over enclosed verandah. Cat shoots out between my legs and takes off down steps. (I have the urge to call the RSPCA but don't. I know Steve didn't mean to lock the cat in. He's always loved the cat.)

9:10 A.M.—Put on pink rubber gloves. (I wouldn't touch anything in that place without my gloves on.) Open up every window and door in the house. Throw every cushion and rug the cat has shat on, and some it hasn't, down into the yard.

9:20 A.M.—Open up huge standing garbage cleanup bag (INVALUABLE for cleaning at the Easterns'). Pick up eleven empty tins of cat food and throw into bag.

9:30 A.M.—Pour half a bottle of disinfectant into a bucket of

hot water and mop the entire front verandah (VERY SATIS-
FYING).

10.00 A.M.—Enter main house and ponder over where to start.
Decide to start in center of house and work my way around until
I end up on the verandah again.

Firstly—Notice that Easterns' living room is incredibly DARK.
Realize that the only light fixture has blown a bulb. Stand two
minutes while eyes adjust to the dark.

Secondly—Start vacuum cleaner and try to clean the cat hair off
the sofa.

Thirdly—SWEAR because bag is full and the suction won't work.

Fourthly—Stand outside trying to empty bag into overflowing
garbage bin. Have mild allergic reaction to dust and cat hair.

Finally—Vacuum (between sneezing fits). Push couch out into
the middle of the room to vacuum under it. Find bits of pizza,
moldy Play-Doh, rat droppings, spiderwebs, AND one tiny pink
sock. (I cry because I can still see her foot in that sock. At least the
crying helps to clear the dust and cat hair from my sinuses. I wipe
my nose on the sock, then I put the sock in my pocket.)

11:00 A.M.—Take all the clothes that were lying on the floor
down to the laundry and put the first load into the machine.
(Throughout the day I fill the Easterns' entire clothesline with
wet washing. Consequently, the clothesline threatens to cave in,
but doesn't dare.)

11:10 A.M.—Put all the shitty stuff to soak in some bleach in the tub. Notice Evelyn's nappy bucket. It is EMPTY. At least I don't have to deal with that issue.

About 12:30 P.M.—Living room in reasonable state. Don't stop for lunch.

Sometime after 1 P.M.—Strip the bed in William's bedroom. Remake the bed and tidy his toys. (Surprisingly, William's room is the cleanest in the house, although I suppose he's been living more or less with Clare these last few months.)

About 2 P.M.?—Find cigarette butts everywhere in Steve and Evelyn's room. (A couple of them have even left burn marks on Evelyn's dresser. The bedclothes are really rancid, so I throw them out the window, and they land right outside the laundry.) Take everything out from under the bed to vacuum. Feel the need to OPEN up every suitcase they have stashed under there. The need to CLEAN and REORGANIZE. Looking. Searching. (Each time I lift a lid on one of their suitcases, my heart is in my throat. I think I get a bit frenetic because I throw a lot of stuff out of that window that isn't laundry. I notice a big pile of *Playboy*s in a corner of the room. I TOSS them out as well.)

Sometime between 3 P.M. and 5 P.M.—Nearly reaching exhaustion point. Slight dizziness from lack of food. COMPULSIVELY clean the kitchen and spend an eternity washing up. (At least the kitchen isn't as dark as the rest of the house. The window looks out onto that old jacaranda tree in the backyard. It must be pretty in November . . .) Notice ENORMOUS SPIDERWEB outside kitchen window while washing up. There is a big blue butterfly caught in the web. Think about rescuing it, but its wings are so tangled and damaged by the web that the kindest thing might just be to leave it there.

Sixish?—PACKING UP to leave when I remember the little sock in my pocket. (REALLY HARD for me to walk into her room. Have been avoiding it all day.) I open the door to Amy's room. The room is full of the last afternoon sun. WARM AND SERENE. Painted a sunny yellow. And those curtains Evelyn ran up on her machine, with the little purple violets . . . I think she must have known that it was going to be a girl. Open the wardrobe and the tears start to stream down my face. All those lovely little dresses, size 00. Liberty print dresses with smocking, fine cotton sunsuits with matching polly hats . . . She'd bought beautiful clothes for her. Open up the drawers. She must have spent a fortune on baby clothes. Everything is either from David Jones or those expensive children's boutiques in Hamilton. Nothing even looks worn. Heart starts pounding. NONE of these things have been worn. Evelyn NEVER dressed Amy in any of these clothes!

GOD KNOWS WHAT TIME!—EMPTY drawers into the cot and RIFLE through the things. (WHERE are Amy's little Bonds suits? WHERE are her undervests? Her waterproof diaper covers? Her nappies? WHERE is the other pink sock? Where are any of the socks for that matter?) The room contains nothing of Amy's. NOTHING at all. SEARCH on the shelves for the little Dalmatian dog I gave her when she was born. (Evelyn used to put it in the pram with her.) Can't find that either. Finally realize that Amy is not lost somewhere in the house. Not misplaced by a mother with some psychotic postnatal condition who has left her somewhere under a pile of clothes. (Ludicrous really. To let absurd possibilities haunt me like that, when the police must have scoured every inch of that house after she disappeared.)

LATE—Realize that Amy could be anywhere, but she isn't in the house. Probably not dead either. (What would a dead baby want with two dozen nappies? Evelyn bought a stack of them. She said she loved babies in real cloth nappies with nappy pins.)

EVEN LATER—Hands shaking. Stand on the verandah sipping a glass of water. Teeth chattering against glass. Holding that tiny sock in the darkness and seeing her face. Get cramps in my legs from standing so still. It is pitch-black, and I cannot see my watch face. My body shudders, and I realize that I have ABSOLUTELY NO IDEA what the time is. For the first time in my life I have LOST TRACK of the seconds and minutes that make up my day.

SOMETIME BEFORE MIDNIGHT LAST SATURDAY—The police station. Renewed affirmations that they are doing "everything they can." Given a coffee that tastes like the polystyrene cup. Don't show them the sock. Keep it in my pocket, covered with dust and spiderweb. Amy's pink sock.

JEWEL
BEETLES

WHOOSH! THE GIRL'S PLASTIC JAR CAPTURED a piece of the scratchy green world on the trunk of the lemon tree.

"Quickly, William. Quickly! Put the lid on. I've catched it in here. See?"

The boy saw. He slid the red lid awkwardly under the jar with his five-year-old fingers. She upended the jar and pushed the lid down. Snap! Trapped.

The children crouched in the yellow-green garden beside the deeper green shadow of the lemon tree. Their heads were bent together, illuminated by the sun and tousled by the breeze. The boy's sandy brown hair entwined with the red wisps that had wandered from the curls on the little girl's head. They were a world in themselves. A child world where the universe ended at the garden fence, and they were a pair of clumsy giants peering through the jar at their tiny captive. The jewel beetle scuttled across the hard plastic, skidding its tiny black feet over the unfamiliar surface, frantically feeling for the bark where it had been attached in the last moment of time.

"It's bwootiful, Sophie. Look how it shines. I see red, green, blue . . . just like the rainbow on the side of a bubble."

"It's a jewel beetle, William. Remember the museum last week?

We saw lots of jewels. They were all in glass cases and lined up. Let's put ours in a glass case too."

"What does a julie beetle do in a glass case?"

"Nothing, silly. It's dead. It just sits still, and you can look at it and see how pretty it is."

"I don't want to put it in a glass case, Sophie. I don't want it to be dead. Let's put it in a box with some leaves and keep it for a pet."

The boy reached up for the jar, but the girl pulled the prize away and held it above her. The jar caught the sun, and the flash of white light made the boy cower and cover his eyes.

"Mom says you can't keep bugs as pets. Sometimes I keep them overnight in my bug catcher, but after that I've gotta let them go."

"I don't want to let it go. It's too bwootiful. Let me keep it, Sophie. Let me put it in a box and keep it at my house. My dad won't mind. Lots of bugs live in our house already . . ."

The girl held the bug catcher up to her face again, and her green eyes were magnified by the curve of the container. "In the museum there was a tea cozy that was made out of beetle wings. They were sewed on with a needle and looked like sparkly flowers. It took lots and lots of beetle wings to make that tea cozy."

"How did they get all those wings?"

"Oh, I suppose they catched lots and lots of jewel beetles and ripped their wings off." She smiled at him and shook the jar a little so that the beetle landed on its back with six brittle black legs flaying in the air. She laughed.

"Gimme that beetle!" yelled the boy, snatching at the jar again in a futile attempt to save the beetle. "I want to keep it!"

"Well, it's my jar," said the girl, narrowing her green eyes and pouting her pink lips. She opened the jar and shook the beetle onto the grass. He scrabbled on the ground to find it, and when he did, he cupped his hands around it and sat holding it protectively under the lemon tree.

"You can have it," she said, looking down the short distance of her freckled nose. "I'm going to catch a bee. Bees are more fun. I'm going to catch one, then it will make me some honey."

She turned and he watched the hot pink shorts and yellow top disappear around the side of the house. He heard her sneakers crunch over the gravel path, and, finding himself quite alone and removed from her bossiness, he picked himself up and tore some leaves from the lemon tree. The sharp smell of citrus tickled his nose as he stuffed the leaves into the front pocket of his navy shorts, the pocket with the Velcro flap. He looked at the jewel beetle one last time and popped it inside his pocket too. Very gently, he patted the flap shut. "It's all right now, bwootiful julie bug. I'll look after you," he said.

It was nearly lunchtime, and Clare was searching for the other melamine Pooh Bear mug in the plastics drawer. She could never find anything in her plastics drawer, and when she'd finished looking, she could never shut it either. There was always a lunch box lid or a drink bottle top wedged at the back of the cabinet. Finally, she fished out the cup and began looking for Sophie's Teletubbies plate. She found it just as she heard Sophie shrieking in the garden. Her heart thumped, and she dropped Po and Dipsy on the tiles. The crack as the melamine broke accentuated the crescendo of the child's cry as Clare ran outside.

"Sophie! What happened?" Sophie was screaming, her face bright red as she clutched her wrist. Clare saw that at least there was no blood. She couldn't deal with blood.

"The bee bit meeeee!" Sophie sobbed.

Clare gathered her child up into her arms. "Show me! Where, sweet pea?"

Sophie flung her wrist out for her mother to see. Clare pulled out the sting. "Don't cry now, Sophie . . . Shhhhh. That's what happens when you try to catch bees in your bug catcher . . . Shhhhh. I've told you that before. Come on inside now and we'll put an ice pack on it. You and William must be hungry. It's nearly lunchtime."

Clare found an ice pack in the freezer, wrapped it in a tea towel, and pressed it over the bee sting with one hand while she stroked Sophie's curls with the other. The attention, more than the ice, seemed to soothe the child and, after a few minutes of this Clare was able to put William in charge of holding the ice pack while she made lunch.

Sophie and William sat around the little children's table. William quietly sucked his blackcurrant cordial through a straw while Sophie, with a tear-stained face, chomped into her cheese sandwich. Clare felt guilty. Perhaps she should have been keeping a better eye on them. Even Sophie's favorite pink cookies, sprinkled with hundreds-and-thousands, didn't cheer her up.

Clare sipped her tea and ate her cheese and vegetable sandwich. William was unusually quiet, his big brown eyes staring intently at Sophie, one podgy little hand resting, ever so lightly, on the pocket of his navy shorts. Poor thing. It must affect him, losing his baby sister and his mother all in one go . . . Clare tried to think of a small treat that might cheer them up for the afternoon. Then she remembered the little bottle of pink glitter nail polish she'd packed away at the back of her cupboard for Sophie's birthday.

"Here," she said, setting the bottle down on the table between the children. "How about we all paint our nails with this?"

Sophie's face burst into a smile. "Pink polish! I've been wanting that for ages!"

"I know. I thought you might like it now. A little treat to cheer you up."

William looked sadly at the bottle. "My dad says that nail polish is for girls," he said quietly.

Clare put her arm around William. His sandy brown hair fell across his face.

"I'll tell you what we'll do. I'll put some polish on your toenails, William. If you put your own shoes on in the mornings, your dad will never even notice. If he says something to you, just say that Clare said it was okay. All right?"

William smiled and nodded, pleased to be part of the conspiracy.

Clare sat out on the front steps with the children and painted their toenails. They smiled to see the glitter sparkling in the sun.

"My toes look like julie beetles!" cried William, jumping up and down the front steps.

"I want to paint my fingernails myself now, Mommy." Sophie grabbed the bottle and clutched it in her hand.

Clare looked at her daughter's determined face. She didn't want a tantrum. "Well, perhaps, if you're very careful, you can paint your fingernails. I'll get you some newspaper . . ." The phone rang. "Don't open the bottle, Sophie. Wait until I come back," she called over her shoulder.

The girl looked at the pink nail polish glittering in the jar. She picked up the bottle and tried the lid. It came off easily. She pulled out the brush. The nail polish clung to the brush in thick blobs and she got more on her fingers than on her nails. She smiled. The hot pink color was beautiful, and she layered more and more on until it oozed all over her hands.

The boy watched her. "I want some on my nails too."

"You're not allowed," she said matter-of-factly. "Your dad

wouldn't like it. Boys don't wear nail polish on their fingernails." The girl shook her red curls to reinforce the point and pushed her tongue out between her lips while she refocused her attention on the task at hand. She finished her nails and looked around for some other body part to paint. She was enjoying herself.

"I know, let's paint your bottom," she said. "Your dad won't notice it under your pants."

The boy contemplated this proposition for a moment, biting his lip. "Okay," he said, stepping out of his shorts and carefully laying them aside.

"You'll have to take your undies off too," she said, the brush poised ready in her hand.

As the boy pulled down his underpants the girl was confronted with that intriguing object which was usually hidden away inside the boy's pants. She stared at it, hanging limply before her like a pale little sausage . . . She began to paint . . .

"Sophie! What on earth do you think you're doing?"

Two startled faces turned toward Clare. The pink-laden brush slipped out of the girl's hand and fell on the step, splattering pink everywhere. Clare gasped. Sophie was covered in nail polish but that didn't concern her as much as William's predicament. His penis resembled nothing so much as a limp little cocktail frank ready for a toothpick and sauce.

THE PRICK

THE PRICK

"SO HOW DID YOU GET IT OFF, CLARE?" WENDY asked, cupping her hands around her mug to make herself warm. She had taken to drinking herbal teas. She couldn't face coffee anymore.

Clare grimaced. "I used nail polish remover."

"Shit!" said Joanna, gripping Sam tightly around the waist. "That must have hurt!"

Clare shrugged. "I didn't know what else to do. I couldn't take him home to Steve like that, could I? What would he think?"

Susan raised her eyebrow. "I hope you tried a good soak in the bath first."

"Of course I did. Sophie was covered in the stuff as well. I managed to get most of it off her using my loofah and some soap. But I didn't want to scrub away at his little penis."

"Well, you have a point there," Susan said as she tipped a spoonful of sugar into her cappuccino and watched the sugar sink into the froth. "He might develop something Freudian."

Clare shrugged. "Anyway, I had a script to fill so I decided to take the kids up to McIntyre's Pharmacy. I thought that maybe old Gerald would be able to recommend something."

"Gerald's a nice fellow, isn't he?" Joanna interjected. "A real gentleman. He always helps me lift the stroller up the steps even though it nearly kills him to do it. How old do you think he is?"

"As old as chivalry and not quite dead yet." Susan laughed.

"What?"

"Never mind, Jo. Couldn't Gerald recommend anything, Clare?"

"No. He wasn't there. I handed my script to some fresh-faced pharmacy graduate. Then I looked around on the natural remedies stand for something that might work on William. I couldn't find anything suitable. I don't suppose there's a big demand for substances that remove nail polish from sexual organs."

Susan began to snort with laughter.

"Why didn't you ask the young pharmacist for some help? I'm sure there must be something a bit gentler on the skin than acetone." Wendy had to raise her voice to be heard over the noise Susan was making.

"Well, I was going to ask him when I collected my script but, by then, William and Sophie were tearing around the shop playing tag. When I told them to stop, they started hanging off me, begging for lollies.

"The young chemist took one look at me, standing there, like a set of human monkey bars, and said, smug as anything, 'Never mind, Mom. Go home and take your Zoloft and have a nice cup of tea.' Arrogant prick!

"I was speechless. The sheer audacity of it! I was so wound up, I just grabbed my prescription, threw my money on the counter, and walked out of the shop. So then I didn't have any choice—all I had to use on William's penis was a big bottle of Revlon nail polish remover."

"I don't get it," said Joanna. "What do you take Zoloft for?"

"Depression," said Clare, looking into her coffee.

 PERFECTLY PEACHY

I DIDN'T KNOW THAT CLARE WAS CRACKED UP too. I mean, she's been taking drugs since Sophie was born. Anti-depressants, she says. Everyone's taking them, apparently. Last week I read all about it in the *Australian Woman's Weekly.* They'd done some sort of national survey. Fifty percent of the women who did the survey said that they were, or had been, "depressed." Chronic, isn't it? Most of those women said that they took anti-depressants to cope. Unbelievable! At least Clare is in good company.

What I'd like to know is, what has she got to be depressed about? It's not like she's fat and frumpy like me, for God's sake. She's got looks and a figure to die for. She's got a wonderful husband and a nice house. She's got Sophie . . . I always wanted a girl. Don't get me wrong, I love my boys till I'm bursting, but Clare's life is, well . . . perfectly peachy.

Maybe she needs a job. Do you think she needs a job? She hasn't had a job since Sophie was born. She ought to go and get some work, or have another baby. She needs something to do.

The problem is that she's too guilty to let herself be happy. Now, I can understand guilt consuming Evelyn. I mean, what sort of life is she going to have when she's finally over her psychosis? The guilt of whatever happened to her child. It's just going to consume her. Perhaps it has already. But Clare? What has she got to be guilty about?

I wonder if it's got something to do with all that trouble she had with Sophie in the beginning. She keeps trying to make it up to Sophie. She totally spoils her, goes completely overboard and always ends up feeling like she's inadequate. You only have to look at the plans she's made for Sophie's sixth birthday party to see that she takes too much on. She's asked the whole class to her house. It's madness. Crikey, twenty-five preschoolers in your house!

I had Jake's fifth birthday in the park, and I only invited five friends. That was enough. I took some games down. Pass the parcel, treasure hunt . . . you know the kind of thing. I packed the picnic basket full of chips and lollies and sausage rolls which I'd heated up in the oven and rolled in aluminum foil. Tom bought a crate of soft drinks from the servo on the way and we had paper plates, paper cups, paper tablecloth (all in Jake's favorite, Thomas the Tank Engine). Throwaway everything. That's the way to go. Fast and easy.

I did take my time with the cake, though. It took me ages to construct that train. I made a jam roll for the engine and two chocolate cakes for the carriages. I iced the engine blue and the carriages brown and I made Thomas's face out of marzipan and stuck it on. It was bloody beautiful! The wheels were Choc-Mint Slices, and the smoke in the chimney stack was made of marshmallows. I was up half the night with that cake. It was a labor of love, but it was worth it. The look on Jake's face when he saw his cake . . . I never knew he had so many teeth! Priceless.

The thing is, I love making birthday cakes. It's no sacrifice for me to stay up half the night making a cake. That's why I said to Clare, after I found out that she was on antidepressants, that I'd make Sophie's birthday cake. At least she won't have to worry about doing that. I'm looking forward to it.

Clare's theme is "garden party." The kids can come dressed up in anything garden inspired: a sunflower, a lady beetle, a bag of fertilizer (ha, ha). Well, I'm going to make a garden-inspired cake using my great-aunty Molly's peach blossom cake recipe. My mother used to bake that cake for my birthdays when I was a little girl. The best thing about that cake was the pink! It's a soft fluffy cochineal pink on the inside, and it's got white frosting with pink sugar on top. I'm going to use marzipan to make lots of little peach blossom flowers to sit in the pink sugar. I've been desperate to make that cake since Jake was born. But it's not a boy's cake.

Do you want the recipe? It might be nice for Laura or Madeline. Have either of you got a pen?

Here goes . . . The ingredients are: one cup of sugar (this must be superfine sugar to give the cake a fine texture); four and a half ounces of butter (okay, Susan . . . it's not a diet cake but it tastes good); one teaspoon of lemon essence; three egg whites (nice fresh ones at room temperature—they whip up better); two cups of self-rising flour; and half a cup of milk, mixed with a little cochineal (go easy with the cochineal, you don't want red, you want pale pink).

Got all that?

Now cream the butter and the sugar and the essence until it's fluffy. Stir in the flour and the milk. Gently. (A little bit of flour, then some milk—you know how to do it.) Then, separate the eggs and beat up the whites until they're stiff and snowy. Fold the egg whites into the mixture with a very light hand and pour the whole thing into a round greased cake tin. (Line the tin with a little baking paper or it might stick.) Pop the cake in the oven at three hundred degrees for one hour, then test it with a skewer to see if it's done.

I like to ice it with a fluffy lemon cream frosting. Sprinkle on a little pink sugar. It's delicious.

Is anyone else hungry? I was thinking that I might like to try a piece of that orange-and-almond cake in the display cabinet.

Just joking, Susan. But really, you've got to admit, coffee's not the same without cake.

ALMOST PERFECT

IT WAS MAY 18. THREE MONTHS TO THE DAY since Amy had disappeared. Clare made the connection, then tried not to think about it. She didn't want to spoil the day with depressing thoughts. It was Sophie's sixth birthday, and Clare had planned a wonderful party. She was determined that, today, everything would be perfect.

Clare drew back the curtains, and a cloudless blue day flowed into the room. This was "winter" in Queensland—cool and sunny. Yawning beside the window, Clare stood contemplating the sharp shadows the house cast on the back lawn. She had always been interested in the visual drama that shadows created, and she longed to paint them, to revel in light bouncing away from the edge of darkness.

With the tiniest sigh, Clare turned her back on the window and looked at David. He was still sleeping—his brown head of wavy hair curled under the eiderdown. Then she noticed the clock. It was seven thirty already. Damn it! She had overslept.

"Wake up, David!" She flung the white quilt back, and he lay there, naked on the bed. He had beautiful buttocks. Not hairy, like some men's, but taut and firm and ivory-colored above his long brown legs. He was mostly legs. Long legs, with well-defined muscles from all the sport he played. He reached out one arm and grabbed her pillow and held it over his head. "No you don't!" she cried, and she leaned over and sank her teeth into his flesh.

"Yow!" He sprung around. "What did you do that for?"

Clare looked at the red mark on his bottom and felt no remorse. It felt good to relieve her tension on his beautiful bottom. She patted the smooth flesh soothingly. "You've got to get up and help me. Please, David." She didn't want to start the day by nagging him. "Have you forgotten? It's Sophie's birthday party today."

David groaned. "What time are they coming?"

Did it matter? She was asking him to get up and help out. "Ten thirty."

"Let me have another half hour then. I'll be much more use to you if I get a bit more sleep." David pulled the quilt back over himself and rolled onto his side, presenting his broad back to her. She didn't like his back. It was resistant, immovable, and lacked the vulnerability of his bottom.

Clare felt annoyed. She tried to relax. She breathed out, like her psychiatrist had taught her to do. Of course, it was the truth. David was absolutely no use to her half-asleep. He was an "evening person." Last night he'd worked late, then watched the football on TV. She'd slept restlessly, waking up when each goal was scored and celebrated noisily, until he'd come to bed at midnight. Damn him! She pulled on her dressing gown, closed the door noisily, and walked out into the kitchen. There was so much to do.

What first? She emptied the dishwasher and opened up the house. Sophie was still asleep, so she couldn't make the beds. Everyone was asleep, even the dog.

The dog. She'd have to do a quick pooper-scoop before she had her shower. Susan always insisted that dog poos in the yard were very bad feng shui, and Molly, being a rather overweight Labrador, was prolific. Clare found the scooper and raced around the yard, trailing her dressing gown through the dew. She'd bought the scooper for herself when she'd been pregnant. It had been a good investment. It was so much easier than using a shovel. She took the scoop into the bathroom and flushed the poos down the toilet. David thought she should bury them. He hated the idea of dog poos in the toilet. "You put so many poos in at once, one of these days it's going to get blocked when you try to flush," he said. Clare pushed down the button and closed her eyes. She pleaded with the cistern to work. It worked. The toilet was clear.

In the bedroom, David was snoring loudly, deep snores that vibrated the skin at the back of his throat and wobbled the air. She opened her drawers, took out her jeans and her purple pullover, and slammed the drawers as hard as she could. David stopped snoring, gasped for air, rolled over, then relaxed himself into his snores again.

Before she showered, she cleaned the bath, the toilet, and the shower recess, then put a new roll of toilet paper on the holder. David must have used the last of the paper last night. He never put a new roll on. Too much effort, she supposed. She always put on a new roll if the old one was finished, even if it was three o'clock in the morning.

She turned the shower on as hot as she could bear and stood under it, letting the water run down her back. The chlorine odors from the bathroom cleanser wafted up through the steam at her feet. She washed her hair, digging her fingers into her tight scalp and releasing the tension there. She felt better for it. She hopped out into the steamy bathroom, rubbed herself with a dry towel, and smoothed face cream into her skin before she dressed. She combed her hair and pulled it back from her face in a tight little ponytail, then she wiped away the mist in the mirror to look at her face.

It was true what David told her. She was attractive. She liked her face. She liked her eyes, brown with black lashes. She liked her eyebrows too, dark and elegantly placed above her brow. Her mouth was a little too wide, but she had great teeth. Her hair, when it was not pulled off her face (David hated her hair like this), had a soft wave, and since she'd seen the first grey hairs appearing two years ago, she'd dyed it honey blond to good effect. Somehow, though, she never felt connected to her own beauty. She bit her lip—beauty was such a transient thing, and when it was gone, what was left? She'd never really felt beautiful, not on the inside. One day, her beauty would fade. Would David still love her then?

David wanted another baby. A sibling for Sophie. "She needs someone to deflect some of the attention. She's far too spoiled," he said. Sophie was six now. There would be a big gap between her and a sibling. But Clare was only thirty-one. She still had a few years to play with. Did she really want another baby? Was it a realistic option, given how she'd been with Sophie? Then again, she needed something to do. The thought of going back to work appalled her. Besides, she'd lost her nerve. She'd spent too long out of the workforce. Maybe university? Some sort of course? Susan was toying with the idea of study again. Maybe she and Susan could enroll together . . .

Another baby. Clare put her hand over her tummy. Would it be the same? If they were to have another baby, she'd have to talk it over with her psychiatrist first. Maybe the next baby wouldn't be as demanding as Sophie. Maybe the next baby would leave her a little space, a little space to be herself. Maybe she could have a go at painting a series of connected artworks. She could gear up for an exhibition . . .

Clare tried to think back to the girl she'd been, a long time ago, before Sophie, before David, before work. She'd always sketched and doodled and colored. As a child she'd had a special spot for drawing that no one else knew about. She'd take a sketch pad and a pencil and climb up on the low roof of the shed in the backyard. Sitting up there, undisturbed and alone, she could sketch the white gums that tossed their leaves in the cobalt blue air or draw more fanciful pictures sprung from her imagination. Once she had won a statewide school art competition. But that was a long time ago, and if her work history was any indication, maybe she didn't have that essential quality to be a successful artist: persistence.

The mist from the shower had dissipated. Clare took her watch from the shelf over the vanity. Shit! It was eight fifteen already! Sophie opened the door and walked in, rubbing her eyes. She stumbled to the toilet and put her plump little face in her hand, snatching a few more dozes. She did a very long wee.

"Mommy, is it my birthday today?" she asked, yawning as she pulled up her pants.

"Yes, sweetheart." Clare turned on the tap so Sophie could wash her hands. Sophie dabbed a tiny amount of soap on each palm and gave her hands a cursory slap under the tap. Clare kissed her red curls. "Happy birthday, big number six."

Sophie turned around and gave her a hug. "Can I have my presents now?"

"They'll be on the table at breakfast. Why don't you go and wake up Daddy. Mommy needs him to help with the party."

Sophie's green eyes grew wide. "Is my party today?"

"Yes, and everyone's going to arrive in a few hours, so we're going to be very busy."

"Can I help?"

"You can help Daddy blow up the balloons and decorate the back deck. Okay?"

"Okay!" Sophie rocketed off to jump on her father. "Daddy, Daddy, it's my birthday and I'm having a party and you have to help me blow up balloons."

Clare heard David yawn. "Come and give me a cuddle first, sweetie," he said. (Any excuse to lie in bed a little longer, thought Clare.) She walked back into the hall. She made Sophie's bed and quickly tidied up her room before hurrying back to the kitchen to look at her list. Susan had helped her plan the party. She'd written up a list of jobs to do and a time frame for everything. Susan had everything organized, from the preparty preparations right down to the distribution of the lolly bags at going-home time. Clare looked at the list. She was behind schedule. She'd have to move fast.

She grabbed the Minties for the lolly hunt and raced down the steps into the back garden to hide them. Molly had done a sloppy poo since Clare's earlier round of pooper-scooping. She would have to ask David to pick that one up before the guests arrived. She sidestepped the poo and ran up the back steps.

She had painted a big sunflower on a piece of stiff cardboard (to go with the garden party theme), and she needed to hammer the cardboard onto the fence. It was essential for one of the games. The children would be blindfolded and take turns trying to stick a little paper bee (with sticky tack on the back) in the center of the flower. The hardwood fence was difficult to hammer into. She struck her thumb twice and swore. She was beginning to feel a little sick from lack of food, but she didn't have time for breakfast. It was nine o'clock already, and she still hadn't wrapped the pass the parcel. (Susan had told her to do this the night before. She'd forgotten.)

When she got back upstairs, she could hear David in the shower. She looked at her watch again. It was nine already. Shit!

Sophie was sitting at the table. She'd helped herself to cereal and there was milk and sugar spilled all around her bowl.

"Sophie, after you've finished your Rice Krispies, will you wrap the pass the parcel for me? I've already wrapped the surprise. See?" Clare held up a little parcel wrapped in bright pink tissue paper. "You just have to wrap the parcel with newspaper and put one of these little packets of seeds in each layer."

Sophie scowled. "What are they for?"

"They're the little prizes you get when the music stops and you have to unwrap a layer."

"At Laura's party we got Smarties."

"Well, your party is a garden party. Remember?" Clare hoped that Sophie would be reasonable. She didn't want to have a confrontation this morning. "We're having little packets of seeds as prizes. Don't you think that will be fun?"

Sophie crossed her arms and leaned back in her chair. "I want Smarties."

"Mommy hasn't bought Smarties for the parcel, sweetheart. We've just got a big packet of them to share at lunchtime. Don't cry now. You've got to be my big helper. Okay?" Clare heard the anxious, pleading tone her voice was beginning to take on. She told herself to stay calm. She had to breathe and stifle her own anxiety. She could handle the situation if she just got her emotions under control. She released the air that had been building up the pressure in her chest. She smiled at her daughter and spoke softly. "Okay?"

"Okay," said Sophie.

Clare muttered a prayer of thanks to whatever benevolent force was at work. She left Sophie to her own devices and took the punch bowl and the cups out of the cabinet in the dining room. Everything was covered in a fine film of dust, so she ran some hot water into the sink and frantically washed the bowl and cups. She flinched at the temperature because she didn't have time to put on rubber gloves.

David walked into the kitchen. Clean and perfectly groomed, with his glossy brown hair combed and slicked back, he looked well tested and completely unruffled.

"I'll just have my cereal, then I'll do whatever you want me to do."

Clare glared at him. It was nine forty-five. She thumped the punch bowl down on the bench, took the frozen orange juice from the freezer, cut open the lid, and banged it hard on the countertop. The frozen juice popped out and skidded across the counter. She just caught it before it hit the floor, getting ice in her nails and sweet sticky juice all over her hands.

"Shit!"

"Honey, don't swear in front of Sophie. You're getting yourself into a state. Calm down. It's only a kids' party."

Clare ground her teeth.

"Have you had your medication yet?"

She hated it when he said that. He was abdicating all responsibility for her moods and implying that her anxiety levels were due to the state of her hormones. She told herself to breathe out, but the air swelled into a tight bubble in her lungs, and the words took on added force to squeeze past the blockage, crashing out angrily. "I haven't had time to have my medication yet!"

"Well, go and take it. Leave the rest of the preparations to me. We don't want your dark cloud spoiling the party. Come on, Sophie, I'll help you finish that, then we'll go outside and blow up some balloons."

Clare slammed the chopping board down on the table and cut the passionfruit brutally. She scraped the pulp into the bowl with the frozen orange juice and added a tin of crushed pineapple. She threw some strawberries into the mixture and placed a tea towel over the bowl. She would add the lemonade and the ginger ale when everyone arrived. She grabbed the streamers and took them out to the back deck for David to put up.

About five minutes before the guests arrived, Sophie asked about her presents again, and Clare went and fetched them from her room. Sophie unwrapped the first present. It was the foldout Barbie house she'd been wanting for ages. Her face lit up. "Can I play with it now?"

"Wait until after the party, Sophie," David said, giving her a hug. "It will take us a while to set it up."

"Why don't you open your other present now," said Clare, smiling in anticipation.

Sophie unwrapped the other present. An exquisite sunflower costume fell out of the soft yellow tissue paper.

"What is it?" Sophie swung the green velvet leaf up into the air, and the bright yellow petals hung down.

"It's a flower costume. You can wear it today. Isn't it gorgeous?" It had cost Clare more than she would ever have admitted to David. She had bought it in an expensive little children's shop in the trendier part of town. She helped Sophie put the costume on. "Look, the leaves are green velvet, and they tie around your waist like this. See? The petals go around your face."

Sophie peeled the petals off and pouted her lips. "I don't want to be a flower."

"What?" Clare was incredulous.

"I want to be a fairy. I'm going to wear my fairy costume."

"But that thing's so old and grubby, Sophie." The fairy costume had long been Sophie's favorite, but it was torn and dirty and covered in grey mildew. Clare would have thrown it out ages ago if she wasn't so fearful of Sophie's reaction. "Besides," pleaded Clare, "it's a garden party, not a fairy party."

"Fairies live in the garden. I'm going to be a fairy!"

David put his arm around Clare and spoke softly in her ear. "I think we'd better let her wear what she likes, Clare. The most important thing is that she's happy on her birthday."

Sophie ran into her room, dived into the dressing-up box, and pulled on the tattered pink netting fairy costume. She pulled on her ballet shoes and ran to her father so that he could help her put on the wings, which were made out of stockings stretched over wire and were, after much use, pocked with holes.

Clare breathed out again. She tried to let it all go. It was better to let it go. They'd all be arriving any minute now. She went into the bathroom to swallow her Zoloft and clean her teeth.

From ten thirty the backyard began to fill with preschoolers dressed as ladybugs and bumblebees, butterflies and flowers.

"How many did you invite?" David asked, as two bright yellow bumblebees, with stripes of black insulation tape, flew past to gather Minties from the branches of the lemon tree.

"The whole class!"

David looked at the small group of parents who had chosen not to drop off their kids and run. They were loitering around the punch bowl, happily oblivious to their children. He wiped the sweat off his brow. "What's next on the agenda?"

"I think it's the 'pin the bee on the flower.' The blindfold is hanging on the fence. Can you organize that? I have to heat up the sausage rolls and cocktail franks."

Joanna was in the kitchen with Susan. They were whispering about something, heads bent toward each other in some friendly conspiracy. Clare just managed to catch the tail end of something Susan was saying. ". . . of course, I tried to help her get organized for it. I didn't want her to be stressed about it, especially now I know that she's on medica—"

Joanna looked up, her face bright red, as Clare entered the kitchen. "Where do you want me to put the cake?" she asked, pretending to look helpless. Clare smiled benignly. They were talking about her. Of course, now she had told them that she was taking antidepressants, she was hot gossip. Oh well, it made a change from talking about Evelyn.

Clare gazed at Joanna for a moment. She looked a little slimmer. Maybe the diet was working for her at last. She did need to lose some weight. She was short. She had short legs and didn't carry excess weight easily. Even so, Clare thought, she had a pretty face, girlish somehow. She needed to do something with her hair though.

"Here's a spot, Jo. Thanks for making the cake. Can I take a peek?"

"Sure." Joanna eased off the Tupperware lid.

Susan gasped, "Wow!"

The cake was a masterpiece. Large and round, covered in handmade pink marzipan blossoms which were set in a bed of fluffy lemon Vienna cream frosting and pink sugar.

"It's lovely, Joanna. Really lovely. You sure know how to bake a cake!" Clare gave her a hug.

"It's perfect!" exclaimed Susan. "Do you think you could do Maxine's for me?"

Joanna laughed. "Sure! I had great fun making it."

"The garden theme's cute, Clare," said Susan. "Mind you,

Laura's costume cost me a fortune." Laura looked exquisite in her bright red ladybug outfit, with its black velvet cap and feelers. Clare wished the birthday girl looked as photogenic for her own party.

Susan looked down into the garden from the kitchen window. "I sent Richard out the back to photograph all the kids when we arrived . . . Why's Sophie wearing that old fairy outfit? I thought you bought a new sunflower costume for her to wear."

"I did!" Clare rolled her eyes. "She wouldn't wear it."

Joanna laughed. "Sounds like typical kid behavior to me!"

Susan nodded. "Yes. Never mind. The birthday child is always a bit testy when the big day finally arrives."

Clare pulled a tray of jelly oranges and a fruit platter out of the fridge. "Could you two help me set the table?"

"Sure," said Joanna, taking the trays.

Susan took the tablecloth that Clare had dug out from the bottom drawer. She was heading for the door when Sophie ran into the kitchen, pulling Laura along by the hand. "Mommy . . . Mommy . . . Laura sat in one of Molly's poos!"

"Oh no!" Susan dropped the tablecloth back onto the bench. She picked Laura up and, holding her out at arm's length to avoid dog doo on her new green floral dress, she raced into the bathroom.

In the end, Clare had to set the table by herself while Susan and Joanna put Laura in the bath. The party table was actually the legless plastic top of an old outdoor table Clare had bought at a garage sale a long time ago. They brought it out for Sophie's parties because it was low enough for lots of kids to sit around on cushions. Clare threw the pink gingham cloth over the table and laid out bright yellow plastic plates and purple napkins. She brought out clear plastic cups with neon-colored straws and three jugs of Kool-Aid, green, red and orange. In the center of the table she put a little green plastic watering can, full of artificial sunflowers. Then she brought out the chips and the Smarties and the sandwiches and the jelly oranges. The table looked beautiful. If only Sophie was wearing her new flower costume, Clare thought. What a perfect photo opportunity it would be. Never mind, Laura would need something to wear after her bath. She'd tell Susan to put the flower costume on Laura. Someone might as well wear it.

Here was Susan now, carrying Laura wrapped in a towel. "Could I borrow some of Sophie's clothes, Clare? I didn't think to bring a change . . ."

Clare grinned. "She can wear that costume of Sophie's if she likes. It's on the bed."

"Clare! Clare!" David was calling her from down in the yard. She put her head over the deck. "What is it?"

David's brow was creased and he looked up at her, speaking in an agitated voice. "Can you ring the poisons information center?"

"Oh my God! What for?"

"Sam's just eaten a packet of those seeds you put in the pass the parcel."

Joanna anxiously called the poisons information service and was told that, to be on the safe side, Sam would have to have his stomach pumped.

"I'm so sorry, Joanna," Clare cried, as Joanna collected her bag and rushed out.

Joanna put her hand on Clare's arm. "Look, don't fret about it. The silly child eats anything. I'll call Tom, and he can pick Jake up. Okay?"

Clare nodded and watched Joanna carry Sam, happily oblivious to future proceedings, out to her car. The car screeched out of the driveway, immediately revealing the extent of Joanna's panic. Clare put her hand up to her mouth. She was close to tears, but she kept telling herself to breathe out. When she turned around, she saw Sophie standing in the hallway, her little arms crossed, a contemptuous look on her face. "I told you we should have had Smarties, Mom!" Clare opened her mouth to respond to her daughter but stopped. Something was burning . . .

THE PARTY TABLE HAD LOST SOME OF ITS AL-lure. The sausage rolls were burned. The cocktail franks were overcooked and had popped out of their red skins, revealing their obscene flesh-colored insides. Even the jelly oranges were a disappointment. They hadn't set properly, and had melted quickly outside. Now they lay in little pools of red, yellow, and green on the plate. And Sophie, when she saw Laura in her new flower costume, burst into tears and had to be sent to her bedroom.

Clare looked at her watch. Thankfully the party was nearly over. Some of the other parents had already arrived to pick up their children and were standing, chatting with each other, around the table. At least the birthday cake looked lovely. Sophie stopped crying the moment she saw the candles being lit. After everyone had sung "Happy Birthday," some of the mothers complimented Clare on the beautiful cake, and Clare had to tell them that Joanna had made it.

"Where is Joanna?" Wendy wanted to know, having just arrived from work to pick up Madeline.

"She's gone to the Royal with Sam so that he can have his stomach pumped."

"Oh!" said Wendy, understanding immediately from the tone of Clare's voice that further questions would not be welcome.

The other parents, overhearing this conversation, momentar-
ily cast a suspicious eye on the food their children were being
served.

At last it was time for everyone to go home. David handed
out twenty-five lolly bags while trying to reassure Tom, who'd
come to pick up Jake after receiving a rather distressed phone call
from Joanna. Sophie and William disappeared into Sophie's room
and promptly shook the entire contents of the foldout Barbie
house onto the floor. Clare, feeling tearful, boiled water and made
herself a strong cup of tea.

One last piece of birthday cake remained. Clare looked longingly at it before sitting down on a cushion, amid the collection
of broken party blowers and orange peels and half-sucked, soggy
chips. She picked up the cake. It smelled lemony. She took a bite.
Soft and buttery, strangely consoling, utterly delicious. The tang
of the lemon-flavored frosting acted as a perfect foil for the sweet
fluffy cake. She took another bite. The pink sugar tingled on her
tongue. She ate it all, and the tears in the corners of her eyes dried
up. She had to laugh. What a disaster!

She heard Sophie calling her, "Mom, we can't put the Barbie
house together by ourselves!"

Clare sighed. She would have to go and help them. David was
still talking to Tom at the front gate. She sipped the last of her tea
and reflected on the chaos of the party. She had so wanted everything to be perfect. To feel that perhaps she was a good mother after all. At least the cake had been good. Better than good. She must
tell Joanna, after she had apologized again for putting inedible
seeds in the pass the parcel, that the cake had been . . . perfect.

SHADOWS

WENDY CHECKED HER CHILDREN ONE LAST time before work. The house was quiet, sleeping, and her rubber-heeled shoes stole soundlessly across the bare pine floorboards. Sometimes, at night, the house had ghosts. Watchful spirits with corrugated shadows moved across the vertical joinery of the walls. Usually Wendy's practical mind ignored the dark shapes that peeped out of the corners of the eighty-year-old house. They were harmless enough and only as real as her mind allowed them to be. To-night, however, these barely perceptible shapes made her uneasy. She spun around and banished the shadows by staring through them. It was a dare. She turned on the light in the kitchen. That was better. All gone now.

In the dim light she saw through Maddy's doorway. Maddy was sprawled awkwardly across her bed, her pillow dipping down onto the floor. Wendy inched the last bit of pillow out from under Maddy's head and straightened it up again. She heaved her little blond daughter back into a more conventional position and tucked her in, as she always did, with hospital corners at the end of the bed. She kissed her soft cheek and turned on the night-light to banish the shadows to the corner of the room.

Daniel had fallen asleep playing his Game Boy, and Wendy unclasped his hands and put the toy on the chest of drawers. She looked at his face, relaxed now in the sleep that only children manage to achieve. A deep, restful sleep that, for a child, takes place in the blink of an eye. A sleep that has no memory. She smoothed back his hair and pulled the quilt around his shoulders. He was growing up. He wouldn't be her little boy much longer. He was scarcely that now, the way he shrugged off all her attempts at affection. And Maddy? She was growing up fast. Faster than she should now that she was modeling her behavior on Daniel's.

Wendy sighed. She felt like she was missing out on her own children. Still, she was missing out for them. When they were born, she and Harry had decided that they were going to give them every opportunity. School fees were expensive.

She picked up a dirty sock, took it out to the laundry, then looked at her watch. Just enough time to hang out a load of washing before work.

It was a surreal experience, hanging up the washing in the night. The house backed onto bushland, and the crisp, cold air was full of the sounds of animals and birds. During the day, they were tucked away in the hollows of eucalypts or hidden in the long creek grass. Now the night was full of the sharp-throated gurgles and clicks of a family of ringtails that lived in an old lilly-pilly tree beside the creek. Somewhere in the long grasses that edged the creek, a nocturnal curlew cried out mournfully. Wendy shuddered. She was edgy tonight, and the birdcall aroused in her a sense of foreboding.

She had heard the curlew cry out before, many times, but she'd only seen it once. It was the night before Amy disappeared. That night it was so hot that Wendy had left all the doors open along the verandah, and just before ten, the strange nocturnal bird had flown into the house. A large brown-and-white-speckled bird with long grey legs and wide frightened eyes. For nearly ten minutes it blundered blindly in the light of the living room. Perhaps the Easterns' cat had chased it in. In the end, Wendy turned off the lights and waited with the shadows for it to find its own way out. It had been an unnerving experience, and Wendy tried to push thoughts of it from her mind.

She was usually a fiercely logical person. Her rationality saved her from being prey to all kinds of waking dreams. She was not one to dwell on life's darker mysteries. She had the perfect disposition to be a nurse. The type of disposition that could witness the gruesome effects of a teenage car crash, then get up the next day and eat spaghetti on toast for breakfast. Of course, that disposition had been finely honed by sixteen years of nursing in big-city hospitals. It had become a habit of hers to separate herself from the uglier side of life. Perhaps this was why, at least in the beginning, she was so pragmatic about an incident that occurred in the week before Amy went missing. An incident she refused to dwell on, despite everything, and one she assumed Steve, in his grief, would have tried to forget.

Wendy was not thinking of Steve as she reached up to peg the last few items on the line. She was staring through the darkness in an effort to see the strange animals and birds she often heard at night. The shadows were too deep to penetrate, and she turned her face to look up at the moon, the full-blown moon, glowing in the sky inside orbits of deep blue. As she looked up, her face cast in the moon's blue light, she noticed the red glow from a smoldering cigarette. Steve was watching her from his back steps. She drew a breath. She dropped the bra she was about to peg, grabbed the washing basket, and ran up the steps. That gave her away. She was still affected by it. Of course, so was he.

As she drove the back streets to the Mater Mother's Hospital, her hands were shaking. How could she have let it happen? She loved Harry. Poor, hardworking Harry, who was so tired from trying to hold down two jobs that all he could do in bed was sleep with one heavy arm across her back. She loved him. She always had. She loved him for his gentleness. For the way his heavy body fumbled apologetically around her in the dark. For the way he loved the kids. The way he involved himself in the children's lives so that she couldn't be jealous, not really, if he didn't find time for her in the hours when their shifts coincided. Still, it had happened. She hadn't meant it to happen but it had. There had been a moment of weakness when the unfocused desire that she always carried had evolved into a hungry, unloving lust. Lust, that was all it had been. She had never loved Steve.

How had she let it happen so easily? During those hot summer months in the Christmas holidays, then in February, when the kids went back to school, Steve was at home. He had taken time off to help Evelyn with the baby, but Steve wasn't much good with children. He didn't seem to understand them.

Wendy knew that Steve's father had been an alcoholic. What was the saying? "An apple never falls far from the tree"? After Amy was born, Steve used a lot of his paternity leave to catch up with his old mates in the pub. Wendy had seen him, a couple of times, stumbling out of a taxi at four in the morning. Being a shift worker, she noticed these things. She also noticed that Evelyn and Steve were fighting. She and Harry could hear them arguing with each other late at night. One day Evelyn confided in Wendy that she was sure Steve was having an affair. In retrospect, Evelyn's insecurity was part of the paranoia that went with her illness.

The irony was, Wendy thought, that Evelyn's accusations probably contributed to Steve becoming an adulterer. Wendy was sure that Evelyn's repeated and bitter reprisals somehow worked their way into Steve's consciousness. Steve was no martyr. If Evelyn kept him out of her bed because she thought he was fooling around, then Steve would have wondered what the point of being faithful was.

One night, while Wendy was hanging up yet another load of washing after dark, she'd heard Steve yelling at Evelyn from the back steps.

"If you're never going to fuckin' believe me, I might as well do it, Evelyn. At least you'd have something real to complain about then!"

And so it had happened one hot February day, when the kids were back at school. That morning, Wendy saw Evelyn pushing tiny Amy up the road in the pram. Evelyn was always pushing the pram somewhere. Sometimes she stayed out for hours. That meant Steve was home alone. Wendy was home alone too. One of her rare days off. She was baking a cake—a big chocolate cake for Harry's birthday—and she was short an egg. She thought she'd just go over to the Easterns' and borrow one, so, covering her mixture with a tea towel, she stepped outside into the fuzzy heat that rose off every surface and sent rivers of perspiration trickling down her body.

Steve was under the house working on a car. He was a mechanic, and he always tinkered with his cars when he was home from work. She saw his feet sticking out from under the chassis. Long, slender feet with soles covered in a soft layer of dust. She stood for a long time looking at those feet, trying to remember the last time Harry had found her feet in bed and tickled them under the sheets with his toes, his gentle precursor to lovemaking.

Steve didn't even know she was there. When he pulled himself out from under the chassis, lying on his back on a little wheel board, the first thing he saw was her slim legs, shiny with baby oil and freshly shaven. And, for no other reason than simply to feel them, as one might feel the rippling flank of a racehorse, he touched them. Ran his hand down them, felt the warm blood behind the skin. Soft. Luscious. Wendy heard herself inhale.

"I . . . um . . . came to borrow an egg. I'm baking a cake . . ."

Steve took his hand away and sat up. He rubbed his steely blue eyes. "Sorry," he said. "I thought you were Evey." He was lying of course, and they both knew it and laughed. Nervously.

He stood up and wiped the dust off his jeans. "Come upstairs, and I'll get you one."

That was the moment she should have gone home. There's always one moment of grace. She didn't take it. Maybe she had meant it to happen after all. She knew what she wanted. She could still feel the sweat of his hand evaporating off her calf. She followed him up the steps, and the sun beat down on her dark hair. It was so hot.

They got to the verandah door, and he opened it. She followed him in and he shut the door. Her mouth was dry as he turned toward her and took her face in his hands and kissed her lips. She didn't back away. She melted around his lips, his tongue . . . Her mouth filled with his saliva. She smelled the grease and sweat in the folds of his neck and shuddered as he pulled off her T-shirt. It was so hot, she wasn't wearing a bra. His lips found her breasts, and he fumbled inside her shorts, pushing down her pants and stroking her buttocks. She felt him press against her. More than anything she wanted to have sex with him. He moved her toward the daybed on the verandah, and she lay down, blushing in her nakedness, her heart pounding in her ears.

In the dim light of the enclosed verandah, he slid on top of her, riding over her. And she could see nothing but his olive skin.

She could taste nothing but his male flesh. She could smell nothing but his strange exciting odor, and just as she broke around him, the verandah door opened. The sun crashed in and there was a shadow standing in the door. There was Evelyn, holding Amy.

REGRETS

LONG AFTER THEY SHOULD HAVE DISSIPATED in the sharp lights of the maternity ward where Wendy worked, the shadows crept after her, hiding in the recesses of deep cupboards full of linen and blankets and towels. She couldn't shake the memory of that afternoon when Evelyn had found her with Steve. Nor could she alter the way the shadows reached out to grasp her and sent icy sensations through her veins. She rubbed her hands together. They were so cold.

Sometime after midnight a baby boy was wheeled into the crèche area. Although he'd been born blue, the doctors had managed to revive him, and Wendy was asked to look after him while his mother slept, recovering from her emergency caesarean. Wendy picked up the little boy, his head still covered in vernix, and cradled him in her arms. His eyes were shut against the world, but his brow was furrowed and worried. He was an old spirit. Wendy had seen them many times, babies who came into the world with an attitude of resentment, almost as if they had been here before and it wasn't their choice to return so easily. He whimpered a little, and she found a bottle of glucose water to give him.

He sucked a while, making the soft little snuffles of a newborn, then, with resignation, he opened his eyes. Piercing, penetrating blue. He gazed at her unblinkingly, and she smiled at him.

She loved this job. She loved babies, even other people's. Somehow her work compensated for the children she left at home.

Usually it was rewarding work. The maternity wards were generally the happiest in the hospital, but when things did go wrong, it left the staff with feelings of desolation, and sometimes guilt.

There was an incident before New Year which had been particularly traumatizing for Wendy. So traumatizing that when another position in a different hospital came up, she took it just to leave some memories behind. She'd been working at the Royal, and a young homeless girl had come into hospital in an advanced stage of labor. It was bedlam in the labor ward that night. The girl was screaming on a stretcher in the corridor, pleading for something to ease her agony. Unfortunately, the girl was fully dilated, and it was much too late to administer an epidural. Wendy only had time to wheel the girl into the delivery room and push the button for the resident doctor when the girl began to bear down.

Wendy had her certificate of midwifery and felt confident enough to deliver. In any case, she hardly had time to think. The girl began to groan, and Wendy saw the baby's head crowning. She eased the baby out, head . . . shoulders . . . and then she knew. The baby was dead.

Nothing can describe the awfulness of those moments. The girl was crying, asking to hold her baby, and Wendy knew that the baby had been dead for some time. She wrapped the baby up, a little boy, ostensibly perfect, and she heard her own voice waver as she asked the girl when the contractions had started. The girl had been in labor for nearly three days.

The resident arrived then, and Wendy just shook her head and gave the girl her stillborn child.

"You've given birth to a boy," she said. "I'm so sorry . . . he's dead." The tears were running down Wendy's face, but the girl sat up and cried out.

"No, you've made a mistake. Look at him. He's perfect! Do something. Make him breathe again!" She began to sob, and the doctor stepped beside Wendy.

"Nurse, could you take baby down to the crèche area and call the superintendent. A report will have to be made. Then clean him up and bring him back to the mother. She can hold him as long as she likes . . ."

It was one of the hardest things Wendy had ever done. She bathed the pale, blue-lipped boy in warm water. She was gentle. He was a full-term baby with a soft fuzz of dark hair, physically perfect but stung by death. Wendy trickled warm water over his stillness. She washed his hair in sweet-smelling shampoo and wiped him dry. Then she wrapped him in a little blue blanket and took him back to his mother.

The girl held her baby well into the next morning, when the doctors gave her a sedative, and she slept. She left the hospital without being discharged, and disappeared back onto the streets before the social worker could ascertain where her family, if she had any, lived. The baby lay in the morgue for a long time before it was buried. Wendy started working at the Mater soon afterward.

On this night of shadows, Wendy took comfort in the fact that the baby she held in her arms was well and truly alive. He finished his bottle and dozed, so she put him over her shoulder and rubbed his back to bring up the wind. He nestled into her shoulder, and she rubbed her cheek on his head. Strange, how her thoughts should so often return to that dreadful experience. Strange how she should feel such grief for that lost baby and allow herself to dwell on that night again and again, when she refused to dwell on Amy's disappearance at all.

Thoughts of Amy she quickly stifled just as one stifles the burning embers in a fire. And yet . . . and yet a shadow remained. An icy-cold blackness reaching though her consciousness, nestling in the corners of her mind. And there was that other thing too. That other shadow she refused to dwell on. A shadow gaining form and flesh inside her body with every minute of every day. She closed her eyes against the tears.

MOTHER LOVE

"DO YOU REALLY THINK IT'S A GOOD IDEA, Clare? It might be quite distressing for him to see his mother in that state." Wendy wrung her hands together under the table.

"I think he needs to see her," said Clare, buttering her fruit toast. She looked at Wendy, saw that her eyes were wide and fearful and tried to reassure her. "He misses her. I know she's totally uncommunicative with everyone else, but who knows? With him she might be . . . different."

"Yeah, maybe seeing him will trigger her maternal side," Joanna chipped in. "Surely she must be worrying about what's happening to William. Crikey, I know I would be! Whatever happened to Amy, she's still got William to look after." Joanna hunted around in her handbag for the Matchbox car that Sam wanted.

"But Evelyn's not like you, Joanna." Susan jabbed her index figure across the table. "She hasn't got the strength to be the quintessential earth mother. Your love for your children is paramount. You'd never lose one of your boys. You'd never give them away. And . . ." She hesitated. "And you'd never do anything to harm your children." Susan brought her coffee mug up to her mouth to hide her face.

It was true, Susan admitted to herself. There was a possibility that Evelyn had done something to harm Amy. She hoped to God that it wasn't so and, with Amy's little pink sock hidden deep in the recesses of her handbag, she clung to that hope. However, Susan was incapable of deluding herself. She knew that Evelyn had a psychiatric disorder. It was no one's fault, just the inevitable outcome of certain genes coinciding with imperfect circumstances. No one, especially not Evelyn, could wage a war against fate.

Even before Amy disappeared, Susan had been aware of Evelyn's volatility. She had watched Evelyn's emotions continually break through her pale, translucent skin. Laughter came easily to her but so did tears. Very early on, Susan had decided that Evelyn was as delicate as a piece of fine china. Susan could see light through her—and dark. It was a shame, she thought, that Evelyn had never learned to control her emotions. This inability meant that she had a weakness, a craze . . . A flaw.

Underneath the table, Sam was crawling around with his favorite car. It was a red ute, and the paint was chipping off. He wound the ute in and out the chair legs. "Brrrr . . . Brrrr . . . Brrum . . . Brrumm." He made the noise with soft wet lips and watched his own spittle spray the side of Susan's red shoe. Up and over the mothers' feet he pushed the ute. One of the wheels caught on Wendy's stocking and made a little ladder as he pulled it off. Wendy tucked her legs in farther under her chair. She wasn't feeling well. Her face was covered in a thin layer of cold sweat, and the saliva was welling in her mouth. She poured herself a glass of water from the carafe on the table.

Susan turned to Clare, who had buttered her toast but seemed unable to eat it. "Do you think Evelyn still loves her children, Clare? Amy is missing. We don't know the extent of Evelyn's involvement in that. And William, poor child, has been dumped on you because Steve isn't able to cope on his own."

"I really don't know. I used to hope she still loved them, but now . . . Now, I'm not sure what she feels. I believe she still cares for William. That's why I'm going to take him to see her. But Amy? Did she ever love her? Perhaps her depression stopped her connecting with Amy from the beginning. There are a few possibilities, aren't there? Maybe she was so depressed she really did do something to Amy. Or—and I know this is the alternative we all prefer—maybe being depressed made her neglectful. She wasn't herself, she left Amy somewhere and someone else took her. I just don't know what to think. The more I turn it all over in my mind, the harder it is to make any sense of it."

Wendy sipped her water, trying to keep the bile from rising. She felt wretched.

"You're no more confused than the rest of us, Clare." Susan swirled the sludge in the bottom of her coffee cup. "God, I wish she would just open up to one of us! I went to see her yesterday, and after ten minutes of my own voice, I couldn't stand it anymore. I don't think I'll visit her again. Sorry, Clare. I would've liked to have helped."

"That's all right, Susan. Thanks for trying, anyway. Perhaps all our good intentions are just too late." Clare leaned back in her chair. She caught her hair in her hands and pulled it back, twisting it into a tight little knot. "The thing is, I know what postnatal depression is like. Lots of women get that—but they get help. They get over it, and no harm is done to their children. But for some reason Evelyn's depression developed into a full-blown psychotic episode. She wasn't herself . . . If only I—"

Clare trailed off, her thoughts focusing on this lost opportunity. She should have done something while she'd had the chance. What had stopped her? Had she really believed that pure exhaustion was responsible for Evelyn's strange mood after Amy was born? Had optimism made her indecisive and slow to help?

Or maybe, she admitted to herself with a twinge of shame, maybe it was a long-harbored sense of resentment toward Evelyn that had held her back.

Wendy got up suddenly. "I'm sorry. I've got to go." She thrust some money down on the table. "Will you fix up my share of the bill please, Joanna?"

"Of course. Are you all right? You look awfully pale."

"Yes, I'm fine. I just need to go home." Wendy barged though the other tables. She caught her long black sweater on the corner of a chair and yanked it free without looking back.

"Do you think I should run after her?" Joanna asked as she stood up. "She looked dreadful. Perhaps I can . . ."

Susan caught Joanna's wrist. "Leave her be. She looked like she wanted to be alone."

"Yes, I suppose you're right," said Joanna, sounding a little unconvinced. "All the same," she said, sitting back down, "we probably shouldn't talk about postnatal depression around Wendy anymore."

Susan frowned. "What I don't understand is why she didn't tell us she was pregnant earlier?"

"I don't know," answered Clare, remembering how Harry had almost tripped over his shopping trolley in his rush to tell her the news last week in the supermarket. "It's not as if Harry isn't excited about it! If I had known earlier, I'd have had Maddy and Daniel over to stay. Given Wendy a bit of a break. I've already got William. A couple more kids wouldn't have made much difference."

"Well, if I was pregnant," whispered Joanna confidentially, "you and Susan would be the first to know . . . after Tom. I'd be that excited about it!"

"Of course you would," agreed Susan. "Maybe Wendy just thought she was finished having babies."

"But she loves babies," Joanna exclaimed. "She works with them!"

"Yes, but a job's different," said Clare. "Wendy can leave those babies at work."

Susan shrugged. "Anyway, I'm sure all this business with Evelyn and Amy has unsettled her. We'll all have to try to be very supportive of Wendy and hope the lightning doesn't strike twice."

Without anyone taking much notice, Sam began to drive his ute out from under the table, pushing it along the path that Wendy had taken on her way out of the cafe. The other patrons shifted their feet to let him past. He was a momentary irritation.

Clare was studying her fingernails with a tired, faraway look in her eyes. Susan leaned over and put her hand on top of Clare's. "You mustn't blame yourself for what's happened to Evelyn. You've done as much as anyone could expect. More. Let's not forget that Evelyn's childhood was a very unhappy one."

"Do you remember Evelyn's mother, Clare?" Joanna asked.

"Not really. I was nearly six when she killed herself. Evelyn must have been four, I think. My memories of her are very sketchy. I remember that she had a rose garden she used to work in while Evelyn and I played in the front yard."

"Is it still there?"

"I think the bushes are still there. Yes. Yes, they are, because when I picked William up the other day, I saw the old plants struggling under a carpet of weeds. Evelyn didn't keep the garden going, but then she never pulled it out either."

"Evelyn found her mother, didn't she?" Susan asked.

"Yes, and that must have been horrible. She was hanging under the house. It was ages before anyone else worked out what had happened. My mother found Evelyn in the rose garden, using one of her mother's shoes to break all the roses. Later, that's how they knew that Evelyn had found her mother."

"Huh?" Joanna looked confused.

"The shoe! That's how they knew. When the police came they noticed that the body was wearing only one shoe."

"Oh, Clare. Don't tell me any more. The whole thing is giving me the creeps." Joanna looked through the cafe window and tried to concentrate on the cakes. Mud cake, macadamia slice, syrup cake, custard tarts, treacle puddings . . . Sam was being awfully good and quiet under the table, she thought.

"Joanna, don't be such a wuss." Susan gave her friend's shoulder a quick squeeze. "Did they ever find out why she did it? Was Evelyn's dad seeing other women or something?"

"No, it wasn't that. It was worse. When I got older, Mom told me that Evelyn's mother had been a victim of incest. Pretty yucky stuff. I never asked for the details, and Mom never offered them.

"My mother tried very hard with Evelyn. She looked after her during the day. She played with her and read her stories until her dad came home. I was incredibly jealous, of course. Those first few months after her mother committed suicide were very strange times. Evelyn didn't speak for weeks."

"That sounds familiar," Susan interjected.

"Yes, I suppose it does. That never occurred to me before."

"When did she start talking again?"

"It would have been the day after my sixth birthday. I remember because Mom and Dad gave me a Cry Baby Sue doll and it went missing. I was always sure that Evelyn took it. Mom asked her if she had it, and she said, 'No.' That was her first word in ages. Mom was so astonished that she didn't question her any further but we all knew she'd taken it."

"Did . . . did she get better after your birthday?" Joanna asked tentatively.

"Oh yes. Mom took her under her wing. She'd always wanted another child. In time, Evelyn seemed like a normal little girl again—almost."

"What do you mean, 'almost'?" asked Susan.

"Well, she had a lot of nightmares. She often stayed at our house and slept in my room. She woke up a lot. Screaming—about spiders in her bed. Obviously, all Mom's attentions weren't enough to undo the damage that had been done."

"Did she ever see a child psychiatrist?"

"Oh no. Her father didn't believe in psychiatrists. They were for neurotic Americans. Australian kids were supposed to get over things."

"But she never did, did she?"

"No, I guess not."

"What an awful thing for a child to live through!" Joanna shook her head. "Poor Evelyn! If only the police could find Amy. I'm sure somebody must have taken her. Evelyn was just depressed before Amy went missing. After she disappeared, that's when she went crazy."

"Joanna!" Susan flung her hands into the air in exasperation. "You have an incredible faith in the goodness of other mothers." Susan lowered her voice and looked grimly at Joanna. "Has it ever occurred to you that Evelyn doesn't want Amy to be found? Don't you think that might be why she's refusing to speak?"

"No. Don't even suggest it! I can't really believe that she wouldn't want Amy to be found. How could you just disconnect from your own child like that? Take William to see his mother tomorrow, Clare. See if that makes her speak again. I don't think I can stand not knowing what happened to Amy."

Joanna stood up to go, then remembered that Sam was still playing under the table. She bent down to extract him. "Sam!" She got up, hitting her head against the table edge. "Where's Sam? I thought he was under here." Susan and Clare sprung out of their chairs.

"Do you think he followed Wendy out to the road?" Susan looked anxiously over the tables but Joanna was already hurtling out of the cafe, tables and chairs clattering together in her wake.

"Sam!" Joanna screamed.

Susan and Clare heard tires screech. They ran out to the road and saw Joanna yank Sam out of the gutter.

The distance between them and Joanna seemed immense, partly because they were afraid to cover it.

"Here," Joanna yelled, putting her small child into Clare's arms. "You hold him!"

Clare's throat was dry, and her heart was pounding. She checked Sam over. Not a scratch. "Is he all right?" she asked.

"Oh yes," said Joanna, rolling her eyes. "He's been sitting there on the road, trying to fish his car out of the drain. That last car had to swerve to miss him!"

Joanna turned away so that the other woman couldn't see her cross herself. She might be lapsed, but once a Catholic, always a Catholic.

"Susan," Joanna cried with renewed vigor, "will you help me find a stick so that I can yank this bloody toy out of the drain?"

Brittle Things

A rainbowy beetle
A brittle thing
Of shimmery wings
Red, purple, and green

Pointed feelers
Feel holes in the
Matchbox blackness
Where life is enclosed

Where a child's eye
Wet and brown
And wide as a river
Peers down

And sees
A rainbowy beetle
A perfect thing
Of shimmering color

Red, purple, and green.

Today he is coming. I do not want him here. There is nothing to be gained. He will not recognize me because I've become so small. If they press me, I will break up into even smaller pieces. So long in the web has made me brittle and dry. Still, she is determined to bring him. There is no stopping her. And, yes, it will be good to see him. I want to see how he has grown beyond me and become her son. That is what I wished for him. That is the plan the spider whispered into my ear that hot day in summer when I saw no way forward.

Do you think I am mad? They say I am ill, that it is because of the baby that I talk to the spider. They are wrong. I have always talked to the spider. I talked to the spider before I met Steve, before I had William, before Amy too. You are surprised? You are surprised that I can say her name now? I can always say her name when I am small. I can say her name because, when I am small, I cannot hurt her and I know she is safe and far away from the web that I bind myself to. Yes, I talked to the spider before Amy. But after Amy, something changed. After Amy, I heard the spider talking back.

I wept when I heard her voice because it had been so long. And it was hers! It was my mother's voice! I knew it would be. She took her time, but she finally answered the question. And the answer was, "For you."

Then I knew. I knew that day what I must do. I must save Amy from the life I lived or she would learn, just as I learned in four short years, how to feel hopeless and joyless and lifeless. How to smile and feel the tiresome pull of muscles obligingly rearranging the facial features so that they resemble happiness. How to walk out in the shrillness of a blue-skied day, with your child's hand in yours, on a day when yellow butterflies are dancing, and feel nothing. Nothing at all. So that when the child turns and says, "I love you," your smile is thin, and although you answer with the right words, the child knows that you are lying.

"For you," my spider mother said. "For you, so that you could grow beyond me. So my moods will not wear you down and disappoint you anymore. So that I may never hurt you, not because I wanted to, but because I feared that I may not have cared if I did."

The ambivalence. That is what scared my mother the most. Not the injection of feeling, but the lack of it. But I have learned a lesson my mother did not. I have learned to feel comfortable with ambivalence. Ambivalence is like floating underwater. It is like the weightlessness of my mother's womb. It is a state in which I have no desire, and I feel no pain. It is not so different from the death that she chose.

That day, the day my spider mother spoke, it finally made sense. I forgave her then, although I remembered how it hurt when she left me. A deep, jagged scar that never healed over, that opened again and again. Every birthday I had. Every time I had to share a party with Clare, even though my birthday was a month earlier. Every time I walked into Clare's house after school and had to wait my turn to tell Clare's mother about my day. On all these occasions it hurt that she was gone. There was always her absence pulling apart the fragile veins of blood that sought to close the wound.

That day, the day she spoke, I decided that her choice would not be mine. I would not become a spider, even though she showed me how. My mother killed herself "for me." She hurt me all the same. And since, in the end, I did not escape my mother's moods but had myself become them, I wanted something better for my own children. I wanted my children to escape my mother's web even if I could not. Only the spider can leave the web.

I can never escape her web. That is my inheritance. She left me tangled, an insignificant insect, in the web she constructed out of the sticky threads of sadness and the sap of desolation. She left me as her unintended victim dangling in her deserted web where thin gossamer threads blew in the breeze. The stray threads bound my body and became my shroud, and I became the beetle, the moth, the fly, paralyzed and numb, waiting for the spider to return and release me. She never did.

I am still waiting in my mother's web, and I take comfort in the fact that I am now so small I hardly matter, even to myself. The web is both my prison and my sanctuary, for I have learned the only lesson my mother ever cared to teach me—"It is better for you that I am gone." And I have improved on the lesson so that my children can be spared the pain of being left.

I have done what I did for them. I could not leave them, as my mother left me, in a deserted web. Amy will never even know I was her mother. And William? For him, I have made myself small. As small as a beetle, quiet and still so that he will not recognize me when he comes. That is all right. That is how it should be. Clare will be his mother now. He deserves a real flesh-and-blood mother, not a brittle, beetle thing.

WILLIAM SLID ON HIS TUMMY UNDER THE BED. Frantically, he groped in all the dark and dusty corners. He must find her. His heart beat double time, and he began to whimper, his bottom lip quivering against the little wave of sound. Somehow she had escaped and scuttled away on her six black beetle legs. A tear slid down his cheek and spattered onto the cold dusty floorboards. His bwootiful julie beetle. Gone. He found part of a Lego rocket ship Steve had helped him make on Christmas Day. The pieces broke as he clenched his fist around them. He found a dried apricot, a Freddo Frog wrapper, a piece of sticky tack fallen off the wall, a Matchbox car with three wheels, but no julie beetle. He heard footsteps down the hall. Someone grabbed his feet and pulled him out, tummy skidding on the floor, Bonds undershirt sliding up under his chin, collecting dust in the folds.

Steve, dressed in his blue overalls for work, crouched over his son. He'd had a shower. His damp hair shone, and he smelled clean. William breathed his father in. He didn't usually smell like that. He usually smelled like grease and petrol and rust. Today he smelled like Imperial Leather soap.

"What were you doin' under there, mate?"

William wiped his eyes with his dusty hands and left big brown marks on his face.

"Lookin' for my julie beetle. She's gone."

Steve put his face close to his son's. He hadn't shaved. William saw the brown prickles poking out all over his father's face. "Listen, William. There's plenty more julie beetles to be had. Why don't you and I go look for some this afternoon, heh?"

"I don't want another one, Dad. I want the one I had before."

Steve lifted his son up and hugged him. God, he loved the little bugger. Funny how just looking after him these last few months had forged a bond that wasn't there before. He sat down on William's bedspread. The red boat pattern was looking pretty grimy. How often had Evey chucked things in the wash?

"You know, Will, I reckon Julie's just gone on a little holiday. Where did you say you found her?"

"In Sophie's garden."

"Well, I bet Julie went back there. She's probably got family to visit. What about, when I pick you up from Clare's this afternoon, we go down to the backyard and see if we can find her. Heh?"

William wiped his nose with the back of his hand and a snotty snail trail appeared on his wrist. "Do you really think we can find her?"

"Sure we can. But we better get you dressed. Clare will be here to pick you up any minute now."

Steve dressed his son in his green Wiggles shirt and brown pants. The pants had lots of pockets. William liked pockets. Once Steve had tied his son's shoelaces in double knots, they walked out to the front yard to wait for Clare. Steve wasn't convinced that letting William see Evelyn in hospital was a good idea, but he'd allowed himself to be persuaded by the social workers, the doctors, and especially Clare. And if there was even a small chance that William's visit might break Evelyn's silence, it was worth it. He, himself, hadn't been to see Evelyn much lately. What was the point? She didn't acknowledge his presence anyway. It was like he didn't even exist. He hadn't existed since that day. The day she found him with Wendy.

Was she punishing him then? Was it all a big farce? Fuck! He'd gone through the denial and the despair, and now all that was left was anger. What had she done with his little girl? Cold-hearted bitch. She should be the one punished, not him. She had all the answers. Of course she did. He wanted to shake them out of her, shake out the blankness in her eyes, shake out the silence and make her blubber. Shit, that's what he would do if only they'd let him.

Clare pulled up in her white station wagon. It was an automatic. A typical ladies' car, thought Steve. He didn't like automatics.

They didn't have enough grunt. Automatics were best suited to women, especially timid, cautious women like Clare.

Clare smiled, and her honey hair fell back from her face as she wound down the window. Steve wondered what hair like that smelled like.

"All ready to go, William?"

William nodded. His sad brown eyes peered into her soft-featured face and she wondered again whether she was doing the right thing. Too late now. It was all arranged.

"Hop in, then," she said.

Steve opened the door and put his son's seat belt on. "See ya later, mate," he said as he hugged him. He stepped back and bent down to talk to Clare through the window. "I'll pick him up at half three. I'll see if I can knock off work early. William's lost his 'julie' bug, and we're going down to see if she's taken herself off on a holiday in your backyard." Steve winked one blue eye. He was attractive, she thought. He had that raw sex appeal that some men possess. He was tall, with a square jaw—strong and yet, somehow, needy . . . vulnerable. Not her type though. She smiled back at him and wound up her window.

She started the car. As she drove down the street she looked back at Steve in her rearview mirror. He was staring after them, reaching in his pocket for a cigarette. He's changed, she thought. Only a little, but still . . . he's different from before.

At the hospital, William clung to her hand, and Sophie began to whine for a treat from the vending machine in the foyer. Clare wasn't sure if she and Sophie should stay in the room with William and Evelyn and the social worker. She wasn't sure if she was up to seeing Evelyn today. Luckily, the matter was resolved by a cheerful young social worker with brown curly hair. The social worker greeted them at the desk and offered to take William in to see his mother and stay with him throughout the visit. Clare smiled gratefully at the young man and ushered Sophie into a little playroom near the hospital entrance, but not before Sophie had succeeded in scoring a packet of Smarties and a Coke from the vending machine. Clare sat down with a pile of magazines and prayed breathlessly that William would cope without her.

THE YOUNG MAN WITH THE CURLY HAIR AND the wide smile took William down a long hallway that smelled like the disinfectant his mom used to put in his bath. He opened a door and led William by the hand into a room. A white room.

"There now. Here she is, William," he said. "I'll sit over here, and you two can say hello. All right?"

William nodded, but his eyes were lowered. He bit his lip. His heart was afraid, and it thumped noisily inside him. There was a woman sitting in the corner of the white room. She was sitting on a green vinyl armchair. William looked at her feet. Only at her feet. He kept his head down low. The woman had his mother's feet, thin and pale. You could see the veins. Blue veins. Blue veins must carry blue blood. His mother didn't have red blood like other people. William's eyes wandered up the woman's legs to where her clothing brushed her calves. She was wearing his mother's night-gown. Soft little lilac flowers. He saw her empty lap and thought he might like to be in it, and he looked up a little more and saw that this woman had hair that was red and wavy like his mother's. There he stopped. He didn't want to look any more. If he looked at her face, he might find that the woman in the corner was not his mother after all.

He walked over to her, slowly, deliberately. He averted his eyes and climbed into her lap. The woman smelled like his mother. She smelled like the vanilla that goes into a cake. William closed his eyes and leaned against her, snuggled with his head in her bosom. Still, he did not dare meet her eyes. He sat quiet, very quiet and still, and he tried to make himself small by curling up into a little ball. He needed to be small, or the woman might ask him to get off her lap. She might say he was too heavy, and the spell would be broken. He would look into her eyes and see that, after all, it was not his mommy, but someone else's. He could hear her heart beating. He could feel the soft rise and fall of her breast. He began to suck his thumb, like he used to when he was a baby. He hardly dared to breathe because he felt himself slowly growing heavier and heavier on her lap. He felt her little bones being crushed under his, and although her arm came up and wrapped around him, it was barely there. The woman barely touched him. She seemed to melt away from him, and he knew. He knew that this woman was too small to be his mother.

A tear splashed on his arm. Was it his or hers? Certainly his eyes were weeping. He wiped them dry, and when he looked out again, he found himself staring at the window, and there, on the white sill, was his little julie beetle. His heart leapt.

"Julie . . . julie beetle . . . I've found you. You were here all the time!" He ran over to the window and gently lifted the little beetle in his hand.

His perfect little beetle. A beautiful, rainbowy thing. The tears dried in his eyes, and he rushed back across the floor to climb into the woman's lap once more. He stared down at the little beetle. "I thought you were gone. I thought you'd run away. But you were here all the time. You were here waiting for me to come and find you. I'll keep you safe now, little beetle."

William held the beetle in the palm of his hand and water splashed down and made a salty pool near where the jewel beetle lay. William looked up. For the first time he looked into the woman's face. He stared into the green eyes, and the green eyes stared back. Tears crept like soldier ants down the woman's cheeks. William drew a breath. It was her. It was his mother after all, and she wasn't small anymore. She was enfolding him in her arms, weeping into his hair, and her bones no longer felt like they were breaking under him. He gasped, and cried out, in surprise and in joy, "Mommy, when did you get here?"

IN PURSUIT

JOANNA GRIPPED THE HANDLE OF SAM'S RED stroller and plunged through the fierce fluorescent lighting of the shopping center. She maneuevred, obligingly, in and out of the throng of people moving toward her, noting the distance she covered by watching the grey marbelite floor roll away in the space between her brown shoes and the black rubber wheels. Now and then she inclined her head upward to stare at the slim ankles of fashionable young women strutting through the center in stylish Italian leather shoes. Then her eyes flickered up for a moment, taking in their perfect figures and their well-cut clothes. She never looked into their faces. But she felt the eyes of these women burning holes into her scalp, willing her to relinquish a small piece of her envy. Joanna refused them. She let them be hungry too.

Sam was getting too heavy for the cheap stroller. The red fabric stretched and sagged under his weight and pulled against the metal screws where it was attached to the frame. The strain of constant overloading from Sam's weight, and also the shopping that Joanna was inclined to hook over the handle, had buckled the frame so that all the lines bent toward the center. Thus Sam had the appearance of being pushed around in a sling on wheels, his bottom almost low enough to trace a pattern on the floor, his body obscured and his blond head leaning unnaturally forward to see out.

The wheels under Sam's stroller-sling squeaked as they turned over the marbelite, but Joanna was so habituated to the sound she only noticed it when it ceased abruptly outside the hairdresser's salon. Vivianne's Salon was outfitted in a 1960s retro style with black-and-white checkerboard tiles on the floor. Black bentwood chairs were upholstered with purple vinyl, and tall aluminum vases of artificial pink and yellow gerberas were placed around the room. Joanna had an appointment but she hesitated at the door. She felt out of place. Somehow the funky decor just wasn't her. Besides, outside Vivianne's, in the mall, was a coffee shop . . .

The smell of coffee beans and the chink of cutlery scooping up cake from china plates made her dizzy with desire. Maybe she should take Sam to morning tea instead. Just a cappuccino for herself but Sam . . . Sam could have a milk shake, and maybe a piece of cake, and maybe she could have just a sliver of his . . . She would have turned and left then, but she caught sight of herself in one of the mirrors in the salon and saw the way the fluorescent lighting in the shopping center slid off her brown hair, emphasizing its drabness. So she pushed Sam's stroller over to the counter.

"Hi, I think I've got an appointment for 10 A.M.?"

The woman at the counter looked up; her eyes were almost violet and outlined heavily in black. She was dressed in a black woolen shift over a tight grey top, and her hair was cut into a jagged black bob with burgundy streaks. She checked her appointment book.

"Let's see . . . Joanna, is it? I'm Vivianne. Come through and take a seat. I'll be with you in a minute."

Joanna pushed Sam over to the chair in the corner and took a box of Smarties out of her handbag to keep him busy while she had her hair washed.

"Here you go, Sam. Do you want some Smarties?"

Sam smiled and grabbed the box. "Marties!" He fiddled with the end until it tore open, and he sat back in his stroller, popping Smarties into his mouth, candy flecks of blue and red and yellow gathering in the chocolate dribble running down his chin.

"What can we do for you today, Joanna?" There was Vivianne. She had pulled up a chair and straddled it backward, leaning over the backrest to talk to Joanna.

"I want something a bit different. I thought I might go for a shorter cut . . . and maybe a bit blonder. Perhaps some streaks? I don't know. What do you think?"

Vivianne lifted up Joanna's light brown hair and felt the texture of it. "Have you ever had your hair streaked before?"

"No."

"In that case the color will need a bit longer to develop. Will that be all right with you?"

Joanna looked at Sam. He'd already finished his Smarties, and he was arching his back, demanding to be let out of the stroller. She undid his seat belt. "Do you have any toys he could play with?"

"Sure. There's a box of toys out back I can bring in. Then he can sit beside you and play."

Joanna stared at her face in the mirror and touched her chin. There was a little pink pimple there. When she'd been applying the Clearasil at seventeen, she'd never dreamed that she'd still be getting pimples at thirty-six. She sighed. It must be hormonal. Her period was nearly due. God, she looked awful. She'd forgotten to put on her makeup too. Picking up her handbag, she pulled out her lipstick and applied it in the mirror. There, she did not look quite so washed-out now. Susan was right. Lipstick was crucial.

Vivianne brought over the toys for Sam. She set up all her equipment on a little black trolley and wheeled it beside Joanna. Taking a black smock off the trolley, she whipped out its folds in the air with a flourish. The smock billowed down over Joanna, and Vivianne tied it up at the neck. She picked up a latex cap and pulled it over Joanna's head like a piece of soft pink flesh. She smiled at Joanna's reflection in the mirror.

"Not very attractive, is it?"

Joanna laughed. "It reminds me of something else."

Vivianne arched her beautifully defined black brows, and her eyes sparkled. Joanna could tell she was enjoying herself. She took out a little metal hook, rather like a crochet hook, and proceeded to hook Joanna's hair through the tiny holes in the cap.

"Am I hurting you?" she asked, when Joanna winced as a tuft of hair was jerked through.

"Don't worry, I'm okay," Joanna said. But her grey eyes were watering.

Vivianne began to pull the hair through faster, and when she was finished, Joanna looked like a balding circus clown and felt like every hair on her scalp had been plucked out. Vivianne painted on the blonding agent then, a thick blue cream that smelled of peroxide and made Joanna's head spin and her eyes water even more. When her hair was completely covered in blue cream, Vivianne tied a little plastic cap over it to keep the cream from running down her face.

"Now," Vivianne said, "it will take about thirty minutes. Can I get you a cup of coffee or tea?"

Joanna nodded. "Coffee, please."

"And a cookie too?"

A cookie? No, a cookie wouldn't do. Outside in the coffee shop, people were eating mud cake, lemon syrup cake, strudel cake with cinnamon crumble topping . . . "Don't worry about the cookie. Just a cup of white coffee. Thanks."

Joanna wiped her eyes on the black cotton smock that was tied around her neck. Reflected in her mirror were the people eating cakes and slices and little tarts. Joanna watched their forks slide through cake and take little morsels of chocolate and pastry and lemon cream up to their mouths. She began to salivate as her eyes wandered ravenously from one face to another. Her hunger met theirs, and they devoured cake together. But it was one face, one solitary face, upon which her eyes eventually came to rest. This face was, at times, wholly or partly eclipsed by the people walking past, and Joanna bent her head at an awkward angle to see it in the mirror.

There was something compelling about it. It was a young face, a pretty face, heart-shaped and framed by a mass of curly hair. But these qualities, while they may have warranted a glance, did not justify such an intense study. What was it? Joanna watched the way the young woman's eyes crinkled with laughter as she bit into a piece of carrot cake covered with cream cheese frosting. It was not a hesitant little nibble or a big gulping bite but a bite that was aware of decadence and committed to enjoying it. Joanna knew what it was that made her stare at this young woman. Hers was the first face Joanna had seen for months that carried no hunger. This young face was satiated . . . full.

The young woman finished her cake and stood up. It was then that Joanna saw that she had a baby with her. The baby had been parked beside her chair in a navy pram all that time, but Joanna had not connected the two of them, which was strange because she always noticed other mothers with children. The baby was cuddling a stuffed toy. It was obviously an old favorite and might have once resembled a bear or a dog, but it was thin in places now, like an empty skin. The child put the toy up to its mouth and sucked it, then dangled it over the side of the pram while the woman—perhaps she was the child's nanny for she seemed very young—struggled to hook her shopping bags over the handle.

The woman pushed the baby around the other tables. It was difficult to get out. There was not much space for prams but, finally, with a big heave, she made it and began to walk away. It was then that Joanna noticed the child had dropped its toy on the ground outside the salon. She got up, still in her cape and latex cap, and walked quickly outside into the mall and scooped up the toy.

"Excuse me!" Joanna began to walk after the girl, and the girl stopped.

Joanna smiled and held the toy in the air.

The girl spun her pram around. "Thank you! Thank you very much!" she cried as she approached Joanna. "It's her favorite. She won't sleep without it."

Joanna bent down and passed the toy to the little girl, who gave her a gummy smile and started sucking on the toy's ear again. Joanna saw that the toy was not a bear at all but a little dog. It was a little spotted Dalmatian dog, just like the one Susan had given to Amy when she was born. The baby girl in the pram smiled another gummy smile, and Joanna swallowed. Probably lots of babies had toys like that. Susan had got it on sale. All the same, Joanna knelt on the floor to take a closer look at the baby.

There was something about the intense green of the baby girl's eyes that made her reach out and grip the bar of the pram so tightly that her knuckles grew white. She tried to sound casual, but there was a note of accusation in her voice.

"Is she your daughter? Perhaps you're her nanny?"

It seemed to Joanna that the girl's dark eyes grew wider. Had she thrown a stone that rippled or was she only imagining it?

"She's mine," the young woman said. But Joanna thought she saw the girl's hands tremble as they reached out to rest on the handle of the pram.

"Thanks for picking up her dog . . . I have to go." The girl tugged the pram out of Joanna's hands and walked away.

Joanna's heart was beating fast. She had to follow her. She ran back into the hair salon, where Vivianne was waiting with her coffee. She rushed past her, knocking coffee onto the floor, scooped up Sam, and dropped him into the stroller. Immediately, Sam began to scream because Joanna had broken the reassuring rituals about getting into the stroller.

"Got no belt on! Got no belt on!"

"Where are you going?" yelled Vivianne, as Joanna tore out of the salon.

But Joanna offered no explanation. She ran through the mall, the black smock swinging behind her, the plastic cap loosening around her head and allowing trickles of blue cream to run down her face. Sam yelled louder in the red stroller, and Joanna pushed through the crowd like a demented woman, screaming after the girl, who was also running now, "Wait . . . Wait!"

The girl weaved her navy pram through the crowd. She looked over her shoulder with wide eyes and saw the woman in the black cape thundering down upon her. She tried to lose her by darting in and out, moving behind the masses of people that swelled in the mall. But the crazy woman, short and round and red-faced, was gaining on her, her screaming toddler in the red stroller serving as a siren to part the crowd. The girl looked around for a way out.

Faces parted in front of Joanna, turning away from the emotion that bulged in her eyes. Joanna could see the girl she was chasing clearly now, turning to the left, toward the exit. Joanna heaved the stroller around the corner but the stroller frame buckled completely under the force she applied and collapsed altogether, enclosing Sam so that he pushed against the sides like a squealing piglet in a bag, with only his feet free. Joanna's momentum continued unchecked, even after the stroller collapsed, and she tumbled over the broken stroller and felt her wrist thud against the wall.

She lay there a moment before the crowd swelled around her again. The people circled her, keeping their distance. Joanna looked from one face to another but, each time she connected with someone's eyes, that person simply turned and walked away.

Vivianne appeared, her hands on her hips, trying to catch her breath. She squatted beside Joanna. "Are you all right?" Vivianne pulled the red-faced Sam out of the broken stroller. He was still screaming, but he was unhurt. She helped Joanna to her feet. "Come on," she said, "I'll help you back to the salon."

Back inside the salon, Joanna kept her throbbing wrist underneath the black smock. She didn't want to admit to Vivianne that she'd hurt it. She was still shaking and clinging tightly to Sam as Vivianne eased off the latex cap and shook her head.

"It's been on much too long. I'm afraid you've lost a little hair, and we'll have to color the rest because the streaks will be far too white."

Tears began to flow freely down Joanna's face, and Vivianne sighed. The only explanation Joanna had managed to give was some far-fetched story about a friend's missing baby, and yet, as Vivianne looked at Joanna, shivering and clutching her little blond son on her knee, she didn't doubt it. Vivianne made up a bottle of ash blond and rubbed it through Joanna's hair. She took her time, massaging Joanna's scalp, easing the taut skin, talking to her soothingly about inconsequential things. And as she chatted, she noted the length of Joanna's forehead, the width of her cheekbones, the line of her chin, and she thought about the cut that would suit Joanna best.

After a while, Vivianne led Joanna over to the sink and sat her down. Joanna closed her eyes as the chair sighed under her weight. Was that baby really Amy? She'd never acted so rashly before. Perhaps she was going mad. She leaned back toward the sound of warm water hissing as it hit the cold porcelain sink. Steam kissed the back of her neck, and she allowed herself to be comforted. Vivianne gathered up her hair and ran warm water through it. Her fingers massaged Joanna's scalp in circular motions, numbing her mind to everything but the sensation of being touched. She breathed in deeply and exhaled.

When the dye was washed out, Joanna sat, with Sam asleep on her knee, gazing at the mirror but not seeing her reflection. Her wrist still ached, especially under Sam's weight. She was beginning to feel that she had acted foolishly. No wonder the girl had run away. She must have looked like a crazy woman hurtling through the mall, her red stroller thrusting through the crowd, her black smock swooping behind her. Suddenly, Joanna felt desperately hungry. She looked at her watch. It had been three hours since she had walked through the door. Vivianne's cheek brushed against hers.

"Well, what do you think?"

Joanna looked at the floor where her hair was cast across the linoleum like shucks of corn. Then she looked at her reflection, and her own grey eyes met the grey eyes in the mirror. An attractive young woman with a modern cropped cut and luminous golden hair stared back, then smashed through the mirror into her consciousness. Joanna gasped. The woman was her, and she was . . . beautiful.

SUSAN

Tell me the time

A preoccupation
With analogue and digital
Measurements

Metal pins striking moments
Cataloging days,
Months and years . . .

Has been mine
Since 6:15 A.M.
February 6
1963

Mother said
I was over
Two weeks late

She was driven to
Distraction

Of course

Her first experience
Of life being
Beyond control

I have spent
My life making up
The difference in time

Tell me the time

I can dissect minutes
I can slice moments
So there are fractions

Available

I have always been
Acutely aware
Of time

I am
What the sharp edge
Slices

Time is
Paper I write
My life on

A valuable commodity

Not to be wasted
Squandered

Lost

Imagine my surprise
My horror
When I found

I had
Lost
Time

Numerals marking
The clock
Had melted

In the desert
Salvador Dali
Has always haunted

Amy had
Fallen . . .

Out

Of time

I searched
Scooped mercury beads
Once held behind glass

Felt liquid metal
Run poisonously
Through my hands

Unable to reconstruct
The numerals
They dribbled away

In pools
Around my feet
A little sock

A little pink sock
Floating in
Silver-grey

I picked it up
Saw other things
Floating past

A book

A graduation cap
A career

All these things
Fallen
From my clock
I'd never noticed
How much time
I'd lost

Tell me the time

How much is available?
How much time do I have
Left to write on?

Shall I tell you the time?

The sharp edge
Slices though
The remainder

At the third stroke
It will be 9:15
Precisely

I do not know why she is always late, but today I will forgive her for losing track of time. I will not order her a flat white. I will let her order for herself. She prefers tea, I think. Still, I am on to my second espresso and it is already 9:25. I will have to have lattes after this.

(Already my
Thoughts are racing ahead
Of my real place
In time)

Joanna was on the phone last night. Sobbing about a baby she'd seen in Westfield Shoppingtown. She must have made a real spectacle of herself, poor thing. I can see her now, thundering through Shoppingtown, her black smock scooping the wind and her head in a plastic cap.

(Joanna, mad mother
My hero
Maternal instincts
Raging
In your
Swollen belly
You pursue offspring
With udders distended
Bursting to suckle
Away the pains
Of your engorgement
But
The milk runs
Into dust)

She would have looked like such a mad cow. It would almost be comic if it weren't such a tragedy.

I WAS INCREDULOUS AT FIRST. I MEAN, AMY IN the local shopping mall. It's stretching probability a bit, isn't it? And if Joanna was running after me with a surge of maternal aggression, I think I'd take off pretty fast too.

She kept going on about the strange behavior this girl was exhibiting and how she didn't like it when Joanna started to ask a few questions. "Well, maybe she had some secrets of her own," I said. "Have you considered that? From what you've been saying, the girl sounded pretty young. Perhaps she's some poor teenager who ran away when she got pregnant. Perhaps she thought you somehow knew her parents and was ready to provide them with some information that she might not have been ready to share." She had to concede that I might have a point.

"But Susan," she said, "what about the toy dog?" I had to admit to her then that my own heart had missed a beat when she'd mentioned the child's toy. But you know, there are probably hundreds of kids in Brisbane that have little dogs like that. They were on sale when that new Disney movie was released. They were everywhere. I picked one up for Amy because I thought it looked cute. "Besides," I told Joanna, "I've been on that desperate search for the imagined before."

(There's a blackness
A dark tunnel
A silent scream
A rope around your waist
Pulling forward
There's no time
No bearing
Nothing to
Cling to
Break the rope
Break the rope, Joanna . . .)

"Look," I said, "I know where you're coming from. I ran straight to the police with one pink sock in my pocket and a story about some clothes and a toy that was missing. I thought I was onto something and that my information would get the police searching again.

"But the truth is, the police already believe that Amy is dead. They can't charge Evelyn because there's no evidence. Anyway, she's clearly mentally unstable. Postnatal psychosis is a pretty extreme illness. People who are less unstable have committed infanticide before. The police aren't expecting to find a live baby.

They've always been looking for a body. And now they've even given up looking for that. They think it'll just turn up, like bodies usually do."

I know the way I put things to Joanna sounded cold and un-feeling, but I don't want her to torture herself over this. This end-less quest for Amy that's consumed us all . . . It's time to end it. We've all got to get on with our own lives . . .

(Got to wind up the clock
Start time moving again
Let the sharp edge
Slice through
And move on)

Don't think that I'm convinced Amy is dead. I know Evelyn. At least I think I do. She didn't kill her baby. She'd kill herself first. And there's a family history of that! But her baby wasn't stolen either, as Joanna would have it. And it's obvious, isn't it? Why Joanna would rather believe that Evelyn's baby was stolen. Be-cause that absolves Evelyn of all maternal guilt and makes Joanna feel more comfortable with the whole wretched business.

(Joanna
Poor cow
Udders bursting
Milk running into
Dust)

Do you want to know what I really think? My theory is that some-how Evelyn adopted her baby out on the black market. Maybe she even did it over the Internet. God knows, it's been done before!

147

Why else would all Amy's everyday clothes and nappies be missing? I bet she bundled them all up and gave them, along with Amy, to some nice childless couple from the U.S. . . . At least, that's the story I tell myself to help me sleep at night.

(Let the sharp edge
Slice through
I am not afraid)

Tell me the time!

Really! A quarter to ten, and Clare's just arriving now!

And Joanna too. She must have dropped Sam off with her mother this morning.

Are you all right, Wendy? You look deathly pale. Would you like a glass of water? You should be well and truly over your nausea by now. You must be about five months along—it's due sometime in November, isn't it?

THE CAUSE OF SUFFERING

"CLARE!" SAID SUSAN, STANDING BEHIND WENDY and gripping her shoulders. "Run inside and get Wendy a glass of cold water. She's feeling dizzy!"

Clare threw her handbag on the table and ran up to the counter in the cafe. In any crisis, Susan always took the lead. The force of her personality demanded complete obedience. Clare grabbed a carafe of iced water and some glasses and hurried back outside.

As Joanna poured a glass of water for Wendy, she tried to remember if she'd ever felt that nauseous during either of her pregnancies. Wendy's health worried her. Perhaps there was something wrong. "Are you okay now?" she asked, after Wendy had drunk some water. "Shall I drive you home?"

"No . . . no," said Wendy as the color came back into her face. "I'll be all right if I sit awhile. I think my blood pressure might be a bit low or something."

"When are you going back to see your obstetrician?" Susan loosened her grip on Wendy's shoulders and returned to her seat.

"On Monday."

"Well, don't forget to tell him about this. You can never be too careful."

"No. I think I'm just a bit stressed at the moment."

"Well, no wonder! The way you work. Night shifts in your second trimester? You must be crazy. What does Harry think about that?"

Wendy put her elbows on the table and cupped her chin in her hands. Her normally clear blue eyes looked bloodshot and sore. "Oh, he'd like me to stop work altogether, but I only work a couple of night shifts a week."

Clare poured herself a glass of water from the carafe. "Can't you find something in the daytime?"

"No, and I wouldn't want to. I like night shift. I sleep much better during the day at the moment. Anyway, it's not work that's stressing me. It's this whole business about Evelyn's baby. Every time we talk about it I . . . I . . . just can't handle it."

"That's fair enough," said Joanna, relieved that there was a plausible explanation for Wendy's symptoms. "The whole thing makes me miserable too and I'm not even pregnant!" Joanna looked at the specials board leaning against the wall—apricot-and-almond torte, that sounded delicious . . .

"Yes," agreed Clare, "those pregnancy hormones must make things even worse for you. I can remember crying a lot before Sophie was born, over all sorts of things."

Joanna dragged her eyes away from the list of cakes. The light skipped over her hair and surrounded her face with a luminous glow. "I used to cry over loo paper ads when I was pregnant with Jake," she reflected.

"Loo paper ads?" Susan raised her perfectly plucked black eyebrows.

"Yes. You know the one! That cute little Labrador runs around the house with the toilet paper and gets locked outside with that last little piece of loo paper dangling pathetically in his mouth . . ." Joanna put her head on one side and stuck her tongue out in an attitude of doggy dejection. "It brought me to tears every time!"

Clare laughed. "Me too! I'm still sentimental about that brand of toilet paper, you know."

"I can't say that ad ever did it for me," Susan said with a bemused look on her face. "I do remember sobbing over some starving Ethiopians once!"

"Well," considered Clare, "you don't have to be pregnant to weep for people starving in the third world."

Susan tapped her fingers on the tabletop. "Just to change the subject," she said. "I've been thinking that next year, I might go back to university and do my master's. All the kids will be at school and I'll finally have some time to study."

"You're serious about going back to university, aren't you?" There was a small note of anxiety in Joanna's voice. The academic world was foreign to her and so far removed from her life, it was as if her friend was saying she was going overseas.

"I've been mulling it over these last few weeks," Susan continued. "I really enjoy research. It was something I was good at when I was at uni. I worked as a research assistant in the English Department for three years before I had Maxine. I think it's time I did something again. If I don't do it now, I probably never will."

"Would you do it full-time?" asked Wendy, wondering how Susan was going to reorganize her life.

"Oh no. How would I manage the children? How would I manage Richard? I'll take it slowly. Part-time study while the kids are in primary school. Then, once they're in high school, I can find a job. Maybe I can even become a literary critic. That's what I always wanted to do—read novels for a living and tell authors what they should have done!" She laughed.

Joanna looked sadly into her glass. She was going to lose her friend. It was beyond Susan's capacity to do anything part-time. She had made a career out of mothering, and now she would make a career out of study. And where did that leave Joanna? The only thing she had in common with Susan was motherhood.

"Well, I admire you," said Clare. "Going back to study after all this time. That takes a bit of courage."

"No. Staying home with the kids takes courage!" Susan's hazel eyes froze for a minute on Joanna's face, then lifted and darted back and forth from Clare to Wendy. She threw her arms wide. "I'm actually giving in. I'm giving in to my longing for some kind of adult life beyond my family. I'm being selfish." Susan squinted one eye, and said, fiendishly, "I'm giving in to desire!"

"But desire isn't selfish," said Wendy. "It's normal to want things. We can't blame ourselves for being human, can we?" Wendy felt her face grow warm, and she sipped some more water.

"I don't know," said Clare. "Sometimes I wish that I could rise above my own longings and just be . . ." Clare shifted in her chair.

"Be? Be what?" asked Wendy.

Clare shrugged. "Be a good mother, I suppose. Like my mother was. I was listening to Radio National the other day. There was a program on *The Spirit of Things* about Buddhism. Buddhists say that desire is the cause of all suffering."

"I think I'd have to agree with that," said Susan. "Do you know, we've all been sitting here rabbiting on for ages and we haven't even ordered yet. How about I go and order the coffees. Let's see . . . Joanna—a skinnychino. Wendy—a chamomile tea. Clare, what will you have? A flat white?"

"Yes . . . umm . . . no. No!" Why not? She didn't have to go along with what Susan usually ordered her. "I'll have a pot of tea. Please!"

THE WORST PART

THE WORST PART IS SLIDING BACK TO THE place where I do not want to be. In this room, where the light is sharp, I am emerging red and raw, a fetus with capillaries branching out underneath a meniscus of skin. Everything ordinary: sight, sound, taste, touch is overwhelming, excruciating in intensity. I squint my eyes because the light is too bright and it encapsulates me in a hard white dome. It blinds me.

Blind people don't see black. They see white. Shapes of objects and people in my room appear as shadows hovering in the light, devoid of color, existing only in relation to the white light that surrounds me. Sound too is hard and white, and silence exists as a ringing behind my ears, filling intervals between crashes and bangs made by teaspoons and cups and venetian blinds blowing in the wind.

When they bring in my food on the tray I can smell the aroma of each ingredient I am served but subtle flavors are overwhelmed by sensations of saltiness, sweetness, and bitterness. I don't eat much. Not because I am not hungry. I pick at my food because the cutlery feels so cold in my hand that I'm afraid the skin on my fingers will freeze and stick.

Now that I have begun the shock therapy, the staff are pleased

with me. They say that the shock treatment and the new medication are making a difference—that I'm about to turn the corner.
And so I no longer hear the spider amid the clamor of other
sounds. I still listen for her, through the ringing, but I know now
that I can no longer live out my life in the guise of a beetle or a
moth, or some other inconsequential insect wrapped up in the
spider's shroud. I am sliding slowly, painfully, into myself and my
other reality. My thread has unraveled, and I am suspended above
the ground, rocking like a pendulum in the wind. I cannot take
refuge in my mother's web anymore, but the web still sticks to the
soles of my feet. Dirty grey strands still hold me, binding my feet,
stifling my growth into someone who is separate from the vision
of the mother that I cling to.

My doctor says that, for a while, the new medication will
make me slow and sluggish. Amid the roar and dazzle of white
light and screaming sound, I sense there are things happening
around me. I see the shadows move, I hear the doors close, but my
mind takes a moment to catch up. Everything is on a delayed
telecast so that I lose my power in time, my power to make moments meaningful, because by the time I realize the moment, it
has gone, and my ability to seize it, to act in it, is diminished.

Today Clare brought William to see me again. She knows
what she is doing. She knows she is breaking me. I do not speak,
but with William I do not need to. There is a bond between us.
He is so different from myself and my mother. A boy-child.
A boy-child on whom I do not fixate my own self-loathing. He
is like Steve, and even now I do not hate Steve as much as I hate
myself.

William climbed onto my lap, as he did the first time. The
warmth from his body was intense, and I fell into it and put my
arms around him. I did not look at the shape in the corner that

was Clare. I did not give her the satisfaction of enjoying her power. I bent and breathed in the deep, pungent odor of William's hair as he sat on my lap, sucking his thumb. He had a yeasty smell, like bread. I breathed his smell in and out and felt my body relax. My consciousness was sliding into my body. Knowledge of myself in the real world made me cry, and my tears ran into William's hair.

William turned toward me, and for once I saw a face that was unshadowed and defined by color. He looked at me with his deep brown eyes. His eyes are his own, they are neither mine, nor Steve's, nor my mother's. They are still deep pools, where his soul floats softly. He wiped away my tears with the thumb he had just been sucking, mixing them with his saliva. He stroked my face, then the shadow that was Clare stood up to come and take him away. I reached out to touch him one last time, but his colors were already vanishing. I saw that he was wearing his old jeans. They were torn and needed mending. His yellow-striped shirt had a stain . . . I reached out to touch . . . but the white light enfolded him. He and Clare were already gone. The door was closed.

I looked at the shape of the door closed to me, and I knew that I was alone. Alone in the white hospital room with the cold steel bed and the smooth linoleum floor. Alone in my body and alone with my grief and my terror. I can no longer feel nothing, and that is the worst part. I can no longer feel nothing, and I find myself aching for more.

RAIN FALLING

"WHY IS MOMMY SO SAD?" WILLIAM'S BIG ROUND eyes transfixed Clare's face as she leaned over him to do up his seat belt.

A frozen moment . . . and then Clare answered him. "She's not well, possum. That's why she cries."

"Did I make her sick?"

"No. No, of course not." Clare pulled the strap tight.

"Did Amy then?"

Clare squatted down on the cold paving beside the open car door and looked up into the pale sober face of the child. The child registered the pause while Clare thought of the right way to answer his question.

"No. No, Amy didn't make Mommy sick. After Amy was born, something got sick inside Mommy's head. But the doctor will make Mommy better, and she won't cry anymore."

"Will she come home then?"

"Yes. When Mommy is all better she will come home." Clare nodded encouragingly and stood up. She closed the door gently and ran her hands through her hair, gripping her skull with her long fingers and massaging her tight scalp. How her head ached!

She sat in the driver's seat, turned on the ignition, and looked in her rearview mirror. The child's anxious face met her eyes, in the smallness of the glass.

"Will Amy come home when Mommy does?"

How was she supposed to answer that impossible question? The child trusted her to make sense of his world, and she was letting him down. Did Evelyn really know what she had done? Clare's voice trembled. "I . . . I . . . don't know, William."

Tears collected along the rims of the child's eyes and poised, ready to fall from his long black lashes. He knew. Amy wasn't coming home. The car pulled out of the car park, and he put his thumb in his mouth and stared out the window. It began to rain. The drops wriggled down the outside of the window, and he took his thumb out of his mouth and traced the patterns they made on the glass. He was quiet and empty of questions.

The car climbed up the hill in the soft winter rain, and Clare took in the landscape as a panacea to the ache in her head. Stepped up the hill, little wooden workers' cottages, painted in romantic colors—pink, blue, and mauve with white trims—leaned into each other, wall to wall, window to window. They were so close together that the occupants could have shaken hands, although Clare doubted that they ever wanted to. Perched along the ridge, on top of tall wooden stumps, were big colonials and Queenslanders with wide verandahs and ample iron roofs. These houses had steep gardens, sometimes terraced neatly against the side of the hill and sometimes full of rambling weeds and self-seeded mango trees. They had city views, and Clare imagined that today the inhabitants could see the small cluster of skyscrapers threaded through drifts of white cloud and, through the fog, the lights of the brewery flashing.

The car wound through the back streets, where the boundaries of city council parks were politely defined by the modest iron fences of postwar homes. They stopped at a traffic light, which blinked one red eye through the mist of rain collecting between the slow strokes of the windscreen wipers. And then they drove on. William saw the corner shop where he used to walk with his mother for Popsicles. He saw the lonely grey gum at the top of his street and watched its torn and tattered coat of bark flapping in the wind. He saw his driveway with one gate open and the other gate leaning against the fence, waiting, as most things in his house were waiting, to be made well again.

Clare pulled the car into the Easterns' yard and parked it out of the rain, in the dark under the house. She climbed out and hunched her back, to avoid hitting her head on the overhead beams, while she opened William's door. "Are you hungry, Will?" William nodded. "Let's go upstairs then. I'll make you a hot chocolate malt and we'll see if there's some cartoons on television. Okay?"

She led the child by the hand upstairs, through the enclosed verandah, which smelled dank and moldy even though Susan had cleaned it thoroughly. She swung open the heavy front door with the stained-glass panel of entwined roses, and they walked up the worn Persian carpet runner into the living room. Clare flicked the light switch and frowned at the darkness. Steve still hadn't changed the lightbulb. She walked into the kitchen and stood on her toes beside the open pantry. Her hand groped across the top shelf and grasped the cardboard casing of a new lightbulb. She pushed a chair into the center of the room, stood on it to change the bulb, then flicked the switch again and watched the hard white light flood the room.

"There. That's better, isn't it?" she said to William, who was snuggled under an old crocheted blanket in a rainbow of colors. She turned on the television for him and watched a cat chase a mouse across the screen. Thank goodness for the distraction of cartoons on wet Saturday afternoons, she thought.

"Now, let's see if I can find you something to eat."

Clare opened the fridge. It was full of dubious-looking boxes and containers from various fast-food outlets around town. She thought, guiltily, that she ought to run up to the corner shop and restock the fridge with some fresh eggs, butter, cheese, and apples. Maybe she should make a double quantity of bolognese sauce tonight and bring it around so that Steve and William could have some supper together . . .

She opened the lid of one of the plastic containers and peered inside. Something vile and green was growing across an ancient take-away chow mein. She recoiled in disgust and threw the box into the bin. Then she pulled out all the other boxes and containers and jammed them into the bin as well. At least there was some fresh milk—but only because she and David were paying for the delivery, and in the mornings, when she collected William, she brought in the cartons from the steps outside.

Clare poured some milk into a mug and spooned in some chocolate malt powder from the tin in the cupboard. The tin was nearly empty, and she had to tip it up to fill her spoon. She heated the milk in the microwave and found a couple of cookies in a jar at the back of the pantry. She took the snack out to William.

He had fallen asleep on the couch with Steve's old tomcat curled up against his back. Clare watched the blue light from the television flicker across William's face. She put the mug and the cookies on the little side table and tucked the blanket around him. The cat was purring, lying on its back and dreaming through its slit eyes. When she breathed in she could smell Steve on the couch—he was the smell of car oil and sweat and cheap aftershave lotion. She wondered if he slept here with the cat, rather than in the big double bed he used to share with Evelyn. Anyway, where was Steve? He should be home by now. He'd promised to look after William tonight while she spent some time alone with Sophie and David.

She went back into the kitchen to make herself a cup of tea and stood looking out the window while the water boiled. The rain was still falling. She shivered. It was cold in the house. She made her tea and stood by the window, holding the mug between her hands, letting the steam warm the tip of her nose.

Clare saw him beside the back fence, digging in the compost heap in the rain. Steve was gardening? She had never seen him working in the garden before. She watched as he lifted the shovel and brought it down again into the soft mulch, twisting it and breaking it apart and loading it into the wheelbarrow. His shirt was wet and it clung to his back so that she could see his muscles ripple under the wet cotton when he thrust the shovel into the dirt.

When he had finished loading the tray, he threw his shovel on top and trudged, with his barrow, around the side of the house. Clare heard the wet leaves squelch underneath his heavy work boots. She finished her tea, put on an old grey coat of Steve's that was hanging beside the back door, and walked down the back stairs into the rain.

The grass was long in the backyard, and it wet the bottom of her jeans. She looked up at the jacaranda tree, which was devoid of leaves or buds, its branches naked and dead against the grey August sky. She walked around it and brushed past the washing, soaked with rain, hanging on the Hill's hoist. Surely he could have taken the clothes down. She had hung them up three days ago, and it had only started raining today.

He was in the front yard, pulling up weeds in the rose garden that had once belonged to Evelyn's mother. He ripped the weeds out of the ground and threw them angrily at the fence so that the dirt around the invasive root systems came away and scattered in the grass. The earth gasped as the weeds were pulled out, and Steve methodically uprooted everything, even the sinewy crabgrass that clung around the root systems of the rosebushes.

She saw that the bushes were old and gnarled but still green. The trunk on each plant was thick and twisted and determined to remain alive, even at the expense of blooms. Clare remembered that pink and yellow roses had poked their heads through the weeds a few months ago, but when she had looked at them closely, they had turned out to be contorted and diseased, brown with decay and covered in aphids.

Several times Steve appeared to cut his hands on the rose thorns as he tried to pull out the weeds wrapped around the old bushes. He wiped the blood onto his shirt. He didn't wince. He almost seemed to enjoy the pain, for each time he cut himself, he attacked the weeds with renewed vigor.

"You ought to be careful with those," she said. "You can get blood poisoning from rose thorns."

He didn't look at her. "Damn things," he said. "Evelyn never looked after them, but she wouldn't let me take them out either. They could have looked nice with a bit of care. They might have bloomed properly, but no, she never let me touch them."

"Why not?"

"Buggered if I know. Something to do with her mother, I suppose." Steve began breaking the hard soil around the roses with the edge of his shovel.

"I've always hated this garden," he said. "It's so ugly. It's like it's . . . got death in it."

Clare moved closer to him and put her hand on his arm. "I've always wondered why you and Evelyn stayed. Here, in this house. It's full of so many bad memories."

Steve threw down the shovel and leaned over to grasp a runner from some crabgrass. He pulled and tore the runner out of the ground. "She wouldn't move. That's why! Once her father died, and the house was left to her, she wanted to stay. At first I thought it was a great idea. The old place had potential to be renovated, and it was debt-free. But Evelyn would never let me change anything. After a while I gave up. What was the point? If she wanted to live in a wreck, that was her problem. I've never been very domestic anyway—as you've probably realized."

"Mmm. I was going to make some spaghetti for tea. I'll make extra and get David to drop it round."

Steve found another runner of crabgrass and jerked it out of the soil. He didn't look at her but focused on the garden instead. "Thanks," he said flatly. "William only gets takeaway when he's with me."

"I've noticed."

Someone walked toward them, sloshing through the wet grass. "Hello, Clare!" called Wendy from the fence. "What are you two doing out in the rain?" They turned to watch Wendy, obviously pregnant now, walking through the front gate. She wore a stretchy black top, and Steve looked thoughtfully at her round belly. Wendy blushed and swallowed. So he was wondering, she thought. He'd never said anything. Good. It was better that way.

"Steve's decided to fix up the rose garden," answered Clare.

"I've always wondered if those plants could be salvaged once the weeds were pulled away." Wendy stood next to Clare, sheltering her with her blue umbrella, feeling the air cool her face back to pale.

"It's hard to grow roses in Queensland," Clare said. "I planted some years ago, but they were always covered in black spot. The climate is too humid here. Roses take a lot of care. I remember that Evelyn's mother was always working in this garden."

Steve pulled out the last of the weeds and began digging in the mulch from his barrow.

"Don't go too close to the root area, Steve! Roses don't like having their root systems disturbed." Clare offered her advice heartily. It was enjoyable, watching Steve do some work around the house.

Steve grimaced and kept on churning in the mulch. He wished the women would go and leave him in peace. He was beginning to feel like a freak. Why did women always stand around watching the moment a bloke tried to do something?

"It's a wonder these plants have survived so long," Wendy re-marked. "They must be a very hardy variety. Every spring they try to flower, but the flowers usually drop as soon as they open." Wendy watched Steve's breath form little white clouds in the cold air as he pushed his weight into the earth. She saw the flesh beneath his shirt and longed to reach out and touch it. Instead, she clasped her hands so they did not give her away.

Steve thrust his shovel deep into the soil, but the blade met with some resistance. "What the hell?" he said as he scooped up the earth.

"What is it, Steve?" said Clare. "I told you to be careful of the roots!"

Steve dropped his shovel on the ground and knelt on the dirt. He brushed the soil away gently with his hand.

Clare and Wendy leaned over him from behind, trying to see what he saw. A tiny hand rolled free of the soil. Its fingers were spread wide.

"Oh my God!" Wendy sank to her knees on the ground and covered her face.

Steve reached into the earth. He fumbled around with his hands, scooping the dirt away, and pulled up the naked body. The rain washed the dirt from the stiff little limbs, and it trickled like blood onto the grass.

Clare could hear Wendy retching over her swollen belly, but she did not move to help her. She stood watching events unfold as if from a distance. She felt nothing, just a sensation of numbness and a strange tingling along her spine.

Steve put his hand on Wendy's shoulder. "It's all right," he said. "Look!" he gently laid the torso on the ground in front of her. "See," he said. "It's a doll. It's just an old doll."

The numbness left Clare. "Let me have it!" she said, leaning over and scooping up the bedraggled doll from the wet grass. As she held it, the rain continued to wash away the dirt. The blond hair had disintegrated and the little holes where the hair had been rooted were filled with dirt. The blue eyes were caked in mud and rusted over; the plastic was discolored, and one hand was missing, where the doll had been struck with the shovel. But it was. It had to be. She was sure of it.

Out of the sensation of numbness grew the rage. The anger surged within her, and when she spoke, her voice was bitter and cold. "It's not just a doll," she said. "It's my old doll. It's Cry Baby Sue!"

IF CLARE HAD SEEN THE FACES OF WENDY AND Steve as she tore out of the garage that day, she would have seen two faces totally perplexed by her behavior. It wasn't like her to swear and curse. And over what? A doll? A decayed relic of a toy with a plastic body that perished as they touched it, pieces peeling off like dead skin.

Clare had thrown the body of the old doll into the car, climbed in beside it in her wet clothes, and sped off up the street as if she were on a vendetta. And indeed she was. After twenty-five years, she finally had the evidence with which to confront Evelyn. Let her try to avoid the consequences of her actions now!

Clare thundered across the car park, her eyes dark and furious, the doll tucked under her arm like a lightning bolt. She still wore Steve's grey coat, soaking wet and smeared with mud and streaks of rust leaking from the sockets of the doll's eyes. The large glass doors of the hospital slid open automatically as she approached the threshold and pushed past a group of visitors on their way out. An elderly woman with a stiff hairdo clutched her husband's arm as she sidestepped Clare, and muttered, "I'm not sure I like the way they let the patients wander in and out these days. That one nearly bowled us right over."

"Excuse me!" The balding attendant at the main desk, peering over his computer, popped up from behind the huge vase of blue irises on the counter. He tried to attract Clare's attention as she passed. "Excuse me," he yelled, waving his hands, "visiting hours finished at three o'clock! You will have to come back!" The flowers trembled, and a deep blue bloom dropped on the floor. There was a chink and a gush of water as the vase spilled its contents over the computer. "Oh shit!" The attendant tore off his navy sweater and started mopping up the mess. "Nurse!"

Clare barely noticed the fuss she was creating. She strode across the white linoleum, with her chin jutting forward, and her shoes trampling mud and dirt into the sterile floor. She reached Evelyn's door and sucked in the air outside before she pushed through.

Evelyn was sitting on her bed. She felt the cold air gush through the open door and turned to stare at the strange apparition wrapped in the thunder cloud and dripping water on her floor. There was a gust of wind, then a streak of lightning cut across the white space and blasted into a million shards at her feet. Evelyn looked down to see what remained at the point of impact. What she saw, rolling across the floor, was the broken head of Cry Baby Sue.

"You DID it?
 DIDN'T you?
 You TOOK her and
 HID her where no one
 would FIND her?"
     The words crack above my head.
     I nod.
     I nod because she needs the truth to stop the storm raging around her, around us both. Yes. Yes, I took her. I took Cry Baby Sue.

     I took her that day when we were small. I plucked her from her box, all new and smelling like a toy store, and still with a tear in her eye. I took her while you were sleeping, and I buried her beneath my mother's roses. That is the place that holds the tears. When I was finished, I washed my hands and I climbed back into the bed beside yours. No more tears for her now.

     Only rain now. Let your rain fall on me and wash away my madness. I have wrapped my madness around myself like a shroud, but I want to be better now. I want to be better for my son.

     She thinks I am playing a game. She thinks it is all a trick. Doesn't she know that underneath I am something splintered and fragmented with brittle plastic bones like a doll buried in the dirt? But even brittle bones can become strong again. Even fragments, no matter how small, can be pieced together and rejoined.

She is trying to look through me with her deep, dark eyes. Like a dog, she sniffs the air between us and tries to smell my emotion. Am I friend or foe? She circles me, all the while fixing her eyes on mine.

She has never looked at me this way before. She always kept her distance, a distance of mind. Something is about to happen. Something is about to change between us. I cower beneath her stare, slip onto the floor, and wait.

The room is quiet. Has the storm gone? Is it safe to venture out and pick up what the storm threw about? I begin picking up the pieces. I order them, in piles. One pile is for shards, tiny broken pieces that only I can see. These are important, for these will slip, with care, into the cracks and chinks that craze. Another pile is for small pieces, little bits that the wind can blow away. The last pile is for large pieces. Everyone tries to fit the large pieces together first. But they won't slide together nicely, they won't lie flat and smooth without the little shards to bind them.

The cloud is lifting now, and her hand slips down and covers mine. Her beautiful hand is like her mother's. I flip it over and trace the lines on the palm of her hand with my finger. Past, future, heart, head. Somewhere on this map of life, her lines and mine must meet and merge. I press my palm into hers and feel the warmth flow through it. A little fragment of myself begins to mend. A little shard binds one piece to the other.

"Why?" she asks. She takes both my hands in hers and looks into my eyes. "Why?" She is searching my face and her eyes shine with tears and I know she has found the small piece of me that is whole and new. "Why?"

I try to find a way to answer her and I grope around the floor and find one rusted eye that has rolled under the bed. I hold it in my hands and wipe it with my gown until I see a tiny piece of blue. There are words. They are hard to sound when you are small. But Clare has come and made me a little bigger, and I try to speak so she can hear. She bends closer. Even though I am shouting as loudly as I can, my voice is still so tiny her ear is against my mouth to hear it.

"So she would not cry," I say. "Like Mother . . . Like me."

CLARE DROPPED EVELYN'S HANDS. HER ANGER was spent, and she left Evelyn on the floor, picking up the pieces and putting them into piles. Something had passed between them, some moment of insight that she needed time to reflect on. She wondered whether she had really heard Evelyn speak or whether her consciousness had somehow deciphered the emotion that Evelyn exhaled.

The nurse was at the door. "I'm afraid I'll have to ask you to leave, Clare," she said abruptly. "You've obviously upset Evelyn, and it's past visiting hours . . ."

Clare drifted past her and walked out though the white hall into the foyer where a technician was trying to fix the computer on the main desk.

She started to drive home, then thought that she would stop for something to drink on the way. It was much too late for tea or coffee, so she pulled up outside a cafe-bar in Paddington. Through the window, illuminated by the warm orange glow of the lights, she could see a group of students, in black jeans and retro seventies outfits, huddled around one of the tables. She walked inside. The students were drinking wine and eating wood-fired pizzas and large plates of potato wedges with sour cream and guacamole.

A skinny young waiter with a black apron wrapped twice around his pelvis sauntered up to her. When he smiled, she could see his crooked teeth. "Can I help you?" he asked.

"I'd like a drink, please."

"We have a ten-dollar minimum order after five. Is that okay?" He put his head to one side and bit his lip, pensively.

She shrugged. "Fine. I'll have a glass of wine, please."

"House special?"

"Umm . . ." Clare tried to think of a name. She wasn't good with wine. She hardly ever drank, but she asked to see the wine list and sat down, in the corner. There was something about the look on his face when he told her about the minimum order—almost apologetic. She looked down at her clothes—the coat, smeared with mud and rust. Of course, that was it! She looked a sight. She hardly looked as though she was dressed for predinner drinks. She took the dirty coat off and hung it over the chair. The waiter came back with the wine list.

"Here you go!" he said, smiling encouragingly. "We've got a mulled wine at the moment. That's nice on a cold evening."

Clare scanned the list. The names, of course, meant nothing to her, and she decided to take his advice. "That sounds good. I'll have one of those."

The waiter walked into the kitchen and came back with the warm wine. It was pungent and fruity, and Clare sipped it quickly. It felt thick, like honey, on Clare's tongue and it smelled of cinnamon. She breathed in the aroma of the spice and threw back her head to drink the last mouthful. Then she ordered two more glasses.

The bulbous glasses rested on the table, full of the warm red wine. She held one of the glasses reverently between her hands, like a communion chalice, and drank the sweet blood. Her head began to feel cloudy, and the students on the next table seemed to shrink into the distance. As the wine filled her body, she felt her muscles relax. What had been taut was soft, what had ached was soothed. Her sense of self became comfortable, small and remote. Here, in this mellow place, she found the courage to know that she was not so different from Evelyn.

Clare thought about her own tortuous thoughts and moods during those first months at home with Sophie. She thought about the day Sophie had screamed for hours and how she had stood on the balcony, looking down. While she was thinking these things, Evelyn's words kept sounding in her ears. "So she would not cry . . ."

Clare picked up the other glass. She sipped the sweet liquid, and it ran down her throat and warmed her chest. Forgiveness. That was all that was required. In the name of the Father . . . In the name of the Son . . . Clare swilled the last mouthful of wine and savored the strange taste of bitter honey. Without ever having intended to, she realized that she had already forgiven Evelyn, the pitiful child-woman kneeling beside the bed, picking up the pieces of the broken doll. Clare swallowed, and the warm liquor ran down her throat and mixed with her blood. Now all that remained was to forgive herself.

Clare left some money on the table and struggled to get out of her chair. She still had to make dinner for David and Steve, and it was late. She stumbled against the table and the cafe's sleek interior bent at an angle in front of her face. The black-and-white tiles floated up to her eyes, and the lip of the empty wineglass on the table tipped sideways and hung before her face like a crescent moon. She sat down again. Bugger them! She would ask the waiter to order her a taxi, and while she was waiting, she would have another drink.

THE GESTATION OF GUILT

WENDY SAT IN THE FRONT SEAT OF HER OLD Morris and jiggled the keys. A wave of nausea rolled up from the pit of her stomach, and she swallowed in an effort to resist the urge to vomit. Closing her eyes, she leaned her head on the metal edge of the steering wheel and tried to concentrate on the cold hard pressure on her forehead, but it was no use. She could not get the image out of her mind. The image of Steve in the rain holding the frail lifeless body in his arms.

She had overreacted, of course. She hadn't realized that the tiny hand in the dirt was only made of plastic. Even when Steve had laid the muddied effigy of the baby beside her, she had swooned when she opened her eyes. It was Clare's dramatic reaction that had made her realize it was only a doll. When Clare had angrily snatched the doll up, Wendy had finally seen that the body was made of dirty plastic, not decaying flesh. The rest of her tears were wept in relief.

The whole episode had made Wendy realize the extent to which she felt responsible for Amy's disappearance. Her guilt had reached the limit of its gestation, and she knew that the time had come. The dark sorrow had finally consumed all the available space in her pregnant body, crushing her lungs and making her wheeze and gasp. It was time to break away from the shadows that pressed upon her, and she knew intuitively what she must do. She must see Evelyn and plead for forgiveness in exchange for the truth.

Wendy sat up in her seat. The nausea had abated. She put her key into the ignition, started the car, and slowly pulled out of the drive.

Steve saw the Morris chug past as he went down the back steps to his workshop. He briefly wondered where she was going. Usually she stayed home during the day, catching up on some sleep before she did her night shift. How did she keep working those odd hours? She was so obviously pregnant now. She'd told him, last week, as they stood in the rain watching Clare tear up the road, that the baby wasn't due for at least another four months. He remembered the way she had emphasized the "four," as if she was trying to convince herself that was the truth. Was it the truth? Steve rubbed his chin and felt yesterday's stubble there.

The truth was that it was the beginning of August, and Wendy was into her third trimester. She was still working, even though Harry had asked her to stop. He had pleaded with her, in fact, because she looked so worn-out. She had dark rings around her eyes, and her skin was pale, almost translucent. Blue veins rode close to the surface and broke into knobbly purple springs on her legs. Even her obstetrician, who saw his patients as incubators rather than women, had registered concern and prescribed an iron supplement for her. Of course the supplement didn't alter her pallor, although it did result in constipation.

Harry had taken the news of her pregnancy so well. He'd been excited. He'd even tried to convince her that they didn't need the money from her job because they could send the kids to state schools.

"We'll never be able to afford three at private school anyway," he said. "There's no point in killing ourselves. We may as well enjoy our family. Perhaps they need us more than a private education anyway," he mused, holding her small hands in his large callused ones.

He leaned toward her, and she crumpled into him. He kissed her then. "God knows, I need you," he said.

Wendy knew in that moment how much she loved him, the security of him and the ungainly gentleness of his large, stocky body. She would never desert him again, and she clung to him and wept tears that came easily to her now that she was pregnant.

She would not give up her job, though. In the end it was he who gave up his second job as a nightwatchman and concentrated on his day job with the city council. He took over a lot of the household chores to relieve her—cooking, cleaning, washing—and as he was not working day and night, he was not so tired anymore. He had time to really be with his family. He had the time and the energy to kick a soccer ball with Daniel and Maddy in the backyard. He had the time and the energy to relate better to Wendy.

Their sex life improved. Harry found her pregnancy particularly arousing. He was turned on by her taut, rounded womb and her bloated breasts, where the warm blood coursed through blue veins close to the surface of her white skin. He loved to rest his head between those breasts, to suckle them and taste the drops of colostrum that leaked out. He loved to cup his hands around them as he rode her from behind. Afterward, he caressed her ballooning belly, kissed her navel, listened for the heartbeat of their child.

Their child. She did not tell him, would not ever tell him, and even now tried to convince herself that there was still a chance the baby could be Harry's.

Wendy did not give up work because she knew that it wasn't the stresses of her job that made her skin pale and sallow. It wasn't the pregnancy that circled her eyes with black rings. It was her bouts of insomnia. She suffered from sleepless nights; she was plagued by shadows that swooped behind curtains and cowered in corners when she turned on the lights.

Wendy needed to work nights to sleep during the day. She preferred the night shifts because she could come home and sleep with the radio on and the window flung open and the light falling down through her hair. Then she slept well and soundly, too exhausted even to dream. But she couldn't always schedule herself for night shift. It interfered with life at home too much. So she often lay awake at night, while the shadows beat their wings in the darkness.

It was guilt that had kept Wendy away from Evelyn, and now it was the burden of that guilt that brought her to the hospital. Wendy turned the Morris Minor into the car park. The engine spit as she turned off the ignition, and in the silence that ensued, she heard her own rapid breaths reach a crescendo as she heaved her body awkwardly out of the car. She steadied herself a moment, holding on to the door, and tried to calm herself. She had to go through with this ordeal. She had to know if Amy was still alive, although she did not know how she would cope with the alternative.

Not knowing was the most difficult thing. That meant being haunted by dreams, and she knew she had to pull herself together so that she could be there for the new baby. When the baby was born, she wanted to see it as a little person in its own right. She didn't want to be forever reminded of shadows, as if shadows had power enough to creep into her womb and gain flesh there.

Wendy lingered for a long time in the hallway outside Evelyn's room. The hallway was lit with fluorescent lights that glared against the walls and ceiling, making everything unnaturally white. But even here, perhaps especially here, the shadows pressed against her back as her hand reached to turn the knob. As she opened the door, Wendy felt the blood rush through her veins and heat her skin. Her lungs compressed in a hard little spasm, and the air rushed out when she saw Evelyn's face.

Evelyn was sitting in a chair, staring through the white light of the hall, aware of a shadow hovering beside the door. Her eyes strained in the glare, and she squinted to make out the features on the face. She saw whose face it was, and her green eyes pierced Wendy's through the white light. Wendy flinched, and Evelyn turned away to look out the window. The sun caught Evelyn's hair so that it shone like copper wire, and for an instant Wendy was reminded of a painting of a sad Madonna with a halo around her head.

Wendy pulled a chair over to the window. She sat beside Evelyn but she did not face her. When she spoke, her words were slow and hesitant.

"Evelyn . . ." She reached out to touch her and saw Evelyn stiffen, so she pulled her hand away again. "I'm so sorry. I didn't mean it to happen. It only happened once . . . We're not having an affair . . ." Wendy tried to swallow, but her mouth was dry. "I love Harry. That day with Steve. It was just . . . It was just sex . . .

"It was the same for Steve. He loved you, Evelyn. He really did. I think that both of us just felt . . . lonely."

Wendy rubbed her hand over her face. She was perspiring although the room was cool. Her palms were clammy, and she wiped her hands over her navy trousers. "So I came today to say how sorry I am and to ask you . . . to beg you to tell me what happened to Amy . . ."

Evelyn turned and fixed her green eyes on Wendy's face,

narrowing them in an effort to bring the face into focus. The pretty features emerged as the whiteness dissipated and Evelyn saw that Wendy was tormented by her own guilt, her mouth contorted, her eyes red and sunken.

"I feel wretched about it, Evelyn. I can't bear not knowing anymore. Please tell me. I have to know the truth. I have to know . . ." Wendy began to sob. "If somehow I'm responsible for her . . . her . . ."

The word formed in Evelyn's mind, the word that would complete Wendy's sentence, and that same word began to choke her like a blob of phlegm until she was compelled to break her silence and spit it out. "Death."

Wendy's jaw dropped, and she began to tremble. Evelyn allowed herself another moment of silence while she extracted her revenge.

Wendy felt the saliva flow into her mouth. She swallowed repeatedly to avoid retching. That one word and the sound of Evelyn's voice after so long . . .

Evelyn waited a moment more. Enough. She let her anger go, and she felt another small part of her brokenness begin to heal. She was still small, but she was growing. All these little shards, shards of brokenness that had the power to wound and the power to bind and repair. She let the jagged edge slide in, and she knew that now she would be heard without the effort of screaming. But after so long, her voice was low and raspy, and she struggled to produce the words.

"Don't flatter yourself. Don't think you're the only one. Don't think . . . I'd kill my child . . . just to spite him."

Wendy sat mutely in her chair, her heart thumping the blood through her veins.

"I hardly want to . . . relieve you of your guilt, but . . . it's time to tell. Not for your sake. For mine. Before . . . I wanted nothing. But now . . . I want to go home. I want to be with . . . William."

Wendy pleaded, hardly able to hear the sound of her own voice over the noise of her heart, "Tell me what happened. Please!"

"She's not dead. Is that the answer you wanted? I gave her away."

She's not dead! Not dead! Not dead! Wendy sucked the words in like fresh air, repeating them in her mind like a mantra.

Now it was Evelyn's turn to consume some of the guilt that had choked Wendy, and tears began to crowd in the rims of her green eyes. "I had to do it. She would grow to hate me, or she would become me . . . I didn't want her to cry anymore . . ."

"But . . ." Wendy muttered, finally able to think of someone else now her own guilt was eased. "But what about Steve? He's so upset. He's Amy's father!"

Evelyn's eyes focused on Wendy's stomach. When she turned to look out the window, her voice was very low.

"He'll have other children," she said.

GETTING ON WITH IT

"WELL, NOW WE KNOW THAT SHE DIDN'T KILL her, we can all get on with it." Susan dipped her Gingernut into her black coffee and bit off the end. Bittersweetness crumbled in her mouth. The bitterness of strong Italian coffee. The sweetness of ginger and syrup. The midmorning sun was hot through her black sweater, so she took it off, her short-sleeved polo shirt revealing thin arms the color and dry texture of flour.

Joanna shifted her chair so that the rubber plant offered her and Sam a little more shade. She clung to him tightly now and never took her eyes off him when he wandered around the cafe. Turning to Clare, who was staring at some tea leaves caught on the rim of her cup, she said, "I know I should feel okay about this. It's a good outcome, isn't it? It could have been worse. But somehow . . . I don't know . . . I feel kind of betrayed."

"Why?"

"Because she gave Amy away to a stranger. How could she do that? Her own child!"

Clare shrugged, leaned over, and poured herself another cup of tea. A woman like Joanna would never be able to understand Evelyn, she thought. Clare remembered what Evelyn had said that day in the hospital: "So she would not cry. Like Mother. Like me." She realized now that Evelyn had acted out of desperation,

not callousness. From the distressed and distant place she inhab-
ited, giving Amy away must have seemed like the only answer. Of
course, Joanna would not see it like that.

Susan tried to jolly Joanna along. Coffee mornings had been
getting very tense lately. "You mean you've never thought that
you'd like to give your kids away, Jo?" she exclaimed. "If I'd acted
on every dark thought I'd had in the last eight years, my kids
would all be in foster care!"

It was black humor, and no one laughed, not even Susan.
Joanna looked despondent. Clare spent the silence that followed
contemplating the fact that today Joanna was holding Sam so force-
fully he was pouting and trying to wriggle out of her rigid arms.

Eventually Clare spoke. "Don't be too hard on Evelyn, Jo.
Remember what she's been through. Her mother committed suicide. Put yourself in her position and imagine how something
like that would affect you. Not just as a child but later on too,
when you became a mother yourself."

Joanna offered Sam one of the sugar packets from the bowl on
the table, and he stopped wriggling. "You know, if I lost my mother
like that, I think I'd try even harder to be a good mother. I'd want
to make sure that my children had everything I missed out on.
Love, security, hugs and kisses . . ."

"Yes . . . of course you think that's what you'd do—it's so
difficult for any of us to understand what she went through. I
grew up with Evelyn, but I never really understood the effect her
mother's suicide had on her. I do remember this, though. Evelyn
was very disturbed after her mother died." Clare felt a need to
explain Evelyn's actions, but it was an effort to find the right
words. She wasn't sure she completely understood the explanation herself. "I don't think Evelyn really grew up after her
mother killed herself. Part of her always remained four years old."

"You mean that she didn't know how to be a mother?" asked Joanna.

"Something like that." Clare mused over Joanna's words. Jo could be very perceptive about the feelings of others, she thought. She was right. Evelyn didn't know how to be a mother. In her heart, she was still an orphaned child.

Susan swallowed the last of her Gingernut. "You've got to admit, Clare, Evelyn's done a pretty good job imitating her mother's madness."

"Yes, I suppose so." Clare drained her teacup and tried to pour another from the little one-person pot on her plate—a few mouthfuls of thick smoky-tasting tea were all that remained. "Where is Wendy today?" she asked Susan. "I was hoping she could tell us the whole story over coffee. She was pretty brief on the phone last night, and I really want to know how she managed to get Evelyn to open up. I've been trying to get through to Evelyn for months!"

"She's at the obstetrician," answered Susan. "I'm desperate to hear the unabridged version too! All Wendy told me was that Evelyn decided to speak when she saw that she was pregnant. How strange is that? After all this time! According to Wendy, Evelyn didn't say much else, only that she gave Amy away."

"What possessed Wendy to go and see her anyway? She's never been to visit before."

"She said it was something to do with being pregnant. The closer it got to her due date, the more she felt that she needed to see Evelyn. My guess is that she wanted Amy's disappearance resolved before her own baby was born."

Joanna perked up a little, and a smile flickered across her face. "Did I tell you that she's asked me to be a support person at the birth?"

Susan was surprised. "Really?" She hadn't realized that Wendy regarded Joanna so highly—hadn't contemplated the fact that the others valued Jo's maternal warmth as well.

"Yes. I'm quite excited about it. I'm already collecting a bag of props."

"Props?" Susan arched one black brow and recalled that Joanna had never experienced natural childbirth before.

"Yes. Wendy suggested a tennis ball for massage, essential oils, some little snacks . . . that kind of thing."

Susan rolled her eyes. "I bet you don't use any of that stuff! A tennis ball for massage!" she scoffed.

As Joanna's face fell, Susan realized, too late, that she had been a bit brutal. "I suppose," she said, trying to soften the blow, "some women find those things useful. Wendy ought to know what she's talking about. She's a midwife, after all . . ."

"Well, I think it's great that you want to help out," Clare said to Joanna. "I'm sure you'll be a very reassuring presence."

"I hope so." Joanna fished the sugar packet out of Sam's mouth. The soggy blue paper burst, and the sugar crystals sprayed across the table. "Anyway," she said, trying to sweep the crystals into a pile with one hand, "thinking about Wendy's baby stops me dwelling on Amy. I know that she was only a few weeks old when Evelyn gave her away, but don't you think she would have felt abandoned? They say that even newborns can recognize their mother's smell. And Evelyn had been breast-feeding her too. The poor little thing would have had to be weaned onto a bottle!"

Susan tried to quell the emotion she heard rising in Joanna's voice. "Don't torture yourself about Amy anymore, Jo. It doesn't help. You'll only make yourself upset."

"But I can't help it!" Joanna cried. "I can't stop wondering where she is. What if she's not being looked after properly? There's a lot of strange people out there, and you'd have to be pretty strange just to take a little baby that someone offered you!"

"Strange or desperate," said Susan, thinking aloud.

"Oh God!" Joanna was getting teary now. "Do you think the police will ever find her, Clare?"

"I don't know, Jo. I really don't." Joanna's distress was contagious. Clare searched in her bag for a tissue.

Sam saw the tears that were beginning to roll down his mother's cheeks. He found a snotty hanky in his pocket and clumsily began to swab at Joanna's face with all the subtlety of a windscreen wiper. Joanna let him do it. Somehow, Sam's childish concern comforted her, despite his cold wet hanky.

"Listen, Jo," said Susan, her face hard, "it's time to move on. We're going to have to accept the fact that Amy might never be found. It's been over six months since she disappeared. Do either of you realize how many missing people there are in Australia?"

Joanna began sobbing then, and Clare was unable to stop the choking noises that came from the back of her throat. Sam found his mother's crying so alarming that he began crying too and others in the cafe turned their heads to see what all the fuss was about.

Susan felt her spine stiffen and the skin beneath her throat grew blazing hot. She managed, however, to keep her own eyes dry. Someone had to stay in control. Public displays of emotion appalled her. Glancing into her coffee cup, she noticed that it was only half-empty. Gratefully, she brought the cup to her lips and swallowed. Damn it! Cold.

CLARE

I DON'T WANT TO THINK ABOUT EVELYN ANY-
more. I don't want to imagine one of the thousands of scenarios
I play over in my mind where I intervene before she has a chance
to give Amy away, to some dubious character in a car with tinted
windows, to some officious-looking woman in dark sunglasses, to
some petty criminal who dabbles in illegal adoptions in his spare
time. I don't want to think. I just want to sit down and have a cup
of tea.

I still have some of the chocolate cake Joanna brought over
for my birthday. I'll cut a slice and make myself a little pot of orange pekoe tea. The ordinary ritual is strangely comforting. I'll
get out my favorite china cup and saucer, an old one of my
mother's with purple violets on it. Tea always tastes so much better out of a china cup. You can't drink tea out of a mug because
the thick rim clashes with the subtle texture and flavor of tea. I'll
occupy myself with teapots and strainers and steaming water and
fine tea leaves swirling in the pot, and I won't think. I won't think
about Evelyn and how I've resented her presence in my life ever
since her mother died and how I felt that she coveted my mother,
my life . . . my happiness.

I won't think about a childhood spent in indignation. All
those birthday parties I had to share with "poor little Evelyn."

The way she crept around our house with a simpering smile and won my parents' hearts, so that I, who had not been through a tragedy, should always be "more grateful and less selfish" and think of "that dear little girl and all she's gone through."

I *should* have been more grateful and less selfish, but I wasn't. I resented her, and the guilt of that resentment weighed me down. When Evelyn figured she couldn't count on my benevolence she learned to play on my guilt so that I would lend her my favorite toys and my favorite dresses and other pieces of my life. She's still playing on that guilt. Of course I will look after William if she is unstable. Of course I will continue to take him to see her when she comes out of the hospital. Of course I will. Why wouldn't I? I'm Clare. My life is meant to be shared.

Forgiveness is what is required. Forgiveness. That is the price of inner peace. That is the insight I gleaned from my transcendental moment beside Evelyn's brokenness. That is how I was able to let go of twenty-five years of resentment toward her and seek absolution in a glass or two or three of mulled wine. Evelyn is a pitiful child-woman. I see that now, and I forgive her constant intrusions in my life. I forgive the way she clings like a helpless infant, and I forgive the way she gave . . . I forgive . . . Oh God! I don't want to think about Evelyn. I just want to have a cup of tea.

My grandmother made tea with every meal, using fresh tank water. Neither my mother nor any of my aunts ever took milk. They all preferred their tea very weak, a subtle orange brew, the color of thin toffee held to the sun. Nothing is as good as tea made with tank water, it's as soft as sunrise. The tea that I pour now, into my cup, is thick town water tea. But it will do. It will help.

I sit on the back deck with my cup and a piece of chocolate cake, and I watch the sun paint the garden with splashes of yellow.

It has been ages since I've done any painting myself. All I have to show for my talents over the last six months are a couple of sketches, in black charcoal. Then again, I've painted nothing substantial since Sophie was born. There always seem to be other priorities—Sophie, David, housework . . . Evelyn. There is never a substantial block of time to get really involved with a serious work of art. That's my excuse anyway. I've always told myself that I would have more time when Sophie goes to school. But now that Sophie is nearly at school, David is pushing for another child.

No other drink can comfort you as much as tea. Coffee can perk you up and give you a buzz, but tea warms through you and lifts your spirits. When someone's in shock, you never offer her coffee, do you. You offer her tea. Today I feel like I need a bit of comforting.

Steve told me, when I picked up William this morning, that since Evelyn was getting better and would eventually be released, he was going to start to move all his stuff out of their house. He was filing for divorce. He told me what he was going to do in such a matter-of-fact way, as if I would never have expected him to do anything else. I guess I didn't. What surprised me, though, was how sorry I suddenly felt for him.

Pity is not an emotion I've ever felt for Steve. I know what he is like. I know he drinks too much. I know he is a womanizer. I know he doesn't help out much around the house. (Mind you, that's a common failing!) But this morning, when he stooped over to lean into the window of the car and looked at me with his deep blue eyes, I felt so sorry for him. There were new lines chiseled in his face, deep lines around his eyes and over his brow.

The hospital has had to stop him seeing Evelyn unsupervised. Apparently, he lost it with her last week, demanding to know who she gave the baby to. She just told him her mind was "fuddled." She couldn't remember. He lashed out and started shaking her so hard that he had to be pulled off her. An understandable reaction, perhaps. This morning all I could see in him was sadness and regret and . . . acceptance. Yes, it was acceptance that I saw in his face. He's given up. Suddenly, I felt how powerless he really was. I wanted to hold him then, just like I hold William when he's sad or upset. But I didn't, and it wouldn't have helped. In the end, Steve has to sort out his own life, just like I have to sort out mine.

My life. This business about Amy has consumed me. It's been a bit of an anticlimax, really, because I was sure that I would be the one to extract the truth from Evelyn. I thought that she at least owed me that much! And being psychotic at the time, no one's going to expect Evelyn to remember all the details, not even the police, though they are looking into the case again.

I think that I'll cut myself another slice of cake, so I walk into the kitchen. A big slice of rich chocolate cake with fluffy, buttery frosting. I'm going to eat it right here, standing beside the sink. (The second piece is always an indulgence and I never allow myself the luxury of sitting down to savor it.)

Perhaps finding Amy doesn't matter so much to me anymore. It's hard to admit thoughts like that. Am I callous to think that finding Evelyn's child no longer matters? But it doesn't, does it?

If Evelyn did—and I believe she did—give her baby away, then imagine how attached Amy would be to her adoptive family by now. Besides, the Family Services people wouldn't let Evelyn have Amy back, even if the police did find her. Strange, isn't it, that just when the police reopen their investigation, I realize it's a lost cause. Susan was right. Finding Amy doesn't matter. It can't matter because, somehow, we all have to get on with our lives.

Susan always tells the truth as she sees it. She can be brutal, but she's never dishonest.

So what does matter? My mind immediately registers the usual answers. David. Sophie. I make myself another cup of tea and feel the soft steam on my face as I sip from my cup. It comes to me then, as the tea fills my empty places, that I matter too. Not just who I am as a wife and a mother but who I am as myself. Clare. Me.

The central core of myself has become wrapped in layers of guilt about being a good wife and a good mother and a good friend. It's time to give up the guilt that makes me recoil at my own selfish impulses and thoughts and explore those impulses and thoughts despite my discomfort. (I usually ring my psychiatrist at this juncture and make an appointment, but it's time to stop making excuses and start being honest with myself.) I am not perfect, and that is perfectly forgivable.

I don't want another baby. Not yet, maybe not ever. I'll tell this to David tonight. I'll ask him to give me one more year to make up my mind. I know he will. (Let's face it, if your wife's been on antidepressants for five years, you have to give her some leeway.) We'll explore our options when the year is up.

I don't want to go back to teaching either, and not because I think that I couldn't handle it. I've spent six years raising Sophie and nearly one raising William. I'm a stronger person now than I was when I started teaching. I'm sure that I could manage the classroom, but I don't want to. I don't want to be an art teacher; I want to be an artist. What was it that made me choose to teach art instead of doing it myself? Was it fear of failure? Did I choose a career where so little of my ego was invested, it wouldn't matter if I failed? I was doomed to fail really, wasn't I?

Anyway, it's not about failing. It's about being true to myself. At the core of myself, I'm an artist. That's who I am. Whether or not I ever produce anything good enough to be hung in a national gallery is of no consequence whatsoever.

My cup is empty. I'll slip back into my housewife role now and begin to tidy up the living room. (Well, who else is going to do it?) Look at this drawing of Sophie's lying on the floor! She does so many. Big beautiful drawings with bright colors that are unadulterated by any shade of blackness. Hot pink, bright yellow, grass green, turquoise blue, orange, and purple.

Sophie seems to work on a series of pictures within a theme. At the moment she spends most of her time drawing pictures of princesses walking from their castles across bridges toward a town. The princesses look like her, with their long, flowing hair colored bright orange. I've always thought that, on some level, the pictures are about her transition from home and preschool to school. Now, when I look at this picture, I realize that Sophie also has a sense of destiny, a sense of purpose in the world.

I owe it to Sophie to find out who I am. No. I owe it to myself, and she will reap the rewards of my discovery. For if I can cross the bridge and discover myself, I can meet her in the world with a smile that comes from the person I really am. Then there will be no resentment, no unhappiness, no unquenchable desire, no guilt for not being the perfect mother.

I used to think that happiness had a price. I paid for my happiness with little pills that were prescribed by my psychiatrist. Well, my happiness does have a price, and the price is my own truth. I know now that I must find the courage to forgive myself for not always being the person that others have wanted me to be. This is the first step. The second is simply to live as the person I am, an artist, and accept that, on the canvas, light is only defined in relation to darkness, and strokes of brilliance are only apparent beside what is mundane.

GROWING BETTER

I AM GROWING IN MINUTE DEGREES. PIECES interlock to rebuild my shattered being. Fragments of loss and loneliness are fused with splinters of desire, and now I am whole enough for my voice to sound as if it is coming from me and not from some faraway place inside my head.

I have stopped thinking about the spider because the bigger I grow, the less significant she becomes. That is how it must be. I must find my own way, or William and I will never be together. So the spider sits in the dark corner of my mind from where my voice used to come, and now it is her voice that is small.

Steve came while I was walking in the hospital garden. He pleaded with me to tell him who I had given Amy to. When I refused, he shook with rage and began to drown in the torrent of curses he yelled at me. There was a sea between us. A whole ocean between him and me, and his voice gurgled under the water. For a moment I wished that I could help him. I wished that I could give him some hope to breathe. But it was too late. Telling him would only ruin things for Amy.

So I lied. I told him that my mind was fuddled the day I gave Amy away. I lied. I told him that I couldn't remember anything about the woman I gave her to. As I spoke, the sea between us dried up, and in the brittle air I saw him come crashing through my words. His body loomed above me before his hands gripped my shoulders, and he began shaking me, dumping my body against his and roaring senselessly in my ears. Some people from the hospital came and led him away.

I watched them drag him away, across the grass, through the sprinklers watering the seedlings that the gardener has planted in the raked beds. There were two broad-shouldered men, but he still shook them off and spit angrily into the dirt. "Bloody bitch!" he swore, and he turned around to glare at me with his hard blue eyes. "Fucked-up bloody bitch!"

How could I tell him the truth? How could I explain that I began to plan her escape from the day she was born? As I held her, I vowed that this child, this girl-child, would not cry. Not like Mother. Not like me. She would be the first to break free of the web. I would find her a new mother. I would release her from my own unhappiness. I would cast her out to set her free.

The day I came home from hospital with Amy I began searching. Every day William went to preschool, or stayed with Clare, I wandered through shopping centers and train stations and parks looking for her. Looking for the one who would be "Mother." It was hot in January. The sun beat an angry rhythm in my head as I walked behind the pram, and Amy was fretful. When I picked her up, she mewed like a cat, and when I nursed her, there was always a layer of salt sweat between us.

I was about to give up, I was about to let the spider mother engulf us both in her sticky shroud, when I found her. She was sitting in a bus shelter, staring into the sun, when I sat down to feed Amy. She had the most beautiful hair. It was long and black and rooted in a widow's peak that divided the white skin on her forehead. She watched me as I nursed Amy. She watched with such longing that the tears lined her eyes and splattered like heavy raindrops onto the concrete floor. When I had finished nursing, she reached out and stroked the soft fluff that was Amy's hair. We began to talk then. That day and other days, meeting each time in the bus shelter near the park, outside Shoppingtown.

To others it would not seem to be a rational, reasonable thing to do. I was aware of that, and so was she. But I was as desperate as she was, and as each day passed I knew that it would be harder to let Amy go. Every day William and Steve grew more attached to her. Every day I sank a little deeper into the greyness of my mother's world. If I left it too long, I would not even have the energy to set her free. I was desperate, and desperation has no reason. It took all my resolve, all my courage, all my love to cut her loose.

I gave her away, and it was done. I was done. Then I didn't even have desperation to drive me. The greyness crumbled into dust, and there was nothing. I was nothing. I was only an absence of feeling—an anesthetized mind. I grew so small, I couldn't even see myself.

But William saw me. He saw me when I was no bigger than a beetle. And Clare saw me. She saw me when I was no bigger than a child. At last she saw me. Something small. But growing bigger now. Filling up with the unenviable desire to want more.

WENDY'S CHOICE

SHE MOVED SLOWLY IN THE SOFT DARKNESS that enclosed her. Encased in her watery world, she stretched a foot or a leg. She sucked her thumb. The deep drum resonated beside her, giving her mother's blood the rhythm of an ocean as it lapped against the vessel she traveled in. She had existed forever within the sounds of her mother's body but she knew her mother no more than she knew silence. She lived through her sensations, and as the vessel that contained her grew tighter, she began to have some awareness of her own edges. She was one with herself. Goddesslike, she expanded to consume the universe until she was the universe, and there was nothing else to be. Was this all? She slid her leg out to feel the boundaries of her existence and felt the hardness there.

WENDY THRUST HER SHOULDERS BACK AND tried to fill her chest cavity with air. The baby was kicking out against her ribs again, and her ribs were splayed and sore. She stood up and bent over her abdomen to search around on her desk for her flashlight. As she bent, her ribs buckled over her womb and ached more. She thought that she would take a walk around the ward. That would ease her discomfort. Perhaps the baby would drop soon, she thought optimistically, although then the pressure would be on her bladder. She sighed. Five more weeks to go. At the end of this week, she would be forced to take her maternity leave. She was not looking forward to giving up her night shifts. Although Evelyn had given up her secret, Wendy continued to dodge shadows. She was still more comfortable sleeping during the day.

Wendy kept her eyes trained on the white ring of light as she walked down the hall. She looked in on 12A. The mother there had given birth just before midnight. It was now 3:00 A.M., and dad had gone home to get some rest, but mom was still wide awake, her eyes fixed on the little boy who lay in her arms. Wendy shined the light on the floor and caught the woman's round face in the fading edge of light.

"Still awake?"

"I can't close my eyes. I just want to keep looking at him."

"I know. That's hormones for you. But you should try to get some sleep. There'll probably be visitors tomorrow."

"Yes." The woman nodded and lay back with her head on the pillow, staring at the ceiling, her sleeping baby cradled in her arms.

"Would you like a sedative?"

The woman shook her head. "Is it all right if I keep him in bed with me?"

"Of course. He's yours. Just let me raise the side of the bed to stop him falling out." Wendy leaned over the bed and, with some effort, adjusted the side rail.

The woman touched her hand, and Wendy saw the whites of her eyes shine in the darkness. "I won't squash him, will I? I won't roll on him if I fall asleep?"

"Of course not." Wendy adjusted the woman's pillow so that it was clear of the baby's face. "There," she said, "try and get some sleep now. He'll have you up in a few hours anyway."

As Wendy was leaving the room, one of the registrars met her in the corridor. "Is it all right if I transfer a young mother and her baby to your ward, Nurse? There are no beds downstairs, and the baby has a bit of croup. Nothing serious, but the mother's so anxious I thought that they probably ought to stay the night. One of the nurses told me that this ward was pretty quiet."

"Yes, just three moms tonight. Twelve F down the end is free. You can put them in there. I'll set up a steam tent for the baby."

"Thanks." The registrar turned, and Wendy fixed her eyes on his white coat as it floated through the muted lighting in the passage. She would have liked to turn the lighting up, but there were rules. It was more restful for the patients this way.

She turned on the light in the room at the end of the hall. Out in the foyer, she found an orderly and asked him to bring up one of the cribs from downstairs. When he had done so, she returned to the room to prepare a bed for the mother and set up a steam tent. Presently, the young doctor came back with the baby. He carried the little girl in and handed her to Wendy. "Mom's on the way up with the stroller and the nappy bag," he said as he disappeared down the hall.

Wendy placed the baby in the crib. She guessed that she must be about eight or nine months old. A chubby little girl with strawberry blond curls and beautiful green eyes.

When she saw Wendy, her face lit up with a wide smile that revealed two baby teeth. She coughed a bit then, but her croup was not bad really, probably nothing that standing in the steam from a hot shower couldn't fix. An overanxious mother, no doubt.

Still, better to be overanxious than neglectful, Wendy thought as she hooked up the tent and the steam began to flow in. She'd seen a lot of cases of child abuse and neglect since she started nursing. Thin, dehydrated children, children with unexplained bruises and bumps, children desperate for love, even from strangers.

Wendy heard footsteps in the room. The little girl rolled over to the side of the crib and held out her hands through the rails. "Mom,mom,mom,mom," she crooned.

Wendy smiled at the child's babble and turned toward the mother. "Talking already?" she said.

The mother's proud smile hit Wendy in the chest and took her breath away. It was her. Wasn't it? The girl whose baby had been stillborn at the Royal last Christmas. Wendy stared at the girl, who bent over the cot, her long black hair trailing down over the rails. It was! It had to be. The girl's pale face was so distinctively heart-shaped and surrounded by long black curls.

Images of that night came back to Wendy. The girl's anguished face, contorted beneath her thick hair as she went through labor. Her disbelief when her baby was pronounced dead. The way she clung all that night and the next day to the still, blue-lipped body of the baby boy. Of course, Wendy thought, the girl wouldn't remember her. During the birth, she was wearing a gown and a mask, and afterward the girl was too shocked to take in anything at all, let alone commit the face of a stranger to memory.

Wendy could feel her pulse drumming in her temples. The noise was distracting, and she felt confused. If this was the girl, then who was the baby? She looked on the chart. The name was printed in black ink. *Gemma Brown. Mother, Helen Brown.*

"Will . . . will you excuse me for a moment?" Wendy stammered.

The girl nodded without looking up. She was humming and stroking the baby to sleep.

The baby curled up in the cot and sucked her fingers, staring intently at the face of the girl.

Was it possible? Could this be Amy? As she staggered up the hall to the phone, Wendy tried to calm herself down and be realistic. There was probably a rational explanation.

Wendy rang her old friend Cath at the Royal. She was lucky. Cath was on duty, attending the phone at the desk.

"What's the problem, Wendy? I thought you'd be on maternity leave by now."

"It's my last week. Look, do you remember that girl who came off the street and had a stillborn baby just before New Year?"

"The one who did a bunk?"

"Yes. That's the one. Could you look up her file for me? I need to know her name."

"Why?"

"I think she's turned up here. She didn't recognize me, but I'm sure it's her."

"Hang on. I'll get the file . . ."

Wendy waited on the phone, her white-knuckled fingers clawed around the receiver.

"Here it is!" Wendy heard Cath shuffling papers beside the phone.

"December 28. The paramedics brought in a young woman off the street in an advanced stage of labor. She called herself Ellen Black, though when she took off, we realized that was a false name . . ."

Cath was still talking but her words blurred together. Ellen? Helen? Black? Brown? It had to be the same girl. Wendy was positive. That face . . . a face like a soft white heart . . .

"Thanks, Cath," she murmured and put the phone down.

If Helen Brown was Ellen Black, then who was Gemma? She couldn't be Helen's natural child because she was at least eight or nine months old. Nearly the age Helen's baby boy would have been had he lived. Of course, the child could be a friend's and Helen could be raising it as her own. There was probably a simple explanation, and really, it was none of her business, Wendy thought. The child was obviously loved and well cared for. She bit her lip and walked slowly back down the corridor to check on them.

Gemma was finally drifting off to sleep, her eyelids growing heavier and heavier. Ellen . . . Helen, whatever her name was, was still humming softly. She didn't look at Wendy. She was totally absorbed in the baby lying in the cot.

"Funny. I never get tired of looking at her. I'm with her every day, and I still can't believe that she's mine."

Wendy swallowed. "Are you a single mom?"

"Yes."

"That must be hard."

"It was at first. I was on the streets for a while, but the Salvation Army found us a place to live."

Wendy tried to control the anxiety in her voice. She knew how to coax information out of people. It was part of her job. "Have you got any support? Someone to look after Gemma when you need a break?"

"One of my neighbors is a family day-care mom and she's been helping me out. She looks after Gem three days a week so that I can go to uni."

"Where are you studying?"

"I'm studying business communications at QUT. Next year, though, I'm transferring to Melbourne. The Army put me back in touch with my parents. They're keen to help out. They say they want to get to know Gemma."

"Haven't they seen her yet?"

"No. I left home after grade twelve. My parents were so ambitious for me, when I got pregnant, I couldn't bring myself to tell them. I guess I thought they'd be shattered."

"But they weren't?"

"They got over it. Now they just want us to come home."

The girl looked at Wendy then. Her blue eyes narrowed, as if she was trying to recall . . . "Do I know you? You look so familiar . . ."

Wendy shook her head. "You two better get some rest. If there's anything you need, anything at all, just press the buzzer."

The girl sat down on the bed and eased off her shoes. "Actually, I was wondering if you could ring downstairs. I think we left Gemma's favorite little toy down in the examination room. She'll want it when she wakes up."

"Of course. I'll ask the orderly to bring it up. What does it look like?"

"Well, it looks very loved!" The girl laughed. "Gemma likes to suck its ear. It's a little dog, a Dalmatian. You know, like the ones in that Disney movie."

"Oh yes, my daughter has that one on video. We'll find it for you."

Wendy recalled that bizarre incident where Joanna had picked up a child's Dalmatian toy in a shopping center, then chased the child's mother through the shops, convinced that the woman had stolen Evelyn's child. All because she thought the toy Dalmatian was the one Susan had given to Amy. The truth was, Wendy thought, Amy had not been stolen. She'd been given away . . .

Wendy felt a roaring in her ears. What if Evelyn had given her baby to Helen? It seemed too incredible to be true, even though Wendy knew that Gemma could not possibly be Helen's natural child. As the adrenaline pumped through her body, Wendy felt the baby kicking against her ribs. She thought of Steve and how desperate he was to find his child, and she knew what she had to do. She went to her desk, picked up the handset and dialed the police. It rang once . . . twice . . . She put the phone down.

Her mind was full of static, like a badly tuned radio station. She should talk to the police, but what would she tell them? That a young woman was here claiming to be a child's mother when she was almost sure that this was impossible? That the baby she had now might be one obtained from a mother during a psychotic episode? If the girl had accepted the baby from Evelyn, that was against the law, wasn't it?

The static grew louder. If Evelyn had given her baby to this girl, was she doing the right thing reporting it? She pressed her palms against her eyes and breathed in. In her mind she heard a voice rising against the noise that sizzled in her brain. The noise subsided, and Evelyn's voice became more clearly defined. "I had to do it. She would grow to hate me, or she would become me. I didn't want her to cry anymore . . ."

Wendy sat down at her desk and tried to breathe deeply. She couldn't betray Evelyn twice, no matter how much sympathy she felt for Steve. Gemma was Amy, wasn't she? Was she going crazy? Oh, please God! But if this was Amy, then at least she was with someone who cared for her, loved her . . . If she didn't interfere, if she left things alone, it might just be enough. Enough to absolve her, in her own mind, and ease the guilt that had immobilized her for so long. It would be enough, Wendy thought, even if it was only an implausible scenario she had dreamed up to suit herself.

Wendy put a hand on her belly and felt her baby kick and sink. The baby was dropping. She took another deep breath as the child sank into the comforting darkness of her womb.

SUSAN

Monday October 7

I think that my life has started again. My own life, sans children, sans Richard. No, I haven't left home. I've found a job. Let me explain.

This Morning: 10 A.M.—I am at university to enroll in my course for next year when, outside the Forgan Smith building, I see a rather LARGE man THUNDERING toward me across the Great Court.

"SUSAN!" he yells. His belly is wobbling like a trifle, and he is waving his pen wildly.

"Bartholomew?" I squint. Could it be? I'm sure there used to be less of him.

He sweeps me up in his embrace and his stomach sends SHOCK WAVES through me.

"Let me . . . Let me look at you." He is red-faced and wheezing, and he holds me at arm's length. "I knew it was you! You haven't changed at all. What have you been DOING with yourself for all these years? You were the best research assistant I ever had."

"Well," I say as I pull family photos out of my purse, "I've had three CHILDREN!"

"Children . . . yes . . . of course. You and DICK, hey?" He winks.

"RICHARD." My voice is flat. Get it straight, fat man. I am the only one allowed to call my husband a dick.

"Oh, excuse me. RICHARD. Children with Richard. How lovely. But you haven't answered my question. What have you DONE with your life?"

Obviously mothering doesn't figure as a LIFE. I smile politely and jab him in the stomach. "Let's not talk about me. Let's talk about YOU."

He grins so that I can see his gold-capped teeth. He likes this subject. (I fight off the urge to make an above- and below-the-belt comment about his obvious overconsumption of refectory custard tarts.) He breathes in deeply and rolls onto his toes so that he grows another inch taller. "Well, actually, I've been involved in a number of LARGE projects for the English faculty. I've written quite a few articles in the last few years. I'm proud to say that I'm the MOST PUBLISHED lecturer in the department!"

"Congratulations!" I look at my watch. TIME IS PASSING and I still have to enroll. I try to end the conversation. "Well, it's been great talking to you, Bartholomew, but I need to speak to someone about my enrollment for next year."

"Enrollment?" He leans backward, pulls in his chin in mock surprise, and now he has three chins stepping up to his face.

I smile. "I want to enroll in a master's—in Australian Cultural Studies."

"Master's, eh? Ever thought about coming back and doing a bit of research work? I really need someone to help me out over the next few months. I've got a very IMPORTANT paper to write."

"Oh, I'm not sure I've got time . . ." I twist my watch on my wrist.

"I could put your name on the paper too. I think it needs a woman's touch . . ."

"What's the project?" I'm genuinely curious now.

"Oh, someone's bequeathed their great-aunt's manuscripts to the university. Poetry, novellas, essays—all unpublished. She wouldn't be of any interest to me at all, except she was a contemporary of some of the GREATS in early Australian literature. She moved in the same circles, but no one ever took her seriously . . ." I see his mind wander, and his hand begins to scratch at his crotch. This is a particularly distasteful habit of his. I avert my eyes, and he relinquishes his thoughts. "I don't know. I think that the stuff really ought to be looked at by a woman. I don't want to be accused of bias in this age of political correctness."

I have to admit, the project does interest me. Why wasn't this woman published? Wasn't her work any good? Was the subject matter too feminine? My mind races through the possibilities. "Well . . . I don't know. It sounds interesting . . . but it's hard for me to work at home with all the kids."

"Oh, you wouldn't have to work at home. You could have some office space . . . Come on. I'll show you." He lumbers off, and I follow him. He's surprisingly fast for someone so large. By the time we get there he's panting and mopping the sweat off his brow with a large handkerchief.

When he shows me my office I'm SOLD. I never knew that I came so cheap, but there is a significant inducement. The desk is under the window and there's a VIEW across the Great Court. I look out across the expanse of green grass, defined as a square by the sandstone buildings that surround it. The court is dotted with small eucalypts rustling their leaves like dry washing. I can see the Forgan Smith building and its tower. On top of the tower is . . . a clock.

A HUGE CLOCK carved eternally in sandstone, with Roman numerals raised in relief on the tawny pink face. Iron hands glide across the stonemasonry, marking every minute and every hour that passes underneath the Queensland sky. I smile. For this I am willing to work alongside the FAT MAN. From this desk, I know assuredly that I will NEVER lose track of TIME again.

6 P.M.—I still can't believe it. Neither can Richard! Not only have I enrolled in a master' program in Australian Cultural Studies, I also have a JOB!!

"But darling, who will make the children's lunches? Who will take them to school?" (Who will BRUSH their hair, WIPE their bottoms, PICK UP their toys, MAKE their beds, DRESS them, FEED them, make sure they CLEAN their teeth . . . ?) He sticks his bottom lip out and looks as lost as a toddler left at day care.

"Richard!" I reply. "I've worked it all out. The course and the research work will only take up twenty-two hours a week. I don't want to be traveling back and forth to university trying to fit everything in, so it will be much better for us all"—(me especially)—"if I can just put in three full working days at university. YOU can take them to school and be a little late. The office will SURVIVE." (Actually I expect that the office will THRIVE and thank me effusively at the end-of-year Christmas party.) "If I go in early, I will be home IN TIME to pick them up, as long as Laura goes from preschool to aftercare. The lunches are EASY PEASY." I lie, but he seems comforted. "I know that you will COPE, I have great FAITH in you."

I give him the Boy Scout salute, and he picks up his newspaper and spreads it between us with a disdainful flick of the wrist. That completes my handover, and I am free.

I am free to continue my life. ABOUT BLOODY TIME TOO!

PAINTING LIFE

CERULEAN BLUE, VERMILION RED, YELLOW OCHRE, turquoise green, magenta . . . The names of the colors, in the half-used tubes, held the same nostalgia for me as names written on the back of a faded family photograph. As I held the colors in my hands and felt the weight of them, I knew that there was still potential there. Most of my paints were still good. A few had dried up because, as a toddler, Sophie unscrewed the lids. These would have to be replaced, but I still had a good blue, a good yellow and a good red—they were the only colors that I really needed. If I added some black or a smear of white I could mix any shade that I wanted. Of course my paintbrushes were a bit scruffy, and I would need some new canvases, but that was okay. I could knock up a few canvases easily . . . in a couple of days.

Upstairs, I could hear my vacuum humming. I'd left it on, as a decoy, while I tried to organize my new "studio." All I needed was a corner of the garage. Then, if I parked out on the street, I'd have some space to paint in. The drone of the vacuum made me feel agitated. I'd left it sitting on the couch, sucking a black hole in the air, and I hoped that it wouldn't overheat. The noise it made reminded me how limited my time was. I needed to get things organized, before *Sesame Street* and *Playschool* finished and Sophie and

William came looking for me. Usually I did the housework while they watched television. The sound of the vacuum cleaner running was our tacit signal that I was incommunicado.

As I climbed onto a stepladder and opened the louvers that ran along the top of the back wall, I felt a warm breeze blowing through the garage. Outside the sun shimmered on the fishbone leaves of the acacias, and I could smell summer in the newly cut grass. I unrolled an old piece of carpet underlay across the concrete floor to keep out the cold, then I looked around for something I could use as shelving. Against the wall I spied the old traymobile my mother had used in the seventies to serve drinks at parties. It consisted of two large yellow trays, one above the other, braced by a frame on wheels. It was incredibly ugly, but useful. I quickly laid my colors, brushes, and palettes out on the top tray. Then I found my old easel and set it up on the carpet underlay.

Against the whir of the vacuum cleaner upstairs, I could hear the theme song from *Sesame Street* playing in the downstairs rumpus room. The music for *Playschool* began, "There's a bear in there . . ." and Sophie called out, "Mommy . . . we're hungry. We want something to eat!"

I put my head out the back door of the garage and shouted toward the house. "I'll bring you something in a minute, sweetheart. I'm not finished the housework yet." Strangely, for once, lying to Sophie didn't tickle my sense of guilt. So, while the vacuum cleaner continued aimlessly sucking air inside the house, I went back to my easel and stood beside it, biting my thumbnail. The paints I longed for were lined up on the tray beside me and, distractedly, I began to finger my brushes. Would I? I hadn't meant to do anything other than set up the space in the garage so that I could use it while the children were at preschool.

Toward the back of the garage, I noticed an old canvas, turned to face the wall. I'd forgotten about that picture. It was unfinished, and it had been months since I'd even looked at it. Casually, I brushed off the cobwebs trailing down one side and watched a spider abandon its hidey-hole and coast on its thread down to the floor. I hesitated a moment and took the painting back to my easel to rest it there.

The painting was a portrait of Evelyn when she was pregnant with Amy. I had started it one afternoon while the children were playing tag out in the backyard. Evelyn and I had just finished afternoon tea, and for some reason I had felt inspired to make a quick sketch of her sitting at the table, her hands on her swollen belly, looking down at her empty plate. A week later I had started the painting, working from the sketch and from memory, always intending to finish the painting as a present for her.

The portrait had been shaping up well until I'd started detailing the face. It was the eyes. I just couldn't get them right, and I fussed over them for ages. Perhaps it was the buildup of paint, or the effect of a wayward bristle on my brush. Whatever the cause, the effect had unnerved me. For some reason the irises seemed to levitate in front of the whites. The eyes I'd painted were like cat's eyes at night. They were disembodied, and they shivered in space. It was a weird effect, and it had unsettled me so much that I put the painting away.

As I contemplated the unfinished painting in the garage, I realized, for the first time, that it was good. Unknowingly, I had captured the emotion of my subject. Somehow I'd painted Evelyn's inner turmoil. It was there in the haunted look in the eyes and in the franticness of the brushstrokes that textured the air around her. Thoughtfully, I squeezed some paints onto my palette and picked up my brush.

I began with her hands. Thin hands with long, tapering fingers clasped together over her womb. To me, those hands seemed tortured by the effort of being still, and I twisted the paint into the canvas with the edge of my palette knife to highlight the tension there. I finished the fingers, the palms, and the wrists, and found that now my own hands were shaking. I had a compulsive urge to complete the picture, and I squeezed out more paint from the tubes. Using cadmium yellow, blended with a little titanium white, I lit the boundaries of the womb beneath Evelyn's shirt and set it crackling with color.

My brush moved more quickly then. Under my furious hand, Evelyn evolved from a two-dimensional image on a piece of tight canvas into a real person with a brittle vibrating spirit. When, finally, I stood back to see what I had achieved, my chest constricted. I gasped at the intensity of the moment I had captured: the moment when substances shook and pulsed before being engulfed by flames.

Perhaps I noticed that the vacuum cleaner was no longer making a steady drone, but I was too absorbed in my painting to register the need for action. I stood back, staring into the colors as they leapt about on the canvas. I could not turn my back on the image, and my face grew hot. My eyes felt like they were burning. Then I noticed the smell of smoke and heard the vacuum spluttering.

VA VOOM! Something exploded, and the house was plunged into an eerie quietness as the circuit breaker cut off the electricity. My heart began to race as I ran out of the garage and took the steps two at a time. Thankfully, I heard their voices even before I opened the door. "Look, William! Mommy's gone up in smoke!" yelled Sophie excitedly.

William and Sophie stood in the living room, watching the flames leap about on the couch where the vacuum cleaner had been resting. They were startled when I appeared and pushed them both back into the kitchen. I grabbed the fire extinguisher that was on the wall, flicked off the latch, and pointed the nozzle at the blazing vacuum cleaner. The foam quickly smothered the flames and soon all that was left was a soggy black mess where the fire had been and the acrid smell of burned rubber and charred fabric.

"What's Daddy going to say about that?" asked Sophie. I couldn't answer her. I was still clutching the fire extinguisher, and my knees felt weak and wobbly. Breeze flowed through the house, blowing the foam from the extinguisher around the room like flotsam. William scooped up a bit of foam in his hand. "Hey, Sophie! It's like bubbles!" he cried. The two children began running around the room, scooping up the foam and blowing it at each other. I put the extinguisher down on the couch and walked back outside. My heart was pounding, and I needed to catch my breath.

"Hey! Where are you going?" Sophie called from the top of the front steps.

"Back to the garage."

"Why?"

"To clear my head."

Sophie frowned, and I realized that she needed a more concrete answer. "I'm going to finish a painting while I calm down."

"In the garage?"

"Yes. I won't be long, then I'll come back and clear up this mess and make us all some lunch. Okay?"

Sophie put her hands on her hips, and I knew from the way her lips were beginning to pout that it wasn't okay. "I want to paint too," she said.

"Me too," said William. "I like painting!"

In Sophie's small pouted mouth there was an attitude of stubborn determination. In William's eyes there was only longing. I sniffed the air. The house was full of smoke. It would be better if we all went outside for a while. "Oh, all right!" I said. "But let me get you some poster paints. You can't use my special ones."

I sent the kids out to the garage, flicked the switch back in the fuse box, and walked through the stinking living room into the kitchen, to make myself a cup of sweet black tea—for the shock. Sipping tea in the kitchen soothed me. Eventually I stopped shaking and took the poster paints out to the garage for the kids. Sophie had already dragged her little pink wooden table into the garage and set it up with paper, some of my old brushes, and a jar of water.

I filled some empty yogurt tubs with poster paint, and Sophie and William dipped their brushes into the colors and began painting with the freedom and confidence so characteristic in children's artwork. I took a deep breath and tried to relax. Now that Sophie and William were occupied, I could return to my painting. The children were completely absorbed in their own art, busily churning out great works and laying their art papers to dry all over the garage floor.

As I considered the painting perched on my easel, I looked at the empty plate Evelyn was staring at and saw that my composition wasn't balanced. You couldn't balance life with nothingness, it didn't work. All the weight gravitated toward Evelyn's eyes, and there was nothing to counter the energy those green eyes possessed. So I began to paint a pear on the plate.

I like painting pears. A pear is a very feminine fruit: swollen with seeds, soft and yielding. Taking out my yellow ochre, I tinted it with some cobalt blue. Slowly, I began to define the rounded shape of the pear. As I painted, I instinctively felt the shape of the pear pulling toward the face of the figure. Under my hand, the pear's stalk quivered and bent like a divining rod toward those powerful eyes. I stood back from my work and regarded it closely, acknowledging the challenge that existed between the woman and the fruit.

William was standing beside me. I turned toward him, and smiled, "Show me your painting." William held it up for me to see. It was obviously a picture of an adult and two children because one stick figure was twice the size of the other two. Evidently pleased with what he had produced, William pointed to a blue and yellow splodge with two green arms. "That's me in the garden," he said proudly, underlining the image with his pudgy index finger.

"So it is. You look very colorful!" I pointed to the larger figure—a blue stick, with a yellow head, on top of a red triangle. "Who's that?" I asked.

"That's you!" he answered, beaming at me with his huge brown eyes.

"Really! And who's the little girl? Is that Sophie?" I traced around a small blue stick, with a purple head, on top of a small red triangle.

William shook his head. "That's my mother." William looked at my painting then. "Have you painted my mother too?"

"Yes," I said quietly.

"Is that pear going to eat her?"

"Pears don't eat people, William!" Sophie stood next to him now, her wet painting in her hand. "Look at my picture, Mommy!" Sophie held her picture in front of my face.

It was similar to the ones she'd been drawing in felt pens for the last few weeks. On one side of the page there was a tall green tower. A yellow bridge curved from the tower door out over a blue river, and on the bridge were two figures, one large and one small. "That's you and me, Mom! We're crossing the bridge together."

Sometimes I wonder if children mean to communicate as much as they do, or if, as adults, we load their words and actions with our own meanings. Who knows? At that moment I felt a great surge of love and, squatting on my heels, I held my arms wide.

"Come here, you two!" I cried. William and Sophie ran at me laughing, almost knocking me over with their enthusiasm. I hugged them tightly, wrapping my arms around them both.

WENDY'S CHILD

ZIP! THE BULGING RED SUITCASE OPENED LIKE a large red-lipped mouth and spit its contents out over the double bed. Baby undershirts and bunny rugs, bodysuits and sunhats entwined like entrails and, smelling like mothballs, fell onto the floor. Wendy stooped to pick them up, fishing blindly for them on the floor, underneath her billowing denim pinafore. Those things would all need washing. It was five years since Madeline had used them, and they had been packed away in a suitcase under the bed since then. As she stood, the blood rushed back to her head, and she felt a wave of dizziness come over her. Still, she kept on. She was nesting.

Being a midwife, Wendy knew all about nesting—the frantic last-minute preparations made by the mother-to-be as the anxiety mounts, heightened by the impending birth. It had taken Wendy a long time to begin her preparations because, throughout her pregnancy, she had never really liked to think about the child she carried. Thinking about the baby always led to thinking about its conception and that nagging guilt that it might be Steve's child and not Harry's.

Harry's surprise when she had told him the news had been quickly overcome by his elation and a certain pride in his own potency. After all, they had not had much of a sex life at the beginning of the year. Even so, she reminded him, they'd had sex on his birth-day. True enough, he'd agreed, but he thought he'd slipped on a condom when things started to heat up. Had he? She couldn't re-member. She blushed now as she recalled that night—Harry's furtive fumbling and her passive acceptance of his overtures. Her growing sense of foreboding as she watched the shadows sliding across the ceiling. Harry's smell mixed with Steve's on her skin. It was possible, she tried to convince herself, that the child could be Harry's. Condoms weren't foolproof, not the way she and Harry used them.

As Wendy sat on the bed, sorting through the clothing, she felt a dragging sensation in the pit of her abdomen. Ligament strain, she told herself, and she stood up and pulled the pram out from the back of the cupboard to prove the ache was nothing more than that.

The pram looked old and tired. The faded navy canvas hung limply over the metal frame, and when she pushed it, the wheels squeaked. As she unfolded the canopy, she noticed that it was cov-ered in dust and a fine sheen of mildew. The pram would need oiling, sponging down, and a spell out in the sun. She'd always told herself that she would buy a new pram if she had another child. Somehow she hadn't been able to get enthusiastic about this baby.

She hadn't even allowed herself to get swept up in Harry's excitement. He had repainted the old wooden crib white and set it up beside the bed sometime ago. She looked at it now, standing on her side of the bed, all made up with Daniel's old blue crib sheets. Harry had done that to see how it looked. When he had finished, he had come to her and covered her eyes while he led her into their bedroom. "Surprise!" He'd laughed as his warm pudgy hands sprang away from her face. "Can you believe that we're going to have someone small enough to fit in there soon?" She had hugged him so that he couldn't see the trepidation in her eyes. That was her penance, she thought. Guilt.

Wendy frowned. Where were the nappies? She had pulled out the entire contents of the suitcase without any sign of them. She must have put them somewhere else. She opened the cupboard again. There they were, at the top, stacked in piles. She pulled over a chair and climbed up, but it was still impossible for her to reach them. The ceilings in their old Queenslander were almost ten feet high, and the top of the cupboard was a lofty prospect. She always tried to avoid putting things there if she thought she would need them. Getting the nappies down would require bringing up the stepladder from downstairs. She considered this for a moment while the pit of her abdomen pulled and strained. The adrenaline shot through her blood, and her heart kicked an extra beat. She bit her lip. It was time to get organized.

Thanks to Harry's recent effort at reorganizing the space under the house, she found the ladder easily, propped against one of the house support. She looked around and saw that Harry's tools were neatly placed up on the board behind his workbench. The old tins of paint were stacked in piles, and the boxes that held who knows what were retaped and pushed out of the way. Harry had been nesting for a while. Wendy groaned as she picked up the ladder and felt a dull ache wrench her lower back. She ignored it. The stepladder wasn't that heavy, and she balanced it against her swollen belly and carted it outside.

She struggled on the back steps. Although it was a lightweight aluminum ladder, the effort of lifting it made her pant, and her overgrown heart strained and pressed against her ribs, knocking the breath from her lungs. Halfway up the steps she took a rest. Long tendrils of sunlight fell down through the swamp bloodwood in the backyard and caught in the strands of her black hair. She felt hot standing outside in the sun, and it occurred to her that it was November now. Her baby would be a summer baby, just like Amy had been.

As Wendy caught her breath, she heard footsteps swish through the long grass down the side of the house and climb the steps behind her. The movie that Harry had taken the kids to see must have finished early. She felt him stroke her hair, and she turned with a smile.

"Steve?" The blood drained from her face.

"I saw you struggling, and I thought . . ." He grinned at her, squinting in the sunlight so that the skin around his steely blue eyes creased and smiled. The dimple in his square chin cast a little shadow on his face.

"Thanks." She let him take the ladder. "I thought you were Harry." Steve's sandy hair had been cut since she had last seen him. Short back and sides. It suited him, and in his white T-shirt and jeans he looked more presentable than she'd seen him in a long while.

Steve passed her, carrying the ladder over his head. He called back over his shoulder, and she saw his biceps bulge as he turned. "You shouldn't be doing this. Not at this stage of the game."

She followed him inside. After being so long in the bright sunlight, the indoors seemed pervaded by darkness. She staggered while her eyes adjusted to the dimness.

His hand was on her arm. "Where do you want it?"

"In the bedroom. I'm trying to get some nappies down from the top of the closet."

It was awkward, having him in the room she shared with

Harry. Her heart thumped against her chest so hard that she thought he would notice her dress shaking. She brought her hands up to her face to cover her warm, red cheeks.

"Are they up there?" he pointed. "Let me get them down for you."

Steve climbed up the ladder and Wendy couldn't help watching his taut buttocks move under his jeans. He retrieved the nappies and passed them to her. She took them, and the tips of their fingers touched.

"Wendy. I need to talk . . ."

"Don't. Please, Steve! Not now . . ."

He saw the pupils widen in her swimming-pool eyes and he was quiet but he moved toward her and cupped his hands under her chin, bringing her face up to meet his. Stroking her warm cheek with his thumb, he searched her face with his eyes. She felt naked before him. With a flick of her head she averted her eyes from his and pulled away, moving toward the bed.

"Thanks for your help. I need to get on with things now." She leaned over and dragged the suitcase off the bed, and it fell down with a thud. Her womb dragged and strained, and she felt something pop. Water trickled down her leg and ran onto the floor. Steve looked down at the puddle forming beneath her pinafore and seemed bemused.

"Wendy," he said lamely, confused. "Have you wet yourself?"

Wendy rolled her eyes to the ceiling and smiled anxiously. "No, Steve. I haven't wet myself. My waters just broke."

The dull aches and pains Wendy had been feeling for hours became stronger and more focused now. Steve brought a wad of towels from the bathroom for her to put between her legs as the fluids continued to leak from her womb. She was embarrassed having him there. They had barely been lovers, and now it felt as if he was witnessing the baseness of her sexuality and the raw power of her womb.

"Could you phone Harry, please?" Wendy asked him, partly to give him something helpful to do and partly to escape the intensity of his stare.

She heard him rifling through the junk that was beside the telephone. "I can't find Harry's mobile number, Wendy! Do you know it by heart?"

"No. It's in the little black book, under 'H'. I hope he's got it on! He's taken the kids to the cinema."

She heard Steve dial the number. She heard the mutterings, the explanations, then she heard Steve say, "Yeah, mate, I'll stay with her until you get back. See you in fifteen."

"You don't have to stay, you know. I'll be all right," she told him when he loitered in the hall. Wendy grabbed hold of the bedpost and breathed through a contraction. "They'll be here soon . . ." she told him, more to reassure herself, as the pain dwindled away. Letting go of the bedpost, she moved toward him to fetch the overnight bag she kept behind the bedroom door.

His hand squeezed her shoulder. "Look, it's okay. I told Harry I'd stay. Here, let me do that!" He took the bag from her. "Tell me what to pack, and I'll do it." His eyes pleaded with her.

It was easier to give in to him. As the vise wrenched her abdomen again, she sent him to the bathroom. "Orange . . . toothbrush . . . soap . . ." She pointed and he began rummaging noisily through the drawers and shelves. "Do you want this green toiletries bag?"

She breathed the pain away. "Yes, that's the one. There's a bottle of shampoo in the shower recess. Throw that in too . . ."

It was weird having him in the next room, helping her to pack her bag for hospital. She shivered. Perhaps he had done this for Evelyn too, back in January, when Amy was born.

While he was in the bathroom, she threw a couple of nighties, some underpants, and some sanitary napkins onto the bed. Harry could bring anything else she needed later. Another contraction gripped her. They were getting closer together now and stronger too. She breathed slowly out as the pain niggled in warning and she breathed in deeply as it seared through the pit of her belly and around her back before dwindling again. She tried to keep the towel between her legs as she hobbled about, collecting the things she needed, but already it was soaked and the waters trickled warmly down her leg and onto the floor.

When Steve appeared with her toiletries bag, she sent him out again to boil water and make a cup of tea. She couldn't think of what else to do with him. She didn't want him around her. It was Harry she wanted.

The Morris pulled into the carport, and she heard the front gate click and swing back on its spring. The kids raced up the steps and through the front door, shoes clattering across the bare pine floors. Madeline ran into the room first, her blond pigtails flying. "Mommy! Is the baby coming out now?"

Wendy nodded. "Daddy needs to take me to the hospital, and it will come out there, Maddy . . ." The pain began to wrench again, and she had to stop talking and breathe again. She stood up and grabbed the side of the bed. The towel dropped onto the floor, and the rest of her waters gushed out, flecked with the vernix that surrounded the unborn child. Daniel and Harry appeared at the door.

Daniel looked at the puddle on the floor and his mother's wet dress and made a face. "Urggh, gross, Mom!"

Harry picked up her bag. "I'll get you another towel to sit on in the car, okay? Steve said he'll stay with the kids until my folks arrive."

Wendy nodded. With Harry's help, she made it to the door. Then she stopped and leaned on the wall.

"What is it? Another contraction?" Harry's round face was twitching nervously.

She shook her head. "Joanna!"

"What about Joanna?"

"I said she could be at the birth, as a support person. Remember?"

Harry yanked his mobile out of his pocket. "I'll ring her, and we'll pick her up on the way through."

Somehow, Wendy and Harry got out to the carport. Wendy looked back toward the house. Steve and Daniel waved stiffly from the verandah, aware that they were outsiders and that this was women's business. They both looked nervous, but Madeline was jumping up and down, waving both arms. "I want to see the baby as soon as it comes out," she yelled.

Wendy pulled the seat belt around her belly and leaned back in her seat. The old Morris shuddered as Harry turned the ignition and jumped backward as he reversed out of the drive.

"Don't bump! Don't bump!" Wendy groaned, as her womb contracted. Harry took one look at her as she breathed through the contraction, then put his foot on the accelerator. Coughing out a big blob of black smoke, the Morris hiccuped up the road and trundled around the corner to Joanna's place.

"We're not going to make it in this thing, Harry," Wendy moaned, as they chugged into Joanna's driveway. "We'll have to ask Joanna to drive us in her car."

"All right," said Harry as he switched off the ignition, and the car heaved to a standstill. He burst out of the car and pulled Wendy's bag out of the trunk. The screen door leading from Joanna's kitchen into her carport swung open, and Joanna raced out of the little weatherboard cottage. She was ready for action, having squeezed herself into a pair of black bike pants and a red top that hugged her ample bosom. She bounded up to the car, beaming with excitement, and tapped on Wendy's window.

"I've got everything you suggested in here," she yelled through the glass, holding up a brown paper bag. "Lavender oil for soothing, a tennis ball for massage, apple juices and high-energy snacks . . . God, you look awful . . ."

"Joanna," said Harry confidentially, "we need to take your car to the hospital. Ours isn't working well. It keeps backfiring, and it's not comfortable enough for Wendy."

"Sure!" said Joanna, helping Wendy out of the car. "You just back the Morris out of the driveway so that we can get out."

Harry turned the key. The car spluttered and coughed, then the engine shut off. "Shit!" Harry turned the key again. This time the engine didn't even turn over. "Not now! Not now!" Joanna and Wendy watched incredulously as the bald spot on the top of Harry's head reddened in frustration.

Wendy clutched Joanna's arm while the child's head rammed against the muscles that held her inside the womb. Joanna's bag of birth aids fell on the ground, and the tennis ball rolled down the driveway into the gutter. Suddenly the way was clear for the child, and the force of the uterus expelled her into the birth canal.

Wendy heard a low guttural noise that sounded like a wounded animal. Was she making that sound? She couldn't speak to them now. She couldn't tell them that the baby was about to be born.

"It's all happening too fast!" panicked Harry. "You help her inside, Joanna. I'll ring for an ambulance."

While Harry fumbled with his mobile phone, Joanna chose her moment and dragged Wendy inside. Just inside the kitchen door, Wendy dropped to her knees on Joanna's linoleum floor. There was nothing else she could do. Great waves rocked and shook her now. Consumed as she was by the force of her own body, Wendy nevertheless thought she could smell something sweet and intoxicating. What was it? Of course, Wendy thought, it was cake. Rich fruitcake had been cooking all morning in Joanna's kitchen until the pungent aroma of plump fruit soaked in brandy pervaded the air. Wendy inhaled the essence of the cake like a drug and pushed.

As the baby moved down the birth canal, her head was squeezed and molded by muscles that forced her through the blackness. Her little heart raced as the pressure built on her skull. She was crowning.

Instinctively, Joanna put her hand on the warm mound that seemed to be rising. "Easy now! You don't want to tear anything!"

With the pressure breaking around her head, Wendy's child felt the air rush against her scalp. One last contraction, and she was propelled out of her mother's body into Joanna's waiting arms. She screwed her eyes shut tight to delay her entry into the world, and with her heart exploding in her chest, she discovered the agony of breathlessness. When she opened her mouth to express the burning inside her chest, her tongue quivered. Then the air rushed in and filled the aching space and, at last, she screamed.

Joanna clasped the newborn girl to her breast and breathed in her freshness. Both she and the baby were covered in the muck and blood of birth, but Joanna didn't care. "It's a girl! It's a girl," she cried.

Wendy, sinking to the floor, wept and laughed at the wailing of her child. Harry, who'd run inside to find Joanna holding the baby, rushed to Wendy's side and helped her to sit up and take the baby in her arms.

"Shouldn't we cut the cord or something?" asked Joanna, looking at the twisted blue umbilical cord, still attached to the baby.

"No," said Wendy, shaking her head. "Leave it for a while. It won't hurt her. The ambulance will be here soon anyway."

As they waited in Joanna's kitchen for the ambulance to arrive, sunlight broke through the nylon cafe curtains hanging in the window. It lit the tiny round face with the soft dewy skin and the open, wailing mouth. Sensing the light, the baby stopped crying, squinting her deep blue eyes. Wendy saw in an instant that the baby's face was Steve's. Still, she smiled and held the child close, undoing her pinafore to breast-feed. Joanna found a cotton blanket and wrapped it around them both.

In the warm sunny room, where the smell of her child mingled with the smell of cake, Wendy experienced an unexpected joy. She put her face against Harry's chest and cried with relief. This was her daughter. Her daughter taken from the dark womb and born into the sun. This child, her child, was not a child of shadows anymore. When Wendy looked up at Harry, she saw that he was weeping too. He bent to kiss the baby's wet black hair. "Beautiful . . . beautiful . . ." he said.

Much later, Wendy was tucked up in her hospital bed, her little room, overlooking the street, crowded with visitors. Harry sat on the end of the bed cooing over his daughter while Madeline kissed the baby's head repeatedly. Musing over Madeline's enthusiasm, Wendy was unable to decide whether it demonstrated sibling love or appropriately disguised jealousy. Daniel sat on the only chair, bent over his Game Boy, his dark brown hair swept forward like the crest of a cockatoo and held in place with gel. He only pretended to be engrossed in his game. Wendy saw his fingers habitually pressing the buttons, but she knew that underneath that crest of hair his eyes were drawn to the tiny person held in his father's arms. Susan and Clare, who'd arrived with bunches of flowers—sweet peas, roses, and carnations—stood, with Harry's mom and dad, at the end of the bed, clucking over the baby.

Usually, Wendy was too much of a pragmatist to celebrate moments of domestic bliss. She enjoyed these moments for what they were, transitory reminders of what mattered in life, then she let them go. She seldom consciously committed special family times to memory because she knew that one memory would overlap another, then another. In the end, all that was important was the emotion these moments invoked—the surge of joy created by Maddy's delicious smile the first day she discovered ice cream, the flush of pride when Daniel brought home his first school merit certificate.

She loved them—Daniel, Madeline, and Harry. She knew she did, but she seldom told herself so. She took them all for granted—usually, but not today. Today her body hummed with love, and she tried to hold the people that inspired that love close—tried to imprint on her mind the scene that surrounded her so that she could recall it in the days to come.

Joanna had left Harry and Wendy to ride ahead in the ambulance while she cleaned up her kitchen and waited for the automobile club to come and move the Morris back out onto the street. Then she'd rushed out and bought the biggest pink teddy she could find. She paraded into Wendy's room behind it, Jake and Sam screaming with excitement in her wake. Wendy said that the bear was "beautiful, " but as Susan remarked later, endorphins were clouding her judgment. The bear was fluorescent, beady-eyed and vulgar. The truth was, Wendy didn't care. She was enjoying the surprising feeling of elation. If she had anticipated having any emotions at the birth of this child, joy had not been one of them. Perhaps it would all work out. Perhaps . . .

There was a knock at the door. Everyone turned their heads at once, and the laughter left the room. It was Steve. Wendy's heart sank. If only he could leave her and Harry alone now that the baby had arrived, she knew she could put the affair behind her. She could make her marriage to Harry work. Ironically, her pregnancy had probably saved it.

Steve hung by the door. He seemed suddenly embarrassed and unsure. It was Harry who jumped up and shook his hand. "Thanks for all your help, mate," he said.

Steve nodded and placed a bunch of yellow roses on the foot of Wendy's bed. "Can I take a peek?"

Wendy bit her lip anxiously, but Harry was full of pride. "I don't see why not!"

Steve bent over the baby, fast asleep in Harry's arms, swaddled in a white cotton blanket. Only her head was visible, and her two tiny hands were pressed up against her face. Wendy watched Steve examine the tiny round face with the little pursed lips. She sensed him agonizing over the urge to take the baby from Harry. She knew how fierce the parental urge was, the urge to unwrap the bundle and pore over its perfection. But Steve only placed a finger inside the palm of the child's hand. Her fingers instinctively gripped his, and Wendy saw a single tear run down his cheek. He looked at her and smiled. "She's a beaut, Wendy. You've done good." He grew bashful then, his cheeks reddening, and he excused himself abruptly and left the room.

When all the visitors had gone, Harry squeezed Wendy's hand. "How sad for Steve. It was nice of him to visit really." Harry bent lovingly over the baby and watched her mouth make little sucking movements in her sleep. "I bet he was thinking of his own daughter when he looked at ours."

CHANGES

IT WAS ONLY MIDMORNING, BUT THE NOVEM-
ber sun seared across the sky. Joanna and the baby sheltered on
Wendy's verandah, where the blazing heat was tamed into a lan-
guid warmth that hugged the house. Outside, on the road, the
heat rippled over the black paving and flashed alongside parked
cars with an eye-numbing whiteness that made Joanna turn away
and blink. She looked up at the corrugated-iron roof above her,
grateful for the shade it offered, noting briefly the sharp edge it
gave to the luminous blue.

While Sam played with a box of Madeline's toys at her feet,
Joanna sat with one hand resting on the pram, pushing it rhyth-
mically up and down the old floorboards. In her newborn pink-
ness, the baby seemed very aptly named. Harry had called her
Rose, after his mother.

Joanna called her Rosie. She felt a special bond with this
baby, a bond rivaled in intensity only by the love she felt for her
own children. Since Rosie's birth, Joanna had watched Wendy
closely, alert to any changes in her moods, ready to rush in and
help the moment she saw that Wendy wasn't coping. Wendy obviously adored the baby, and a strong relationship between mother
and child seemed to be developing. This in itself was reassuring

and would have been enough to set Joanna's mind at ease if it weren't for an undercurrent of anxiety Joanna detected in Wendy's manner. She couldn't decipher it, and so she stayed vigilant. She couldn't let Wendy sink into the same quagmire of postnatal depression that had claimed Evelyn and Amy.

At the first faint whimper, Joanna seized the opportunity to gather the tiny infant in her arms and pat her while she drifted back to sleep. Although it was hot, she held the baby upright against her body, and the perspiration that ran down her neck mingled with the moisture already on the child's skin. Rosie wore only a cotton vest and an enormous white terry nappy that came down to her knees. Her scrawny newborn legs stuck out like two pink knitting needles slid through a ball of white wool. Her thin arms hung droopily over Joanna's shoulder, and her head nestled under Joanna's chin. As if to ward off the world and all its associated discomforts, her eyes were screwed shut, her brow furrowed and creased like a cranky old woman. She had not grown into prettiness, yet Joanna thought that, next to her boys, Rosie was the most exquisite baby she had ever seen.

Wendy walked out onto the verandah with a heavily laden tray that clattered as she walked. On the tray there was a jug of iced water, the ice cubes already shrinking, a plate of teddy-bear cookies for Sam and a pot of brewing coffee. Wendy sniffed the strong aroma that was released from the fresh coffee grounds as the hot water seeped through them. She hadn't been able to appreciate either coffee or tea when she was pregnant. The smell and the taste had made her feel incredibly nauseous. Now that Rosie was born, she could enjoy her coffee again. The nausea was gone, and when she could avoid thinking about Evelyn, Amy, or Steve, she could relax and revel in her baby. The delight she felt when she looked at her tiny child, snuggled against Joanna in the shade of the verandah, was quite astonishing. It was, however, a tenuous pleasure tinged with a fear of being found out.

There had been moments in the last three weeks when she thought that Harry could not fail to notice Steve's legacy in Rosie. Wendy saw it, and she did not doubt that this was Steve's child. She saw Steve in the shape of Rosie's face and the spacing of her eyes. She saw him in the squareness of her jaw, the dimple on her chin, and the ridge across her nose. How could Harry not see it? The child was created in Steve's image.

Thankfully, Harry noticed nothing. In fact, as each day passed, he found a new likeness in Rosie to himself or to his mother or father. "I think she's got my hands, Wendy. Look at the breadth of her palm. And those feet! With those narrow feet, she's going to have trouble buying shoes, just like Mom." Wendy had not seen Harry this happy in a long time. She rejoiced in his ignorance and vowed never to tell him her secret. What good would it do? Since Rosie's birth, their marriage was better than ever.

Soon, she hoped, her worries would cease. Harry had found a new job, one that paid better, in Melbourne. The family was moving, and this chapter in their lives would close. Wendy eased the plunger down in the glass coffeepot. The plunger pushed the grounds to the bottom, straining the liquid of its bitter sediment. As she filled two large mugs with coffee, she wondered how she was going to tell Joanna.

It was best, she decided as she watched Joanna lay Rosie back down in the pram, to be blunt and casual. It was not such a big deal. Not really.

She swallowed and took a breath. "I haven't told anyone yet, Joanna. Not even the kids know but . . . Harry's found a new job.

The pay is better, so I won't have to work so much. Not while Rosie's small anyway."

Joanna was only half-listening. She was paying more attention to the little smiles that flickered briefly on Rosie's lips. Most people said that a newborn's smiles were wind, but she'd never known an adult to smile with gas. It was a moment before her mind processed what Wendy had said. "That's great!" she replied, her eyes still intent on the child in the pram. "I'll be able to pop over and see you more often then—help out a bit with the baby."

"Well, no. No, you won't."

"What?" Joanna was perplexed. She looked apprehensively at Wendy.

"The job's in Melbourne, you see. It's all a bit of a rush. Harry starts in a fortnight . . ."

"Oh!" It was a small word, spoken softly, but it conveyed to Wendy some of Joanna's bewilderment. "He starts that soon?"

"I'm afraid so. They needed someone who could start working before Christmas."

"What about you? When will you leave?" The tears were already lining her eyes. She couldn't help them.

"I'll stay on here, with the kids, until the house is sold. Then we'll go and join Harry. The real estate agent was here this morning. I've already started packing."

"I guess, after so long, there's a lot to pack."

"Yes. And with Rosie taking up so much of my time, I thought I'd better make a start . . . Oh Joanna! Don't!"

It was too late. The tears burst out of Joanna's eyes and ran down her face. When she spoke, her voice wobbled.

"It's . . . not just . . . your news . . . It's everything!"

Joanna's face was going blotchy and red, the cumulative effect of emotion and weather. She wiped the tears from her eyes with her palms. "Everything's . . . different now. Amy disappeared and Evelyn went crazy and since then nothing in my life has felt right. Now you're going away, Susan's going to work and Clare's all wrapped up in her painting . . ."

Wendy poured Joanna a glass of water and pushed it across the table. "I know. It's been a really tough year. But things can't be like they were . . ."

"Why not?"

Wendy noticed Sam's wide eyes. He'd stopped playing and was watching them now. Curious. She lowered her voice, but she couldn't quell the agitation that was rising in it. "Things can't be like they were, Joanna, because of everything that's happened. Our happy little mothers' group began to fall apart the day Amy disappeared."

Joanna looked blankly at Wendy, unwilling to admit the truth in what she'd said.

Wendy became more emphatic. "Amy was missing, Joanna. None of us knew what had happened to her. For months and months we lived with our worst nightmares. You don't wake up from a nightmare like that and forget it ever happened. Can't you see? It's changed us! And perhaps . . ." Wendy continued, thinking aloud, "and perhaps that's just as well."

"But losing Amy didn't change me!" wailed Joanna, a thread of clear mucus dribbling from her nose. "I felt it too. I felt it, but I'm still the same. Aren't I? I'm still fat, sloppy old Joanna who bakes cakes and does coffee . . . Except now there's not going to be anyone to do coffee with!"

Joanna put her hands around her water glass, and her knuckles grew white. Her voice was desperate. "Why can't you stay? I'll help out with Rosie. I'll look after her while you work. Tell

Harry to stay here. He can find another job . . . one in Brisbane. Tom might know someone who . . ."

Wendy put her head in her hands. God almighty! Why were some things so hard?

"Joanna! Stop! I can't stay here in Brisbane. I can't live next to Evelyn anymore. It would be too awful . . ."

"But why?"

"Because I'd have Rosie, and she'd have no one."

"You can't help that!"

"No, I can't. What's done is done. But don't you see? I don't want Evelyn to be reminded of what she's lost every time she sees me with Rosie. And I . . . I don't want to be reminded of Amy every time I see Evelyn. I just want to go away, Joanna . . . I have to go away."

Joanna was silent. So that was what was eating at Wendy. That was the anxiety she couldn't explain. Now that Wendy and Harry had made up their minds to leave, what could she say to stop them? Impotent words whirled through her mind like wind in a bottle. There was nothing she could do, and maybe it would be selfish to try. Maybe it would be better for Rosie if the whole family made a fresh start.

The baby began to cry and Wendy picked her up and undid her blouse to feed her. At first Rosie sucked hungrily, trying to bring the milk down. Then, as the milk began flowing more steadily, her feeding became more relaxed, settling into a familiar pattern—suck, suck, suck, pause . . . suck, suck, suck . . . Joanna stared at Rosie while she nursed and wondered what it would have been like to watch her grow up. Wendy focused her attention on the baby, but her face was flushed, and a tear trembled on the edge of her jaw.

Sam clambered onto Joanna's knee and began whining for a

cookie. Automatically, Joanna took a teddy-bear cookie from the plate on the table, snapped off the head, and pushed it into his mouth. Rosie was dozing at the breast now, and Joanna saw that while she had been feeding, the milk had dripped from Wendy's other breast, leaving a small wet circle on her blouse.

Joanna pulled her car keys out of her handbag and picked Sam up to leave. "I'd better go," she said as she walked past Wendy. Then, at the top of the front steps, she turned around and tried to smile. "Come over tomorrow night. Bring Harry and the kids around for dinner before Harry leaves. Tom will want to say good-bye."

Wendy looked at Joanna and nodded. "Okay. Thanks, Jo."

Joanna braced herself for the heat and then, with Sam on her hip, stepped out into the sunshine that bled down the front steps.

A SHORT TIME LATER, WHEN WENDY WAS BURPING Rosie over her shoulder, Steve ambled through the front gate, his hands wedged halfway into the pockets of his tight jeans. Wendy stood up, frantically trying to do up the buttons on her blouse with one hand while she held Rosie to her with the other.

"Steve!" The anxiety in her voice was enough to unsettle Rosie, and Wendy had to sway back and forth on the verandah, at the top of the steps, to hush her.

"I just came to tell you that I'm moving out," Steve said, standing on the bottom step. He offered her a half smile, and, as he tilted his face, the verandah roof sliced it with shadow.

"When?"

"Tomorrow. I've bought a worker's cottage over in Red Hill. Somewhere for me and William to live once Evelyn comes home."

"I see." Wendy was still swaying, even though Rosie was quiet.

"Evelyn can keep the house when she gets out of hospital. It's hers anyway. She can do what she likes with it. I won't be sticking around to watch."

"Actually, we're leaving too," Wendy said, clutching her baby a little more closely to her chest.

"Selling up?" Steve raised one eyebrow.

"Yes. Harry's got a new job in Melbourne."

"All of us running away." There was resignation in his voice.

"Something like that."

"Listen, Wendy, I think . . ." Steve moved up the stairs and reached out to stroke Rosie's head. Wendy stepped back and Steve's hand fell through the air. "I think we need to talk."

"Please, Steve! Just leave it be. We have to move on now."

Steve stepped up to Wendy. He stood over her and she looked into his eyes. They were deep blue like the darkest part of the ocean, and she felt herself falling through them, drowning under the weight of the lie she needed to maintain.

His hands were on Rosie. He was lifting the baby upward. Wendy's arms dropped to her sides, and she felt the wrench and emptiness as Steve held Rosie to his chest. Steve peered into the child's deep blue eyes, found the dimple on her chin, and traced the ridge on her nose. Wendy sensed the force of Steve's resolve looming before her. She held her breath.

"She looks like—"

"Harry's mom," Wendy cut in sharply, feeling the air rush back into her lungs. "She looks just like Harry's mom, even down to the dimple." Wendy stood her ground and pulled Rosie from his arms. "She needs a nappy change, I think."

"Let me do it," said Steve. "I can still remember how."

Wendy shook her head. "No!" she said, turning Rosie away from him. "No, I'll change her."

Steve put his hand on Wendy's shoulder. "Wait!" He reached out and touched Rosie's fuzzy hair. His hand lingered too long over her little head, then, taking his time, he stroked her plump cheek.

Wendy stood rigid, avoiding Steve's eyes while he scrutinized every aspect of the child's face. She held Rosie tightly, unwilling to let him take her in his arms again; anticipating that, in a moment, he would lay some claim on the child. In the shade of the verandah she waited. As the sun climbed over the verandah roof, the moment she dreaded passed.

Steve leaned over Rosie and kissed Wendy lightly on the cheek. "I only wanted to say good-bye," he whispered, and his breath curled inside her ear. "Good-bye and good luck—with Harry."

EXCUSES

JOANNA STARED THROUGH THE COLD FOG OF her deep freeze. Wedged somewhere in the mist, among packets of frozen peas, fish fingers, and icy poles, were the cakes she had made over the last ten months. She pulled a few out, chipping away the ice so that she could read the labels—pumpkin syrup cake, rich choc-mud cake, hummingbird cake. She selected the hummingbird cake to defrost. It seemed the right sort of cake for summer. She would ice the cake and take it over to Evelyn's house. Clare was picking Evelyn up this morning. William had a day off preschool to bring his mother home.

Joanna sighed. She could never excuse Evelyn. Her conscience prickled because, in her heart, she knew that she ought to forgive her. As if a traumatic childhood weren't enough to cope with, Evelyn had developed a postnatal disorder that had distorted reality and prevented her from connecting with her daughter. Even so, to Joanna, giving away your child to a stranger was unconscionable, and she wasn't sure she was going to be able to relate to Evelyn anymore. She was only going to Evelyn's homecoming today because Clare had insisted.

"Evelyn is going to need some support now she's home," Clare had said. "You were her friend, Joanna. She needs to know that you still care about what happens to her even if you don't approve of what she did."

Susan had coaxed her too. "Come on, Joanna. You don't have to stay long. Just put in an appearance. Bring a cake!"

It was the thought of cake that had persuaded her really. She was dying to eat one. Just one little piece of cake to fill some of the emptiness. Although she hadn't persisted with the aqua-aerobics class, she'd been dieting for nearly a year now and had still only lost a few pounds. What would it matter if she gave herself a treat?

Joanna parked outside Wendy's old place and slumped forward to stare at the house through the car window. The lurching carport that Harry had built looked lonely without the Morris for company. A real estate agent had driven a SOLD sign into the ground beside the carport, and it careened sympathetically to the left. Joanna cast her eyes over the verandah, which was without the familiar paraphernalia of potted geraniums, kids' toys, and wicker chairs. In the family's absence, the house had lost its allure. It was a discarded shell.

In the end, Wendy had left quickly, as soon as the sale went through. She'd left without a proper good-bye, just a hurried phone call with the baby crying on her shoulder. Joanna would miss Rosie. She had seen her born. She would miss Wendy too, she thought, although Wendy had promised she would be in touch. Perhaps Joanna and the boys could visit them in Melbourne, once they got settled. As much as Joanna hated the way things had worked out, she couldn't begrudge Wendy and Harry's decision to move. She hadn't seen them so happy as a couple in years.

Joanna unfastened Sam's seat belt. She put him on the footpath and went back to the car for her Tupperware cake carrier.

"Picky-up!" pleaded Sam, throwing his arms up into the air.

Joanna balanced the cake carrier on one hip and hoisted Sam
onto the other. Laden with child and cake, she trudged down the
footpath, through the Easterns' untidy yard, where car parts were
littered like dog bones around the house. Puffing slightly, she
walked up the steps, leaning her body into the wall because the
missing balusters under the handrail unnerved her.

William's little face with its big brown eyes met her at the
door. He smiled at Sam, and Sam pulled away from her hip. She
put him on the ground. William led Sam by the hand to the end
of the enclosed verandah, where he had a track set up for his collection of Matchbox cars. He showed Sam how to send the cars
down the track. They picked up speed in the loop and rocketed
off the end, smashing into the sided walls that enclosed the verandah and chipping away the finish. Joanna watched the boys playing for a moment. She glimpsed the sliver of sun that squeezed
through the slightly open window, drizzling light onto the boys,
before breathing deeply and walking inside the house.

The women were out back, in the kitchen, the only other
place where the light could penetrate. The kitchen was tidy. The
benches were clear, and someone had put a bunch of blue aga-
panthus flowers near the window. Joanna guessed that Susan had
come early to clean up the house. Evelyn sat with her back to the
window and the flowers. Her auburn hair was swept back and
tied at the nape of her neck with a black band. She looked pale
and thin but . . . peaceful.

Evelyn looked up at Joanna. "You've changed your hair," she
said. "It suits you."

"Thanks," said Joanna, smiling too quickly. She put her cake
down on the table. "Shall I boil water?"

Clare rose. "Don't worry, Joanna. You sit down. I'll make us
a pot of tea."

"Is there any coffee?" asked Susan.

"I'm sorry, Susan, the canister's empty," said Clare.

Evelyn craned her head toward the pantry and furrowed her white brow. She seemed agitated. "Steve probably used it all up," she said, biting her lip. "He's a bit of an addict."

"Never mind." Susan put her hand on Evelyn's arm, "I shouldn't be so fussy anyway. Tea will be fine. It's been ages since I've had a cup."

Evelyn smiled thinly. "Good. Well, let me do something . . . We need some plates for this lovely cake of Joanna's . . . and some cake forks . . ." She pulled away from Susan's grasp and busied herself in the cabinet, clattering around after crockery.

Susan raised her eyebrows at Joanna and looked at her watch. Strange how time labored in these awkward circumstances. Barely five minutes had passed since she'd arrived, but she felt she had been sitting at this table for hours, searching her mind for trivial topics of conversation in an attempt to avoid the silences that were too meaningful to bear.

Evelyn returned with the plates and the cake forks, and as Joanna sliced everyone a piece of cake, Clare arrived with the loaded tea tray. She put Evelyn's best china cups on the table and her pretty floral teapot as well, the one that always stood on the shelf with its matching sugar bowl and creamer.

Evelyn reached out and touched the smooth glazed surface of the teapot, tracing around the purple pansies with their yellow centers. "You know, I don't think I've ever actually used this teapot. It was my mother's . . ."

Clare's jaw dropped. "Oh, I'm sorry, Evelyn. Would you like me to get out another one, the brown pottery one perhaps?" She lifted the pot off the table.

Evelyn held up her hand. "No, no. Don't worry. Pretty, isn't it? I don't know why I've never used it before. You know, one of the few memories I have of my mother is her yelling at me. 'Don't touch that pot! You'll burn yourself!'" She laughed, and her face blushed. "I guess I've never touched it since."

The other women laughed too. An anxious little sound that was swallowed up by the dark house. Clare poured the tea.

Evelyn held the delicate handle of her teacup in one hand and looked over the rim with her green cat eyes. "It's a bit like a wake, isn't it?"

Joanna coughed on her cake, and crumbs splattered over the table.

Susan leaned toward Joanna, and whispered, "Are you all right?" Joanna nodded and took a swig of tea.

Evelyn bit her lip. "I'm sorry, Joanna. I shouldn't tease. I guess you've all got questions."

Susan swallowed her tea so quickly it burned her throat. She shook her head. "No. Don't feel you have to explain anything. I'm sure you're tired of talking about it. Anyway, none of us really knows what you went through . . . do we, Joanna?" She gave Joanna a nudge. Joanna shook her head obediently.

Evelyn sipped her tea. She felt Clare's eyes on the place where her lips met her cup. Her lips began to tremble, and the tea trickled down her chin.

"There is something I'd like to ask." Clare adjusted the clip she had in her honey blond hair. Joanna watched Clare's hands. She had beautiful hands, slender, with long fingers. "I need to know if there was anything I could have done to help. Could I have stopped you giving her away?"

Evelyn placed her cup on its saucer and looked down into the emptiness it held. Somewhere, beyond the emptiness, she found the words to appease Clare. "Don't blame yourself. You had no way of knowing how sick I was." Her voice was very soft, and it traced the fine gold rim of her empty cup. "None of you need to feel guilty. I carry enough guilt for all of us."

Joanna was savoring her last mouthful of cake; she swallowed quickly, regretfully. "Do you? Do you really feel guilty about it, Evelyn?"

"Joanna!" It was Susan who snapped, trying to ease the force of Joanna's words, but it was too late.

Evelyn's fingers clenched the handle of her cup, and her nails dug into the palm of her hand. She forced herself to look Joanna in the eye.

"Of course I do." The words came out smoothly, convincingly.

Joanna sighed inwardly. She would overlook this deviation from maternal love and responsibility, but she would never forgive it. Never.

William ran in, with Sam following. "We're hungry," said William. "We want a piece of cake."

"Cake, peeze," asked Sam, holding out his hands.

Joanna cut two huge pieces of cake, which she placed on paper towels. She told the boys to go out onto the back steps. They carried their cake out triumphantly and sat, devouring the bits closest to the frosting and scattering crumbs down the stairs. They laughed.

Evelyn smiled at them. She was aching to hold William. She was hungry for his sweet sweaty smell and the gentle pressure of his body as he leaned against her. She wanted him to sit on her lap and lean in close so that she could put her hand on his heart and feel it beating against her palm. But she didn't want to make him come to her. She would wait. He would come. There would be time. She would make it up to him, the time they had lost.

Susan looked at her watch. Clare had mentioned that Steve was coming to the house to pick William up. He had custody of William now; Evelyn was only allowed supervised visits with her son.

William came inside, his mouth circled with yellow streaks of frosting. Joanna cut him another piece of cake, and he climbed up on Evelyn's knee to eat it.

Susan and Joanna cleared the table and took the cups over to the sink. Outside the kitchen window, Joanna could see that the jacaranda tree was covered in clusters of mauve flowers. Summer came to the Easterns' garden, if not their house, she thought.

Susan lifted her pink-gloved hand out of the suds in the sink and motioned outside. "Have you seen the size of the spider's web out there? I've never seen such an enormous construction."

Joanna saw the threads that ran from the jacaranda tree to the eaves. She saw how the web was designed. It lay in the path of the sun so that every butterfly or bug or beetle that traveled in the sunbeam became ensnared in the sticky threads. She watched the sunlight run along the fine threads and saw how the shadows bent behind the web. Out on the street, a car pulled up.

Steve appeared in the doorway. His steel blue eyes shone out for William, and the little boy clambered off his mother's lap and ran into his father's arms. Steve scooped the boy up and hugged him. He looked over William's shoulder, and the light faded from his eyes.

"You got everything you need, Evelyn?"

Evelyn nodded, her eyes downcast, and she made her hand into a fist under the table. "When can I see him again?" she asked.

"Tomorrow. All right?"

Evelyn nodded.

"Is that all right with you, Clare?"

"Yes, I'll come around with Sophie in the morning, and we'll stay as long as William's here."

"Good. There should be a social worker coming along at about ten."

"I'll be here, Steve," said Clare firmly. "But on Thursday you'll have to organize the social worker to come early. I've got some things of my own I want to do."

Steve looked a bit bewildered. It was unlike Clare to be anything less than accommodating. For a moment he rested his cheek on William's head and wondered if Clare might still change her mind and save him the trouble of organizing the social worker.

Clare read the astonished look on Steve's face. He was so used to her picking up the slack for him without complaint. Well, he would have to get used to her being a bit more assertive. She would continue to watch over William, of course. He'd crept into her heart. However, she wasn't going to put herself out simply to suit Steve. He'd never been a conscientious father, but he had custody now, and she'd do whatever she could to ensure that he started taking more responsibility for his son.

Finally realizing that Clare wasn't going to adjust her plans for his sake, Steve hoisted William higher onto his hip and decided to leave. "Okay, well, we'll be off then. Got to straighten up Dad's new patch, haven't we, William?"

William didn't answer his father. "Can we get McDonald's for lunch, Dad?" he pleaded.

"I've already bought some bread and ham for lunch, William."

"Pleeeaase, Daddy!" William squeezed his father around the neck.

Steve prized his son free. "Oh all right, you win!"

Joanna laughed. "You're a pushover, Steve. How's the work on the new house going?"

"Oh, a little more paint, and we'll be done, won't we, Will?" Steve placed William back on the floor. "Go and say good-bye to your mother."

William ran and hugged Evelyn tightly and Joanna wondered for a moment which one of them was the child. Evelyn seemed dwarfed by her son, small and withered. Joanna saw tears in her eyes and looked away.

While Susan and Clare walked out to the car with Evelyn to wave her son good-bye, Joanna lifted the remains of the cake into her Tupperware container. There were still three large pieces left. The passionfruit frosting oozed over the plate. She scooped it into her mouth with her fingers. The thought occurred to her that she ought to show some restraint. After all, she'd had one piece already, that should have been enough.

It wasn't enough. That strange emptiness gripped her, and she knew she couldn't bear it any longer. She had to consume that cake. Sweating and salivating in anticipation, she began to break off small pieces of cake and eat them. These made her mouth water even more, and her stomach began to groan. So she broke off bigger pieces and stuffed them in her mouth. Big, buttery pieces that surrendered sweet banana and tart pineapple flavors onto her tongue. She filled her mouth with cake and felt the soft texture press against her cheeks before she swallowed. She licked off the frosting like a child, and with her teeth she crushed the passionfruit seeds, which cut through the sweetness and tingled her tongue. She devoured all that remained and a sensation of warmth spread inside her. At last, she was full, and it was as if her whole body was glowing. Her flesh was plumped out with ecstasy, and the tiny beads of sweat on her white skin swallowed all the sunlight in the kitchen until she glowed. She glowed like a huge golden orb.

As Joanna pushed the last piece of cake around the plate to scoop up the frosting, she laughed because she didn't feel guilty. Not at all. No, she felt good. Really good.

Later that night, lying beside Tom's warm body, she dreamed. She dreamed she was a Gypsy queen riding out across a barren country. The moon rose, and she gathered its light in her cloak until her cloak shone silver in the darkness. Then, with a feeling of jubilation, she cast off her cloak and tossed the moonlight onto the road behind her and continued riding naked, into the night. Her round belly shimmered with its own ethereal light as her horse thrashed beneath her, casting pebbles and stones into the grass with its sharp hooves. She could have ridden across all her dreams on that horse. Instead, she woke and rolled on top of Tom and the moonlight slid under the curtains and kissed her buttocks silver as she writhed.

 THE END OF CRAVING

IT STOPPED! THE CRAVING FOR CAKE. QUITE suddenly. As if I hadn't been dying for it all year. As if I hadn't started drooling every time I smelled a piece of chocolate cake or apple tart or ginger snap at the Vista Cafe. As if I hadn't got up so many nights and baked in the altogether with only moonlight to guide my hands as they creamed and folded and beat.

I suppose Clare's shrink would say the craving left me after I ate all that cake at Evelyn's. That day, I gorged myself until I glowed. I ate and ate until the urge to eat was extinguished. Catharsis—I think that's the jargon. And that weird dream! "There's something Freudian in that!" Susan said, when I told her about it. "Something about sex and horses and the liberating experience of female masturbation." Shit! If Susan's brain gets any bigger, it's going to explode.

Anyway, whatever my dream means, when I wake up the next morning, after that day at Evelyn's house, I'm not dying for cake anymore. I wake up with semen from Tom all wet and sticky between my thighs and while I'm having a shower I think about what I'd like for breakfast. Porridge. Would you believe it? A big bowl of steaming porridge with brown sugar and real milk. Not thin watery blue milk. Not milk that looks like it could have come from my own tits. Real whole milk. One hundred percent homogenized, pasteurized whole milk.

So I hop out of the shower, dry myself with a big fluffy pink towel in the steam of the bathroom, and rub baby oil into my skin. I oil myself all over until my skin is shiny soft and sexy . . . Yeah, sexy. I don't need to weigh myself to know how sexy I am. I don't need to put so much as one foot on the scales and dream of how sexy I could be if I just lost nine or ten more pounds.

When I go back into the bedroom, Tom is sprawled naked, on his back, under the sheet. The sheet is propped up over his erection, and he's snoring. Every time he snores, his bent thingo trembles under the sheet like a miniature Tower of Pisa in a quake. That makes me laugh. I chortle as I reach for my bike pants and T-shirt, then, when Tom snorts in his sleep, I change my mind. I put on my new denim skirt instead and the floral blouse, the one that Wendy sent me, as a present, from some swanky boutique in Melbourne. I put on some strappy black sandals and some lipstick and I bend like a willow from the waist and brush my hair from underneath to give it some volume and shine. When I stand up my head is spinning but I see myself in the mirror.

I study my reflection, taking a minute to form an objective opinion as I turn about and crane my neck to look at myself from every angle. Okay, I'm no supermodel. But the outfit is flattering, the hair is well cut, the face is attractive, and the skin is strangely luminous, almost transparent. A smile wider and whiter than a crescent moon shines out of the mirror at me. Hell, I actually look good. Better than good. I look gorgeous! Not surprised gorgeous like I looked that time in the mirror at Vivianne's salon. That was like looking at someone more attractive trying to be me. No, this time I'm just looking at me, and I like what I see. I really do! I like the ash blond bob and the voluptuous boobs under the gauzy purple flowers. I like the denim skirt and the way it hugs my big bottom at the back. I like the bare legs and feet in the black sandals, and I like the way my skin glows.

As I spin around in front of the mirror, Tom wakes up and winks at me in the glass. He wolf whistles. "Come here, big babe!" he says, real low and drawling like an American movie star. He throws off the sheet and flings his arms out wide so that the black hairs in his armpits fan out. The sight of him there, the naked fleshiness of him, sets me off laughing again and I pick up a pillow and throw it right at the Tower of Pisa. "Not now." I giggle, as Pisa subsides. "I'm going to make some breakfast for me and the kids."

I stand out in the kitchen and turn on the radio I keep on the counter. Some soppy song from the eighties is playing, and I hum along while I stir the porridge. I don't feel like cake, even though the freezer is full of it. Full of mud cakes, orange cakes, syrup cakes, fruit cakes, and all the other midnight cakes I've made. Even I don't know exactly how many cakes I've jammed in there and I decide to take stock after breakfast.

Jake and Sam shuffle out of their bedroom in their blue pajamas, sleep still crusty in their eyes. They haul themselves onto chairs and lean their elbows on the kitchen table, holding their heavy heads in their hands. I ladle out the porridge, thick and creamy, from the pot, sprinkle it with brown sugar, pour in milk and place it in front of them. Jake pouts at the porridge. He doesn't really want to eat it, and he keeps reminding me that porridge is for cold days. Sam is happy enough though. "Is this what Goldilocks eats?" he asks.

When the boys have eaten, they run into the backyard with a football, then I hear Tom in the shower. I sit down in the kitchen and eat my porridge while I read the Saturday paper. Gee, it tastes good to eat something other than dry cereal with skim milk. My stomach feels warm and comfortable and after one bowl I'm full.

Sometime later that morning, Tom goes out to do the shopping. He kisses me and takes the list I have stuck on the fridge with the purple dinosaur magnet that Jake made at preschool. Jake made that magnet out of salt dough, painted it himself and gave it to me for Mother's Day. It's getting a bit moldy now. Salt dough doesn't last forever, especially in this humidity. I like to keep it there on the fridge anyway. It makes me happy, looking at it, because I remember how happy Jake was when he gave it to me. I remember the way the smile spread across his face and joined his two dimples together like a dot-to-dot.

By the time Tom goes to the shops, Jake and Sam are playing with their Duplo in the living room. They're making a city, and they've piled up all the cushions from the couch on the floor to make a mountain. I watch them crawl along the floor, making wet truck noises, with their little blue pajama bottoms in the air. They're absorbed in their own world, so I go back to the kitchen and clear off the countertops to make room for my cakes.

The cakes are stored in the deep freeze. Tom invested in the huge freezer years ago so that we could buy bulk meat, but I've never bought much meat to put in it. I could never bring myself to store half a frozen cow or pig in my tiny kitchen. When Susan comes over she always says that the freezer is bad feng shui. It takes up a lot of space, and it needs an ugly black extension cord to connect it with the power supply.

As I open the freezer, a cloud of cold air blows in my face. I can't see. I feel a bit like that character in Jake's storybook who stands at the entrance of a mysterious cave and peers inside, holding a candle up to the darkness. For an instant, he can't see anything, then . . . Abracadabra! The treasure is revealed. When the fog clears, I admire my hoard of cakes, each one tightly wrapped in Glad wrap so it glistens. Then I haul the cakes out of the freezer and sort them on the bench into three magnificent piles.

In the first pile I put all the morning-tea cakes. Light, wholesome creations, perfect for a semivirtuous midmorning snack: banana bars, carrot cakes, blueberry muffins, date rolls and light fruitcakes. In the second pile I stack the afternoon-tea cakes. These cakes are made from slightly richer batters with stronger flavors to tempt a jaded palate. There are chocolate cakes, coffee cakes, syrup cakes, and butter cakes flavored with lemon peel, orange peel, or pure vanilla essence. In the last pile are the special-occasion cakes. These are the kind of cakes I used to dream about—rich, decadent, and seductive. Most of these cakes are stored in separate pieces and tightly wrapped in several layers of plastic and aluminium foil. Three tiers of chocolate fudge cake wrapped and ready to be drenched with port, sandwiched with cherries and cream, and drizzled with melted chocolate. Two layers of hazelnut meringue, languishing for poached pears and Tasmanian double cream. A rich shortcake base in a tart tin waiting to be filled with lemon curd and topped with blueberries . . .

I call in the boys. When they see my stash piled up on the counter they just stand there with their tongues dangling and their eyes wide. "Are we going to eat all of those?" Jake asks, pointing toward the great stacks of frozen cake. I'm quiet. I don't know how to answer him. I guess I've never thought about what I'm going to do with my cakes. I've hoarded them desperately for months but now . . . Now, I don't need them anymore.

I smile sheepishly at Jake and feel like a greedy child caught with a fistful of lollies. While I think about what to do next, I ask the boys to choose one cake for morning tea. Of course they pick a chocolate cake. I zap it in the microwave to defrost it and whip up

251

some chocolate butter frosting to spread over the top. Then I make myself a cup of tea, get the boys some milk, and we sit at the table together, eating cake. It feels good, the three of us sitting together in the kitchen. I watch the boys devour their cake, and I smile at the crumbs that stick in the corners of their mouths and the frosting that smears across their cheeks. They guzzle down piece after piece while I eat my cake slowly, as if I've already had enough.

Habitually, I pick up the last crumbs of cake with the tip of my finger. "Would you like to earn a bit of pocket money?" I ask my boys before I put the crumbs into my mouth.

They nod, and the cake billows in their cheeks as they grin.

"I'd like to," says Jake.

"Me too!" yells Sam, sending cake and spittle all over the table.

"Right then, you two," I say, standing up, "go and get dressed. We've got some work to do."

The boys slide off their chairs, race each other down the hall, and dive into their bedroom. I hear their drawers thump open as they pull out their clothes. While they are busy, I get organized.

Half an hour later we set off up the street. Outside, the air is blazing hot, and the sun is still climbing high into the blue. Jake pushes his little wheelbarrow, stuffed full of cakes, in front of him and Sam rides along the footpath with more cakes in the trailer behind his plastic tractor. I walk behind them, a purse slung over my shoulder, pushing the laundry trolley in front of me. The wicker clothes basket in the trolley is loaded high with cakes. It doesn't take Jake and Sam long to sell my cakes to the people who live on our street. Soon they have pockets lumpy with coins. By the time we get to the end of our street, we've sold twenty-five cakes and made over sixty dollars.

I'm on such a high, walking outside in the sun with Jake and

Sam, that I don't feel at all self-conscious pushing the cake-laden laundry trolley up the street. I just laugh when a mob of young blokes in a hotted-up Falcon drag past, hanging out the windows, hooting and yahooing.

We walk around the block and the cakes are selling well. After two blocks, the boys have so much money weighing down their pockets that their pants begin to drift down their backsides, and they have to keep hitching them up. Because it is such a hot day, other people's garden sprinklers seem inviting. Once, after I check that the grass on the footpath is free of bindi prickles, we stop our procession to get wet. We take off our sandals and run through the edge of a sprinkler watering someone's front lawn. We must look a bit odd, I suppose, the three of us, but the boys are screaming with laughter, and I don't care.

By the time we get to the Easterns' street, there is only one cake left, a coffee cake with caramel frosting. We all stand at the corner on the dry grass under the street sign while I think of reasons not to give the last cake to Evelyn. There's a moving van down the road parked in the driveway of Wendy's old house. The boys, who are truck crazy, spot it and plead with me to take them down there.

We abandon the little wheelbarrow, the laundry trolley and the tractor and walk down the hill. Jake and Sam walk hand in hand, and I carry the cake. Two stocky men with broad shoulders and big thighs are carrying a piano into Wendy's old house. They waver on the stairs, and the piano hits the step and roars. All the while, the kids belonging to the new family are running up and down Wendy's old verandah playing tag among the packing boxes. Jake and Sam look done in, and they sit on the footpath and watch. I'm exhausted too, and I sit on the grass with the coffee cake in my lap.

Midday sun pounds down through my white canvas hat, and I feel the frosting on the last cake getting soft and sticky. It seems a shame to waste it. Jake and Sam look too exhausted to sell any more cakes, and in this heat, the frosting won't survive the walk home.

"Come on, boys!" I say, standing up and brushing the grass off my denim skirt.

"Are we going home now?" Jake asks, looking hopeful.

"In a little while. I just want to give this cake to William's mommy first."

I like to think now that I decided to give the last cake to Evelyn as a token of my enduring friendship, but that wasn't it. I simply couldn't bear to waste my baking. So I lead the boys through the gate, dragging their feet and with pockets weighed down with booty. Then I tell Jake to look after Sam as I sit them in the shade of a crooked lemon tree near the rose garden.

I feel awkward as I climb the front steps. Though the house is all shut up, when I knock on the brown door I hear a little rustling noise that tells me Evelyn is moving about. The sound she makes is barely perceptible and, if I did not know that Steve had taken the cat with him, I would have thought she was the cat, pattering across the floor. I hold my breath while she undoes the deadlock. The door opens the width of the safety chain and I see half of Evelyn's pale face peer outside. It takes her a moment to see me through the midday glare, and she squints through one green eye to cut the sun.

"Joanna?" she whispers.

"I thought you might like this." My voice seems loud and booming. I hold up the cake so that she can see it through the crack.

She looks puzzled, but she opens the door and stands in front of me in her old terry cloth dressing gown. She seems embarrassed and tries to smooth down her hair, but the auburn locks coil under her small hands and burst free like wire springs.

I try to speak softly. She looks pathetic and kind of small. "It's a cake," I say. "The boys and I were selling them. We've only got one left. You can have it if you like. A gift."

Her lips twitch nervously on one side, trying to make a smile.

"I made it myself." She doesn't move. "Something to have with your afternoon tea." I nod encouragingly as her too-thin, too-white hands reach out and take the cake.

"Thank you," she says, bringing the cake across in front of her chest. "Would you like to come in?" There's a pause. "I could make tea?"

I step backward, stumbling down the top two steps. "Oh no! The boys are with me . . ."

She nods and retreats back into the darkness. "Maybe another time . . ." she says. "Thanks again." The door closes between us, and I'm still standing on the steps. My heart is thumping as I turn and begin to walk down to the boys, then I stop, on the middle stair, turn around and walk up to the door and knock again.

She opens the door and I stammer, before I can change my mind, "I'll come back by myself. At three." Something about the way she looks at me makes me feel like I'm talking to a child. "You have a shower and get dressed. We'll share the cake for afternoon tea. Okay?"

She nods and smiles, and there's an emotion on her face I can't read. Relief?

As I walk home with the boys, I'm shaking my head. Why did I say that? It will be torture! Evelyn and me sitting in her dark house, staring into our teacups and not knowing what to say to each other. Am I out of my mind?

Perhaps not. As I gaze at my boys my anxiety fades. Sam's chubby little legs pummel the pedals on his plastic tractor and the front wheel scratches noisily along the pavement. Jake trundles along behind his wheelbarrow. His ears stick out under his cap, glowing pink as the sun shines through them. They look like the insides of the pipi shells I held up to the sky as a child. I'm sublimely happy this afternoon, just being with my boys. The satisfaction I feel is hard to articulate but I have a kind of revelation, as I'm walking home, that it's got something to do with Evelyn.

Don't get me wrong, I still think the choice she made was crazy. Yet, deep down, in the pit of my stomach, I know she did that crazy thing for the right reasons. She wanted to find someone who would do what she wasn't able to do. She wanted to find someone who could mother her child. Evelyn's going to be okay. She really is. And so am I.

I'm the lucky one, really. I'm a mom. I used to qualify that phrase with the word "just." Whenever anyone asked what I did, I would say, "I'm just a mom." It was like an apology for not being someone more important, more intelligent or more sexy. Being a mother's not easy. Sometimes it's like being at the very bottom of the heap. Susan knows that. Clare knows that too. But hell! Evelyn gave away her own child, her precious blood, because she wanted to secure for Amy the love that she, herself, had been denied—the love of a devoted mother. Strange though it may seem, now I know this, I feel better about myself. And the best part is that I can eat my cake but not crave it. I'm not dying for it anymore.

BREAKING THE WEB

THE SUN IS SOAKING THE CURTAINS. IT IS SEEP-
ing through the loose cotton weave and making tiny squares of
pure gold. The gold dances on the edge of my darkness. I kick
away the sheet and stand in the darkness, in my cotton nightdress,
with bare feet pressed against a warm floor. I move over to the
window and find the center, where the curtains meet, and pull
them apart. I hear the metal rings rip across the track as the blue
day washes in.

The blue sky washes through all my days, but William is the
one who brings other colors into the house. When he comes to
visit with Clare, his red shoes run up the front steps and splatter
across the floor like disappearing paint. He jumps into my arms,
and I swirl his colors, green and red and gold, as I spin him around
myself. He is a fluid rainbow, and he pulls me outside into the garden, where the sun paints away the shadows and puts a splash of
yellow behind every blade of grass.

Clare sets up her easel and poises her brush in readiness, and
we run through the grass, William and I. I am a child with him,
bare feet sinking into coolness, hand held in his as we climb the
jacaranda. Skin on rough bark, toes curled against gravity, heart-
beats rushing through our ears. It is January, and the leaves on the
tree are unfolding, filling spaces vacated by purple with luminous

green. We reach out to the lower bough and pull against it, scattering the last purple blossoms to the ground. They spill over the grass, and we jump down into a sea of purple and laugh. We laugh as we throw the soft petals over our faces and feel splashes of coolness where they fall.

Then we lie down. We lie on the ground and the sun trickles like honey into our mouths and we taste its sweetness. We fill ourselves up with it, and somewhere we can hear bees. We are full of honey, and the bees think we are flowers and frisk in sharp circles around us. We are still. We are so still that we can see through their brittle wings and marvel at their perfect bands of yellow and black as they dart in and out of the flowers that have fallen on us. William squeezes my hand, and we jump up and are off again. Running.

Running so fast our chests ache and heave with our breath. We are running to get to the hose, and William gets there first and sprays ribbons of water everywhere. I dart in and out of the ribbons, soaking my clothes, my hair, and I laugh. And he laughs as I pull the hose from him and put my thumb against the spray and make a million tiny droplets in the air that arc into a rainbow. William runs through the rainbow, and there are two rainbows dancing before me, dancing colors of green and purple and blue.

Clare sees the colors and captures them on her canvas, dipping her brush again and again into the liquid tones to paint William and me together. She paints William dancing through the water across the grass and he is vivid and full of brightness. And she paints me. She paints me small on the canvas, like him, in watery colors, reflecting his joy.

When we are wet, the colors run and pour through us, and I am happy. I am happy because I know that, one blue day, when I don't see William, if I close my eyes, I will still see a rainbow arcing behind my eyelids. Then I will remember how my world is colored in different hues when we are together.

On blue days, when William is with Steve and I am by myself, I circle the house, standing in the little chinks of light between windows and under doors where the sun oozes through. I push my face against the light and close my eyes and think of him, and I can see rainbows. Sometimes it is not enough. I want to hold him. I want to be with him. My son.

There is a hunger in me that only ceases when he is with me. A hunger for him. For the color he carries into my life. He pulls me outside into a kaleidoscope world where colors rocket like beads into patterns of joy, and I become the child that I never was. Each time I am with him I grow up a little more. It is then that I realize he is the one who will give me the courage to leave this web. He is the one who will make me want to go. He will help me to say good-bye to the spider and put her to rest forever in my dreams.

Strange how I let her suspend her web over my life. Strange how I let what she did to herself, and to me, spin out into my life with my children. Things could have been different if I'd let her go before Amy was born. But I clung to her like a desperate child. My mother became someone I needed to emulate if only . . . if only to believe that she loved me once, some long-ago yesterday.

Yesterday I brushed down the web that hangs outside the kitchen window. I brushed down the web by climbing up into the jacaranda tree and leaning out with a broom. My heart was beating so fast I thought I would drown in the sound of it. I leaned out as far as I could, still holding the branch with one hand, and the broom shook as I knocked apart the sticky threads. The spider scampered under the eaves. She will build her web again. It does not matter.

One day I will break apart the real web. I will break apart the sided walls that wrap around the house and I will not have to steal slivers of sun. I will stand on the verandah with Steve's mallet, and I will feel its weight and the thrust of its power as I gather all my strength into it and hurl my heart with it high into the air. The force of the blow, as the mallet descends, will shatter the wall into fragments at my feet. Into fragments on the wind. Into fragments in my mind.

I will not stop. I will not stop until all the false walls are shattered and all the ugly windows are broken away. I will persist until there is nothing left but the low railings that were built around the verandah in the beginning. Then my house will expose its real face to the street. The shroud will be gone, and the true front door, with the stained-glass paneled roses, will swing open. I'll stand at the threshold and let the colors of the day wash through me. Then I will close my eyes and allow myself to see her little face. And I will know. I will know that I have realized my dream for her because I desired her happiness more than I desired my own.

Amy. My daughter. The daughter I gave away. I will see her face in the fragments of dust that float forever in my mind, and I will see her smiling. Always. She is smiling with her beautiful mouth that looks so much like a rosebud, and her green eyes are crinkled up with joy. She is clapping her chubby hands and laughing. She is laughing and holding out her arms. How I want to gather her up and hold her, even in my mind. But I will not. I will not ever break the family I have created. Will I? A moment's hesitation, and Amy's face begins to disappear. The feelings well and churn inside me, and I let them go. Jealousy, desire, love . . . hope.

Hope. I keep this longest and cup my hands to hold it. All at once I see them together in my mind. Together. One beautiful little face, so familiar to me, smiling and pressed against another. The face of the woman I gave her to. I remember her now, and in my mind she is laughing. Tears falling, eyes smiling, long black hair shimmering with sun. She can never thank me enough, she says. She can never repay me for this gift. Her arms are extended, shaking in anticipation, aching to hold what has hitherto been denied. As I hand over my child, the greyness is already encroaching. It takes all my strength to place my child in her arms. Then there is a moment of elation. A moment of such acute joy that it is incised in my mind. That is the moment when I realize I have set Amy free. I have freed her by giving her away. And I have given her to love. For she will be loved by this woman. This woman with the heart-shaped face.

ML

5/05